ENOUGH TO GO AROUND

Tanya Savko

Kova Publishing
PHOENIX, OREGON

Kova Publishing
PO Box 1222
Phoenix, OR 97535
www.kovapublishing.com

Publisher's Note: This is a work of fiction. Names, characters, places, and incidents are a product of the author's imagination. Locales and public names are sometimes used for atmospheric purposes. Any resemblance to actual people, living or dead, or to businesses, companies, events, institutions, or locales is completely coincidental.

Cover design by Toni Tesori
Cover photograph by Tanya Savko
Book Layout ©2013 BookDesignTemplates.com

Enough to Go Around/Tanya Savko. -- 1st ed.
ISBN 978-0-9817868-2-7

For my dad, Michael, who would have loved it

God grant you many years!

—OLD CHURCH SLAVONIC SONG

God strike you dead with lightning!

—OLD CZECHOSLOVAKIAN CURSE

CHAPTER ONE

If they make me go it will be the death of me.

Anna Sopko hoisted herself up out of her sagging, old, floral print couch and hobbled over to switch off the as-old TV set. *Don't they realize that?*

She walked down the dim hallway toward her bedroom while straightening her baby-blue fleece robe. Her slippers shuffled across the parquet floor. She remembered picking it out as the three-bedroom house was being built in 1969, almost twenty years ago. And it was fine that so many years had passed and the flooring had not changed. Nothing that truly matters is affected by the passing of time, Anna thought. Not love. Not faith. Only the scratched-up floor and my old bones. And what did they matter?

She passed the hallway full of old framed photographs – her wedding, her three children's graduations – and stopped at the door to her room, trying to recall what it was she had been going in there for. The laundry. Anna had lately been plagued by episodes of forgetfulness – forgetting her phone number when asked, forgetting to turn off the oven, and sometimes, which deeply concerned her children, forgetting to eat. She passed it off as "just being old," but it bothered her, too, more than she wanted to admit.

And the worst thing was the thought of going to live in a retirement home, as her children wanted her to do. "You'll be safer," they kept saying. But she had always been safe! She crossed an ocean at seventeen and kept herself safe then. Her husband had died seven years ago, and she had been safe all this time since. A retirement home might keep her body safe, but not her spirit. She was too independent for that. Didn't her own children realize that?

Michael, her husband, would frequently forget things in the years before he died. He would go to the door and just stand there, not only forgetting what he had come for, but where he was. In the 1970s doctors told Anna that he was senile. Now, thinking of her recent forgetfulness, she wondered if she was going senile too. But she didn't go out for a walk around the block and tell the police officer who found her three hours later that she was going home to Czechoslovakia.

She could never understand why her husband had wanted to go back. That place was nothing but a blurry black and white photograph to her. She had come to America sixty-two years ago and never returned. Her memory of Czechoslovakia was like a dream lost upon awakening, and she liked it that way. Anna could easily remember her childhood when asked, even better than she could remember her last meal sometimes. But she preferred to let her past stay where it was, in elusive shades of gray, like a charcoal drawing, smudged and imperfect. Maybe Michael had wanted to go back because his past wasn't like hers. He didn't owe any explanations to anyone. He hadn't left a jilted lover (that she knew of). He hadn't watched a sibling die, knowing he was responsible. He hadn't felt that pain.

Anna sighed, more from exertion than emotion. She struggled with her cracked, white plastic laundry basket as she began walking to the garage. Recently her son Peter had again tried to convince her to let someone come in to do the housekeeping, and she again refused. Now, trudging down the hallway, she began to realize that he was probably right. But it was happening so quickly! Wasn't it just a few months ago that she went camping in Yosemite with her daughter Anya and her family? Or was that the summer before?

She set the laundry basket down on the floor of the kitchen and opened the door to the garage. Anna braced herself against the cold darkness. With her foot she pushed the basket toward the washing machine, visible from the pale daylight streaming in through the ground-level wall vents. She glanced around the two-car garage as her eyes adjusted. They roamed over stacks of boxes filled with musty clothing, books, magazines, her husband's unfinished woodworking projects, children's and grandchildren's toys, once-used exercise equipment, and God knew what else. No car. That had been sold last year when she reluctantly admitted that her reflexes were probably no longer quick enough for driving. She hated that someone, usually her son, had to drive her to do her grocery shopping.

I don't want to be like Michael's mother, bothersome, taking up space and time in my children's home. They finally get their children in college, and I come along so they can take care of me, when they want to go on a cruise. How bad will it get? How soon? Will they have to help bathe me like I had to do for Michael?

A lump formed in her throat as she remembered caring for her husband before his death, watching him deteriorate more each day. She could feel the creaking of his bones as she helped him to get in and out of the tub. Sometimes, he was like a little boy as he sat there and whined when soap got in his eyes. Sometimes he cried, but not from the soap. And she cried with him.

She poured too much powdered soap into the washing machine, and then she realized that there was already a load of clothes in there, ready to be transferred to the dryer. *Damn it.* Since she could pull the clothes out easily, she figured they hadn't been sitting there too long. Piece by piece, she shook the soap off onto the cement floor, then put the clothes in the dryer.

Anna put in the new load to be washed, started both the washer and dryer, and went back into the house. She stood in the kitchen, deciding if she should eat something. Was it time? Did she need to?

A loud thump came from her bedroom, like something had been knocked over. A chill spread through her. She could hear rustling sounds; someone was definitely in her bedroom. She bit her lip as her mind raced.

Anna felt clammy as she realized it was not one of her children. Something drew her, almost hypnotically, down the hallway. She had to know; she had to see with her own eyes. She stood transfixed in front of her bedroom door, with no thought of what to do.

God protect me!

Anna never really looked at the young man. She felt herself go numb as his form appeared in front of her, toe to toe as he stopped short, startled for a second. He didn't seem very tall, but even someone shorter than herself would have alarmed her, terrified her as much.

He took a small step back, but Anna didn't notice. She couldn't yell, couldn't say anything with her tongue thick and cold, her entire body frozen, unaware of her heart thumping fanatically.

Scream, why don't you?! Help! Oh, God!

She managed a mere gasp as the young man in a low-brimmed baseball cap yelled, "Get out of the way!" He clamped his free hand on her shoulder and shoved her down to the floor. Her knees buckled and she crumpled to the carpet, coming down hard on her right hip. Pain shot through that side of her body, up to her shoulder, down, hitting her elbow, and then spread to the tips of her fingers.

Anna grimaced and moaned. Then she opened her eyes to see the back of the young man – his blue jeans and black T-shirt – as he opened the front door and slung a black canvas backpack over his shoulder. He ran out, leaving the door wide open. Sunlight poured in through it, almost reaching the hallway where Anna lay, her body heaving with sobs.

Oh, God, he will come back!

As she cried, she tried to keep herself from reaching hysteria. Willing her shaking arms and rubbery legs to move, she began to crawl out of the hallway. She wanted to close the front door – *bolt it* – her one protection from another attack, but the phone was closer.

She sat up a little with her legs bent under her, picked up the receiver, and punched the number four button on the memory-dial phone that her son had bought for her and shown her how to use. Her gasping had subsided somewhat, but her hands still shook.

"Peter...Peter..."

She needed his comforting voice, his stable presence. He would know what to do. He was a lawyer! Her loving, intelligent, accountable son would help her. "Ma? Ma! What's wrong? Are you okay?"

Hearing his voice brought an emotional swell to hers; she felt the consuming fear again as she stumbled over words. "Come quick! Someone robbed me...he - "

"You were robbed! Are you *hurt?*"

Anna swallowed and took a breath before answering. She remembered the searing pain in her hip and leg but didn't want Peter to worry. She hoped that the pain (and her fear) would eventually go away. "I'm okay, but I'm scared. I don't know what to do. He was in the house –"

"He was in the house! Is he gone now?"

"Yes, but I'm scared, Peter. Will you come?"

Peter assured her that he was on his way, and she felt the sobs coming on again as she struggled to hang up the phone. The pain in her hip surged and she collapsed, slumping between the couch and the coffee table.

*

Fifteen minutes later Anna jolted back to consciousness as her son lifted her and said, "Ma...Ma – it's Peter. Are you all right? Let's get you up here on the couch. Ma? Can you hear me?"

Anna opened her eyes, shocked to find herself on the floor, and then images of the robbery flooded her memory, as definite as a wave when it finally crashes on the shore. She glanced at the front door, which was now shut, and then rested her eyes on the familiar face of her middle-aged son. He lifted her from the floor to the couch and sat her upright. She winced from the pain in her hip.

"Why didn't you go next door?" Peter coughed and loosened his necktie as he sat down next to her.

"I just...couldn't...move, Peter. I was so scared!" Anna grimaced and put her face in her hands as she cried.

Peter reached over and took her hand in his. "I know, Ma. It's okay now. It was a very scary thing to happen, but it's over now, and you're all right."

Anna's voice halted through her sobs. "We lived in Los Angeles for forty-seven years and nothing like this happened before!"

"I know, Ma. We were very fortunate. But now, we'll just install bars on the windows and some other type -"

"It doesn't matter! It could happen anywhere! Not just in the house – on the street, in my own neighborhood!"

"Ma, tell me what happened. Just start with that and we'll go from there."

"It's just, when I think of what could have happened..." she cried, filled with fear.

"But it didn't, Ma, it didn't. Just...take a deep breath. Come on, breathe with me now." Peter took her hands, looked into her eyes, and guided her through a calming breath. Anna looked at the concerned face of her second child, round and smooth like her husband's had been when he was younger. Peter had his father's deep, soulful gray-blue eyes and bald head. In fact, he looked so much like Michael that she let herself believe for an instant that it was her husband holding her, soothing her. He was there and he was not senile; he was strong and he was looking into her brown eyes. Just for one cherished moment. *Yes, Michael, I feel better now.*

"I was in the garage doing laundry," Anna said, "and when I came back into house I heard noises coming from bedroom."

Anna closed her eyes and told him what she had heard, the thumps and rustling sounds. She could visualize so many things with her eyes closed – all the painful memories she tried so hard to forget. Her sister pitching head-first off the roof and Anna saying she didn't know what happened. *Accidents and death, loss and loneliness.* She wanted to confess to the only one who needed to know the truth, someone she hadn't seen in sixty-two years. *Guilt and shame. Fear.* The memories ran through her mind in quick succession, like the cars of a midnight train.

"Mm-hmm. Then what?"

"I started to walk down hall and then all of a sudden he was right in front of me, and...he -" Her voice halted. Anna realized that, although painful and frightening, the burglary paled in comparison to any other traumatic event in her life. This time, her father was not beaten by soldiers and taken away. This time, villages were not burned. Siblings didn't die. Yes, she was afraid, but that was all. She didn't want to lend any power to that lousy fool who had dared to break into her home and steal from her. He wasn't worth it. He was nothing.

"It's okay, Ma. Just tell me."

"He said, 'Get out of the way,' and he pushed me down and ran out front door and left it open. And then I was in pain and scared, so I crawled to phone and called you."

"I'm so glad you're okay, Ma," Peter said, embracing her. He asked about her injury and suggested going to the doctor, which Anna declined. She didn't want to take up any more of his time. "Well, I'm going to go have a look in the room. You just sit here; I'll get you something to drink." Peter walked into the kitchen and poured a glass of water from a pitcher in the refrigerator. He took a sip as he walked back to his mother and handed her the glass. Then he headed down the hallway toward her bedroom.

Oh, what did that worthless bum take?

"Ma," she heard Peter call out. "I'm trying not to touch anything, in case the police want to get fingerprints. But it looks like he went through your jewelry box, and some clothes are on the floor in front of the closet. For some reason he must have taken your old mink stole because it's not where you usually keep it. He stole the stole - sorry. And it looks like he took some jewelry. I don't remember all that you had, but I don't see the ruby set – the ring, necklace, and earrings. Did you happen to see anything he took with him?"

"No, Peter; it happened so fast. He was wearing blue jeans and black T-shirt, I think. And that's all I remember..." Her voice trailed off as she remembered opening the presents Christmas morning in 1938. She had treasured her mink stole for fifty years. Michael had saved his paltry factory worker earnings to buy it for her. She had worn it every Christmas, every anniversary, including their fiftieth, eight years before he died. It soothed her every time she'd touched it in the seven years since. Every time her fingertips lingered on the silky brown fur. Every time she felt that divine connection, that link with the good life, the satisfaction of achieving shared goals, the remembrance of a determined love.

"He had no right to take it," she mumbled, tears pooling in her eyes.

Peter, standing by the phone, hadn't heard. "Okay, Ma, I'll call the police now." She heard him flip through the pages of the phonebook and pick up the receiver to dial out. He coughed and said, "Hello. I have a burglary to report..."

Anna leaned over to set her water glass on the coffee table. She began to wring her hands and bite the inside of her bottom lip. The buzzer went off inside the garage, signaling that the clothes were finished in the dryer. Anna glanced at the door leading to the garage as the buzzer stopped. In the space of fifty minutes since she had put the clothes in the dryer, she had gone from the strong, independent seventeen-year-old immigrant to a frail, vulnerable seventy-nine-year-old who needed to move to a retirement home to be safe. There was no escaping it now, the hopeless inevitability of complete dependency.

"He had no right to take it," she whispered.

*

Peter Sopko figured his mid-life crisis had finally hit. He hadn't bought a red sports car, he hadn't had an affair with his secretary, nor had he quit his job to backpack around the world. He had no inclination for clichés. He was just a crazy fool who decided to take his sixteen-year-old daughter, nine-year-old son, two-year-old grandson, and their nineteen-year-old Czechoslovakian cousin to Disneyland for the day. His wife of twenty years was at home having a nervous breakdown. And after an hour at Disneyland alone with the kids, he was ready to join her.

"Leif!" he admonished the tow-headed toddler who had run after some pigeons. "Hold Grandpa's hand! You don't want to get lost!" Then Peter turned around and called, "Kat! Joseph! Danika!"

"We're right here, Dad," his daughter Kat, short for Katya, said in an exasperated tone. Her blue-lined eyes glowered at him from beneath her California Angels baseball cap, and he realized that she no longer had to look up at him when she made eye contact. "We followed you when you took off after Leif."

"Oh. Good," Peter said, feeling a headache coming on. He coughed a little, his "nervous" cough before speaking in an awkward situation or when under stress. "Okay," he continued, catching his breath. "What would you guys like to do next?"

"Autopia!" Kat said at the same time that Joseph said, "Peter Pan!"

Peter had hoped, foolishly, he realized, that seven years would have been enough of an age difference between his two younger children for the older one to concede to the younger one, but in fact it was usually the other way around. Kat, the only athletic one in the family, was fiercely competitive. She did not see her younger brother, a Lego-building daydreamer, as one to be coddled but one to be conquered. And someone who would rather read *The Lion, the Witch, and the Wardrobe* did not bond well with someone who would rather be at the batting cage. Joseph was content to entertain himself in his room instead of fighting to watch a TV program that was on at the same time as one that Kat wanted to watch. At first it bothered Peter that his younger son was so compliant, his daughter so demanding. Was that sexist of him, or just concerned? And he certainly saw to it that Joseph got to choose occasionally and Kat couldn't override him. But would Joseph grow up to be subservient? Would Kat grow up to be self-absorbed?

Peter turned to his daughter while Leif pulled on his hand. He braced himself and wished that his older son, Leif's father, had been able to come. Crowd control with an active toddler was something he wished he had not taken on. "We're already in Fantasyland, Kat, so we might as well do Peter Pan first and then go over to To-morrowland to do the Autopia and the Rockets -"

"– and the Submarine!" Joseph interjected with excite-ment. Peter noticed that his son's sandy blond hair needed a trim.

"Whatever," Kat scowled. She shoved her hands in the pockets of her puffy pink ski jacket and turned to her third cousin. Three years apart, they looked like sisters with their long, straight blond hair, gray-blue eyes, and slim physique. "Joseph always gets what he wants," Kat mumbled, rolling her eyes.

Peter opened his mouth to object when Danika stepped forward and gestured to Leif. "He is same as the little boy...I am nanny for," she said in her soft, accented voice, smiling. "You want I watch him? I bring cookies!" She gestured to her denim purse.

"Thank you, Danika," Peter answered, relieved. Danika had come to the United States four months ear-lier to visit family and find work to do during her six-month stay. She had studied English for three years in high school, and Peter could hear the improvement in her language skills every time he saw her since her arri-val. She had been shy and reticent then, reluctant to speak for fear of saying the wrong thing. Now, she was still quiet, but she spoke more freely and showed a little con-fidence. She loved the two children, a three-year-old boy and a one-year-old girl, that she watched for a wealthy couple in Brentwood.

Danika squatted down to Leif's level and said, "Hi, Leif. You want to play with me now?"

"Want cookie!" Leif said. His little blond head bobbed up and down, answering *yes* to himself.

"Okay, Leif can have cookie, but Leif stay with Danika. Okay?" Danika pulled a plastic bag of vanilla wafers out of her shoulder bag, and Leif continued bobbing his head as he reached for the cookies.

Thank God. "Okay, let's go get in line for Peter Pan," Peter said as he put an arm around his children and began walking with them. He felt Kat recoil from his touch and decided to talk to her later. Now was not the time. One thing he had learned in his years of being a family mediation counselor and divorce lawyer was that timing was everything. Timing and attitude. And lately he couldn't stand his daughter's attitude.

Why do I come here every year? Why do I come at all? I loathe this place. This isn't the way to bond with the kids. I'm paying a small fortune to be a referee and give myself a migraine.

Peter wished he could be home reading. His favorite spot in the house was his papasan chair with a beige twill cushioned seat in the small library he had set up on the stair landing. He loved to be splayed out in the chair, his feet propped up on the matching footstool, a good book in one hand and a glass of red wine in the other, with the sun streaming in through the vertical blinds behind him. He would much rather be there on a Saturday afternoon than standing in line for hours with a surly teen girl, a distractible boy, a rambunctious toddler, a foreigner learning to speak English, and a hundred thousand other people. It served no purpose for him, other than to get the kids out of the house so that his wife could rest.

Theresa. His wife of twenty years, with her honey blonde shoulder-length hair and willowy figure, her perfect picket fence of teeth that he rarely saw anymore, her startling green eyes that no longer captivated anyone, was not at the top of her game. She hadn't been for years, but it had recently gotten worse. He figured it was depression, but he couldn't figure out why or what to do. She had good days and bad days. The good days were manageable; she got up and made breakfast for Joseph, who was in fourth grade, and got him out the door in time for the school bus. She chatted with Peter about inconsequential things while he ate breakfast and got ready for work. Then she watched their grandson while their nineteen-year-old son and his wife, who lived in the first floor of the Sopko's tri-level home, went off to their respective jobs. On the bad days, she stayed in bed while Peter made sure that Joseph and Kat got up and ready for school. Then, according to their older son Mike, Theresa would drag herself around the house in a baby-blue fleece robe (by coincidence alarmingly similar to the one Peter's mother wore), curl up on the living room couch, and stare at the wall. Mike would venture in with Leif, set him up with the Disney channel on TV, and put a pile of toddler books and snacks near Theresa. He'd tell her that he was going to school (he took classes at a local community college), that Leif was going to watch TV, and he reminded her when and what to feed him. Could she function well enough to take care of a toddler for several hours? Her bad days, which used to only occur about once a month, were now occurring more frequently. Peter, with work and household duties, was too preoccupied to do anything, even though he knew that something needed to be done. Where was the witty, well-read paralegal he had fallen in love with? Theresa had quit work two weeks before Mike had been born and never went back. She said that she wanted to be a stay-at-home parent, that she felt strongly about doing it and claimed she never regretted it. But twenty years was a good chunk of time. Time enough for the first child to grow up and have a child of his own. And Theresa was helping to raise him.

It was the right thing to do, they felt, to allow their son and his then-girlfriend, Heather, to live with them after the baby was born. There was no way two seventeen-year-olds could make a home for themselves in Los Angeles County, continue to go to school and work, and take care of a baby. And they were good kids. Even good kids have sex when they're in love. Even good kids who were raised going to church, as Mike had been. Of course, when he turned eighteen, he stopped going. But Peter didn't hold it against him. In fact, he secretly wished that he could do the same. He'd gone to church nearly every Sunday of his life and questioned whether that made him a better person. He wished he could go on a "church sabbatical" for six months, just to see if he missed it, to see if it made a difference in his life. He believed in God and appreciated how blessed he had been with his home, his family, and his ability to provide for them through his work. He was thankful for his health and that of his loved ones. But he saw so much hypocrisy in these religious people who sang at church and dropped their collection envelopes in the basket and then cursed each other when they cut each other off in the parking lot, trying to leave church as fast as they could. Peter, through his job, knew what they were like all week long – yelling at their spouses and kids, gossiping about the neighbors, telling racist jokes, having affairs, driving drunk. He thought about the cases of molestation and rape courtesy of the parish priests. Peter was reaching a point where he still believed in God but no longer wanted to be affiliated with the Catholic Church. But he couldn't stop going. How could he explain that to his mother? She wouldn't understand. For her, there was no separation between God and the Church. God *is* the Church.

Theresa would understand, probably, if he talked to her about it. But they didn't really talk anymore. They just went through the motions of their lives. Monday through Friday: get out of bed, get the kids off to school, go to work or stay home with a toddler and do housework, prepare dinner together, watch a little TV, go to bed and read, then sleep. Saturday: yard work and running errands, maybe a family outing, maybe sex before bed, if the outing hadn't made Theresa too tired. Sunday: church, then visiting family throughout the urban sprawl of Los Angeles County. Both Peter's mother and his older sister lived within twenty-five miles of them, as did Theresa's sister and their families, and their parents. Christmas was a mad scramble of church, coming home to open the rest of the presents (they allowed the kids to open two gifts before church), and then traversing no less than nine different freeways as they made the visiting rounds with their relatives. Every year they did that, every year they went on a family ski trip to Mammoth Mountain, and every year they went to Disneyland.

As Peter and his children boarded the Peter Pan ride, he thought how ironic it was that he should share the name of the fictitious boy who never wanted to grow up. That now, as he grasped at holding his marriage together and being a more involved father, all he wished for was to be a kid again, to only be concerned with getting his paper route done and doing his homework, to play with the dog and not have to worry about a depressed wife and an aging mother who was not taking very good care of herself. The thought had occurred to him that his mother really needed to go into a retirement home to be safe. And if she forgot to eat, there would be someone there to feed her. He was relieved she had not been severely harmed during the break-in.

The ride came to its jolting conclusion and the three hopped out to look for Danika and Leif, who would be waiting near the exit. Kat, much to Peter's relief, actually allowed a smile to cross her now brace-free teeth, and she walked next to him, weaved her arm through his, and in a sing-song voice reminded him about the Autopia being next.

"Yes, honey," he said and kissed the top of her head. And then he saw Danika. Her eyes were watery and red-rimmed. Her chin trembled.

Oh, God, Peter thought. *Where's Leif?*

CHAPTER TWO

Theresa Sopko slowly emptied the dishwasher, almost methodically. It was usually her daughter Kat's job, but Kat had a science project due tomorrow, and Theresa wanted her to focus on getting that done when she got home. Besides, what else did Theresa have to do? Blow her grandson's nose again? Sit on the couch and watch *Sesame Street*? Get a life? Apologize to her sister? Go back to bed?

The latter choice was tempting. Sometimes it felt like an effort just to move, to pick up the spatula and open the drawer and put it in. She could barely stand at the kitchen sink and stare out the window watching the breeze rustle the large crinkled leaves of the hibiscus plants that covered the fence. Immobilized, she watched the droplets of rain slowly darken the cement patio, wishing she could just lie out in it, feeling the cool wetness saturating her skin as she breathed in the scent of dust off the leaves and from the barbeque that had not been used in months.

Leif, her grandson, had come down with something during the night, her son Mike had declared as he handed him off before leaving for class. Of course he did, Theresa thought. Poor baby got lost at Disneyland two days ago and then was taken for a hike out in the cold the very next day. But she merely clucked and assured Mike that she would take care of him. And he appeared hesitant as he looked at his son and looked at her. Time stopped and in that second Theresa knew that he wasn't sure if his mother was in a good frame of mind to care for a sick toddler. Her own son doubted her.

She looked away for a second, then held eye contact with Mike, which was difficult considering that he was several inches taller. And it was not lost on her that the tables were turned, that he was no longer the teenager who'd stayed out too late or dented the car. He was not being taken to task. She was. So she looked into his eyes for that moment, cradling a sick, whining child, just like the three sometimes-sick, often-whining children she'd lovingly raised, and that was all she had to do. He felt what she conveyed with her eyes: *Do not doubt that I can do this.* He knew and she knew and nothing needed to be said. Mike kissed her cheek and Leif's wispy blond head and went out the door, reminding her that Heather, his wife, would be home by 5:30.

Theresa began putting the silverware away. Leif had eaten an orange and crackers for lunch and was now taking a blessed nap. He had required constant attention, as she expected, and it had taken every ounce of energy she could muster. There were women – celebrities, lawyers – who began having children at the age of forty-seven! She figured it wasn't so bad for them because they had nothing to compare it to. How did they *do* it? Well, they had nannies and maids. She had forgotten about that. She briefly wondered what that would be like. And a chef! Might as well dream big while you're dreaming.

While putting the knives away, she saw the little spreading knife, the one with the metal floral-designed handle that matched the old silverware set. It made her want to cry, and she had no idea why. Frequently during the past two years (yes, she realized, since Leif's birth), she would feel like crying for no reason. It would consume her, made her gasp and bite the inside of her lip, trying to hold back the tears. She often chewed the inside of her lips, a habit stemming from childhood. But this, when the crying jags would come, was a severe bite, a clamping down, a holding on for dear life.

She had been like that since she could remember.

The second of three children, with an older sister and a younger brother, Theresa had always been accused of being melancholy. People – relatives, kids at school – were forever asking her, *Why do you look so sad?* Even as a child she grew tired of the question, the supposition and inference that she was deficient because she was not bubbly and ridiculous, and later she became outright exasperated about it. But, she realized now, there had been an element of truth to it. Her first major depression had occurred at age ten, when her little brother Mark, then six, found her curled up in the bathroom, crying. He looked at her and began bawling, howling as he ran out of the room. And she didn't know why she was crying! She never did! Looking back, she decided it must have been caused by the onset of puberty, but still. She didn't know anyone else who responded to it like that.

It didn't help matters that her father, the youngest son of Irish immigrants, was prone to mood swings exacerbated predictably by alcohol. He was not physically abusive, just easily angered. Theresa recalled him punching a hole in the wall to kill a spider that her sister had been afraid of. *Daddy, there's a spider! Come quick!* After her third request, he entered with a scowl, and Bridget pointed to the wall. *There's your damn spider,* he yelled after throwing his fist through the thin wall, then stomped back out of the tiny room that the girls shared. They quietly cried about the hole, the undeserved blemish on their small sanctuary, as much as they cried about the yelling. He would save them, but they would have to pay. Then, without prodding or nagging on anyone's part, the following weekend he quietly fixed it while they were out grocery shopping with their mother. Their father put up billboards for a living, so he had access to the tools and materials necessary to do the job properly, leaving only the faintest trace of the offensive hole. They came home, helped unpack the groceries, and went to their room to read when they noticed the smell of fresh plaster and discovered the patched hole. Their father, they surmised, was at the bar, and she and Bridget looked at each other knowingly. It was an unspoken belief between them that it would be best not to acknowledge the fixing. Best to leave it a "mystery." An unexpected act of contrition.

Leif stirred then, sniffling and crabby. She had finished putting the dishes away a while ago and tore herself away from staring out the kitchen window to go and get him, to keep her unspoken promise to her son. Too much in her family went unspoken, she realized with regret. *Why don't we just say what we're thinking and feeling? Why don't we acknowledge it, celebrate it, accept it? It's as if in speaking our truth we give it life, and we're too afraid to do it, too afraid to let it be. Too afraid of our own vulnerability.*

Theresa went into the living room where he slept on a green-flowered comforter that had been folded in half on the floor and picked up her little grandson. She held him close, nestling his body into her front.

She eased herself into the brown upholstered rocking chair, the same one she had rocked her own three children in, and proceeded to rock in slow, grand, undulating movements. It was as soothing to her as it was to him, and together they relaxed into her hypnotic rhythm. She hummed a made-up tune, the same one she had hummed to her children years ago. It was sweet, high and low, lilting but serene. Leif settled into her shoulder.

The living room of her tri-level home would not be on the schedule of any holiday open-house tour of homes. It was usually in some state of disarray, although at least the furniture, a cognac leather couch and chair with a shiny black coffee table and matching end tables, was up-to-date, thanks to a shopping spree last year during one of her "energetic" episodes. Breathless and smiling, she had charismatically explained to Peter, invoice in hand, that their home was in dire need of some updating, *especially* the furniture. They still had the same particle-board bedroom furniture from when they were first married, for God's sake! Definitely time for updates! Peter was not easily convinced, but at least he didn't make her return anything, as he had with the diamond and sapphire necklace that one time.

But the wallpaper in the living room was getting dated, the geometric print with metallic backing. And she never liked the cream-colored painted bricks around the fireplace. They still had the huge, old built-in quad style stereo instead of the newer separate components that the kids were buying. Mike had one, and Kat was saving her allowance and gift money for her own. The TV wasn't very old, so at least there was that. And they were all thrilled with Theresa's recent purchase of a VCR, even Peter. It seemed that these days that was the only thing he enjoyed – watching a movie on the VCR. That or reading, as long as wine was involved.

She had to admit that Peter had incredible patience with her, though. She'd been in a depression again, for over a year, almost as bad as when she had postpartum depression with all three of the kids and needed medication. She probably needed it now but was holding out, trying to prove to herself that she could beat it on her own. She loved her children and her grandson! Why should taking care of them as babies cause her to pitch headlong into this churning, roiling blackness of despondency? And then, like clockwork, as soon as she took the medication she was catapulted out of the depression and into this state of extreme energy, in which she became the bubbly, ridiculous person she eschewed in adolescence. She would buy things they couldn't afford and didn't need, like the ill-conceived, flat-bottomed fishing boat for Peter and the kids. Peter had never fished a day in his life and had no desire to. That went back, along with lifetime gym memberships and a down payment on a timeshare in Florida.

Sometimes her energetic phases lasted longer, such as during her college years. She was a good student, very productive even though she liked to drink and go out with friends, got by on little sleep since she was working in a bakery while taking a full load of classes. She graduated with honors and received an Associates of Applied Science degree in Paralegal Studies at Berkeley College, then moved back to southern California to work. She loved her single life, often indulging in shopping sprees, excursions to the day spa, or impulsive weekend trips to New York City. She had a few affairs and a couple of one-night stands, but where was the harm? Life was to be enjoyed.

She spent eight years swirling through this flighty yet productive phase, periodically getting too bubbly and ridiculous but not realizing it at the time. Usually about five days would go by and she'd be back home, physically and mentally, taking stock of what she'd spent, where she'd been, whom she'd slept with. Most of the time there wasn't too much damage control to be done. Except, to her deepest chagrin, for the night with Bridget's fiancé. No amount of apologizing could undo that. No amount of self-flagellation could make Theresa forget. But she shamefully got on with her life.

Somewhere near the end of those eight years she met Peter in court and knew that she wanted to be with him, craved his stability, his steadfastness, his love. They went out to dinner and he sent flowers to her office. He took her to Chatsworth Park for picnics and they would lie on her father's old plaid wool blanket and feed each other grapes and look longingly at one another. She loved his soft blue eyes and baritone voice and his analytical mind.

They married a year later, and Mike was born a year after that. Thus ended her eight years of being a single professional woman and began the almost twenty years of being a stay-at-home mother. The occasional bouts of medication made her feel better, but then she felt wired, unable to focus properly during the day or fall asleep at night, with the random thoughts racing through her mind. She didn't know where they came from; it almost seemed that she had accessed someone else's thoughts, for they were not hers. Fleeting, nonsensical, relentless. Her brain constantly hummed while she tried to sleep, until the baby woke up and it didn't matter. She went on like that for months until she stopped taking the medication. Then she'd be all right until she felt the urgent need to revamp her wardrobe or add to their record collection or liquor cabinet. She drank more during the energetic phases, wanted to go out to dinner, have sex more frequently. Her senses were heightened, like everything was right at the surface of her skin. But she never cheated on Peter; they had both seen the demise of too many marriages, and she had no desire to do that to him, nor to herself.

Not surprisingly their sex was different during those times, and it was almost as if Peter felt uncomfortable with it. Or maybe he was uncomfortable with her. Usually they had sex with a dim light on, because that felt right to Peter, to keep things simple and emotionally accessible, superficial. "You're too pretty to have the light off," he'd say, wooing her with a thinly disguised compliment, even though she knew he meant it. But when her senses were heightened, she wanted to have sex with the light off. Peter protested not being able to see her, and she told him, "Sometimes I like to feel the darkness around us. Like we're in our own little world, just our bodies, surrounded by emotion, surrounded by fate." The mention of fate seemed to make Peter nervous. He let her have the lights off, but it was the fastest sex ever.

Rock, rock, rock. She hummed, more for herself than Leif, who had fallen back asleep. She couldn't stop rocking; something in her propelled her to continue, even though she could have easily gotten up and put Leif back down on the blanket. She had been off track for so long, and recently it was getting worse. All her life she felt like everything was outside of her control, and on top of that, now she felt like she was losing her already fragile identity, if it was not already gone.

*

Danika Zarachnak had learned all sorts of American phrases in the four months since she had immigrated. She learned "I'm just pulling your leg" meant that the person was joking, although usually in a way that would make Danika look foolish. She learned to "have butterflies in your stomach" meant that you must be nervous, but it was said in a way that made whatever Danika was nervous about look trivial. "Fuck you" was easy to learn, of course, especially when *not* to use it. But the phrase that she now knew the best was "you have your hands full." That's what neighbors would say as she took the two children in her charge, three-year-old Eli and one-year-old Brittany, for walks to the local park. And there was always the underlying tone of "better you than me," but it took Danika a while to figure that out.

She knelt down on the beige carpeted floor of baby Brittany's room to change her diaper, mindful to put her on top of the changing pad, as the children's mother, Lisa, had instructed her to do. "She's too big for the changing table now, but we want to make sure the carpet's protected." Lisa hadn't taken into consideration that while Danika was changing Brittany on the floor, her big brother might decide to push the pink wooden rocking chair over to the changing table, climb up on it, and stand to reach the pink ceramic flower vase on the shelf above the table. Lisa hadn't instructed Danika what to do when that happened. If she got up to take the vase from Eli, he might drop it onto the baby before she had a chance to get to him.

Not that he would intentionally throw the vase on the baby. Eli loved his little sister and would readily plant kisses on her, take her hand and show her things. But Eli possessed an intense combination of curiosity and high energy, and a lack of awareness typical of most three-year-olds. "Flowers!" he exclaimed, as if he'd procured them at long last. He held the spherical vase with both hands and sniffed the yellow tulips as Danika gently suggested he put the flowers down; they were not toys.

I must be "multi-tasking," she thought as she quickly taped the sides of Brittany's new diaper without looking at it.

Eli laughed and tried to jump up and down with the vase in his hands, his brown curls bouncing on top of his head. "Flowers, flowers, flowers!"

"No jumping on the table, Eli! Stop!"

Water, of course, sloshed down the side of vase and he dropped it. It ricocheted off the side of the changing table and onto the floor, inches from Brittany's head. The contents spilled out, but the carpet had softened the blow to the ceramic, and the vase was intact.

"Flowers fall down!" In a tone suggesting that his work there was done, Eli turned and began his quick descent down the rocking chair.

Brittany, still on her back as Danika threaded her legs into her lavender fleece pants, craned her neck to see what had happened, as oblivious as her brother to how close she had come to sustaining a good blow to the head. She rolled over and stood up as Danika adjusted the waistband, and squealed with delight as she followed her laughing brother out of the room.

"Gaaahh!" Danika growled. She did not feel that she had any particular gift with small children, especially after what had happened with Leif at Disneyland. All she knew now was that she didn't want to have any for a long time, making a mental note to ask her boyfriend where she should go for birth control pills. They'd used condoms the few times they managed to have sex, but she didn't want to take any chances.

Danika popped her neck and went to go get a towel. She knew she should bring Eli back to make him help clean up ("He's old enough to learn the consequences of his actions!" his father, Ben, had instructed her when she had mentioned that Eli found it funny to throw food on the floor), but she could just do it faster herself. And nothing had broken, so there was no need to tell Ben or Lisa and risk being lectured.

They were lovely people, really. They did have high expectations, but Danika would expect that of what her boyfriend called "Hollywood People." They were TV producers, and she had been their live-in nanny for the past three months. She had her own bedroom and bathroom, and her own TV. She had weekends off and was given $500 a month for spending money. They provided meals for her and made her feel like a member of the family. She didn't know how she was going to tell them that her Visa had expired.

But her boyfriend knew, and he could help her. One Saturday about two months ago, on her own at Venice Beach, she walked into a Mexican restaurant, and there was Eddie Montoya, waiting tables and looking quite debonair with his slicked-back short hair and inviting smile, his crisp white shirt and his deep brown eyes. After she had eaten her chicken enchiladas, which he had recommended, he asked for her phone number. She told him about her living situation and that she was an immigrant. He said that he understood; he was one, too.

As a child, even a toddler, Danika used to take off down the street. She knew she wasn't running away, she just wanted to go somewhere else. Her earliest memory was at the age of three when a loud plane flew over her head while she was out playing in the backyard, and she had shouted, "Airplane! Airplane! I want to go on airplane!" Sixteen years later, she was on one bound for New York.

Her grandmother, Olga, had told her stories about her Great Aunt Anna who went to America – New York – at the age of seventeen, by boat. And she got married, had children, and eventually owned her own business. It was always Danika's dream to follow in her great aunt's footsteps, to go to America and be successful. To live the American Dream that she'd heard so much about.

A textbook middle child, Danika had to fight for attention, and was an average student in school. Her parents, Magda and Thomas, loved her as well as her older brother and younger sister, but seemed more interested in their jobs. Both being math teachers, they were colleagues, and they tended to focus more on their own relationship than their children. They supported Danika's plans, even helped to pay for her airfare, but the only thing they ever encouraged her to do was math, which she was disinterested in. Danika often had great difficulty saying no to dares, such as running through a local field and slapping the cows on their haunches, or walking her bicycle up a large, steep hill, upon which stood Saris Castle, and riding the bicycle straight down, resulting in a concussion. Jumping off the roof of the family's townhouse on a dare at the age of eleven had not deterred her from future ill-advised ventures. She broke her ankle and hated not being able to walk while healing.

Danika didn't really think of herself as so much of a daredevil, although her family and friends did. It was more a need to be active, to be doing something, going somewhere, "living on the edge," another phrase she'd heard people say in America. She could understand Eli's energy, his need to climb and jump, to smell the flowers on the high shelf; she was not so different.

And where was Eli? She quickly finished blotting the carpet and picked up the vase to refill it in the bathroom. The two curly-headed cherubs were in Eli's room, playing with his train set. Danika returned to Brittany's room, picked up the flowers and reinserted them in the vase, which she returned to the shelf as she heard the phone ringing downstairs.

Eddie!

She leaped over the child-proof gate at the top of the split staircase and rushed through the spacious home to pick up the phone in the kitchen before the answering machine got it. "Davidson residence," she greeted, as Ben and Lisa had instructed her.

"I'm looking for a very sexy young lady," Eddie said with a bad French accent.

"I'm sorry, but you have the wrong number," Danika said, smirking.

"Danika, it's me!"

"I know. I said a joke about your joke!"

They laughed together, something she enjoyed about him. Then he asked her how her day was going, and she told him about the vase fiasco. She reminded him of the

Disneyland scare and suggested that she should find another type of job, even though she loved the kids.

"Danika, you don't realize how good you've got it. Most illegals are standing in parking lots waiting to get picked up by contractors, or cleaning their houses while the wives lay out by the pool or go get their nails done. You should be grateful."

She didn't mean for it to happen, but defensiveness surged within Danika. "It's not my fault! You know what happened and why I am now illegal! This was not in my plan! You should be supportive!"

"You complain too much. I'm supportive, but you're so self-centered! You're too concerned of what others think about what you think you should do, which is why you came here in the first place."

She didn't know all of what he said, but it didn't sound good. "You're talking too fast and I can't understand you! You do it to make me feel stupid!"

As Eddie began to object, Danika hung up the phone and wiped away frustrated tears. How could he do that to her? Say such things? Last week he had told her that he loved her. And she had said the same in return. But now she wondered, slumped on the beige tile kitchen floor, feeling hopelessly stuck, feeling like a failure, how much was love and how much was need? Where did one end and the other begin?

CHAPTER THREE

Anna remembered the first time she saw the Statue of Liberty. It was not a drawing, nor a photograph in a newspaper or book. It was with her own eyes. And she was not yet two years old.

They were leaving, not arriving; she and her parents and older brother John were on their way back to Czechoslovakia, although it would not be called that for another seven years. It was 1911 when they left the United States. Her father had been a coal miner for five years where they lived near Lansing, Pennsylvania. Labor strikes hit one after another, and they feared for their jobs and the hard-earned money they had saved. He had also been told by a doctor that he needed to get out of the coal mines to save his ailing health, to potentially, hopefully, reverse the debilitating effect on his lungs. So they packed up their meager belongings, took the train to New York, and boarded a vessel headed for their old home. Anna watched as the big statue got smaller and smaller while they steamed away. She knew that she saw it; she could still see it in her mind's eye. People – including her own children – told her that she only thought she remembered it because she was actually remembering pictures she had seen of it. How could they say that to her? They did not know her mind, they were not in it, remembering. They only focused on the fact that she forgot about a doctor appointment a few days ago.

They think because I forgot something so recent that I could not possibly remember something so long ago. But I do. They do not know what it is like to remember everything, both the happiness and the pain. To remember the details so vividly that to remember is to laugh again, or cry. To remember the Statue as it faded into the horizon, and my mother weeping, and being too young to wonder why, so I wept with her. That is what I remember. Not a drawing, not a photograph. My own memory.

Her eldest child, her daughter Anya, was coming over for a visit that afternoon. It was common for people of her ethnicity to name their firstborn children after themselves, the mothers as well as the fathers. But she and Michael did not want exact duplicates. It was so confusing! There were already so many Johns and Michaels and Annas. They decided that a little change would be good. Every one of their friends was so surprised when they did not name Peter after Michael, but they accepted it when Michael explained that he wanted to name his son after his father. Anya was similar enough to Anna that no one had questioned it. They named their third child Marya, after Anna's sister who had died at the age of thirteen in Czechoslovakia.

Anna's memories of the old country were vivid, but dark. Everything was dark; even the snow had shadows. The raw memory of the break-in that had occurred two weeks ago was dark like that. She shuddered thinking of it, the violence of it, and how it reminded her of violence she had witnessed as a girl in Czechoslovakia, when it was still called the Austro-Hungarian Empire. She remembered in the middle of World War I, in April, 1915, when the Hungarian police came to take her father away to force him to be a soldier. They were peaceful people, living in small villages in the Carpathian Mountains with their own small family farms. Each family had a couple of cows, some chickens and pigs, and they grew wheat, cabbage, and potatoes. Her father, Michael Petrovich, was the mayor of the village and raised work horses to sell. He kept two so that they had colts every year. Her father's frame was characteristically short and hardy, as were most of their people – Rusyn, they called themselves. They were hard-working, not the "lazy gypsies" they were mistakenly called by the Hungarians. In early 1915, they started running the Rusyns out of their villages, taking the men for soldiers and leaving the families unprotected. Some of the villages were burned.

She remembered the night that her father was taken, when she was five years old. The Hungarian police loaded up horse-drawn wagons with munitions and kitchen material, and as her father was saying goodbye to them, kissing them and telling them to be brave, the police hit him with a club, making his knees buckle as he fell to the ground. Anna cried out and her mother screamed. The police grabbed him and dragged him up until he could walk. When they reached the wagon that he was to walk beside, her father made the sign of the cross on himself and the police hit him again. Anna cried, feeling her father's pain, and her own fear. Then they were forced to march. Her father and the other men went one way, and Anna, her older brother, their mother, and baby sister went with the rest of the women and children in the opposite direction. The darkness of that night echoed in her mind.

As Anna sat on the couch crocheting a blanket, waiting for Anya to arrive, she thought of her own children. Anya had taught her to crochet when she had the twins and stayed home with them for three years. Anna loved to knit slippers for all of her family every year for Christmas gifts. She knit blankets when all the subsequent babies were born (Anya's twins received theirs later) and knit sweaters for birthdays. She loved to do it; it was a creative outlet for her, stress release, even. And what she made served a purpose. Now that everyone was grown and had their own families, and since Michael had died, she needed that. There was no one else to take care of.

Anya had been a model child. They never had any problems with her. She helped out with household chores, she took care of her younger siblings, she was a good student, and she was the only one of Anna's children to learn Slovak, to care about learning it because it was part of her heritage. Peter and Marya could not even pretend to be interested. But Anya learned; she was always compliant, respectful. She loved reading and went to college to become an English professor. She married Tom Reilly, an economics professor, twenty-six years ago, and they had the twins, Claire and James, who were now twenty-two. James was in grad school to be an accountant, and Claire was a fledgling reporter who lived with Marya, her aunt.

Marya. How could she have two daughters who were

so different? Marya complained about the simplest of chores, she wanted to play outside instead of playing dolls with her older sister, and she never seemed satisfied with anything except sleep. That child loved to sleep! She loved to climb trees and play baseball with the neighborhood boys. Maybe that was why she slept so much – she wore herself out playing outside all day long. In school she did the bare minimum that she could to receive mediocre grades and didn't find her niche until her junior year of high school, when she started writing for the school newspaper. She got her degree in journalism and was now an editor for a newspaper in Tucson, Arizona. Eight years younger than Anya, she was still single, and seemed happy that way.

Peter, her only son and middle child, had been a well-rounded sort of boy. Like Anya, he was usually compliant, and often played the role of peacemaker between neighborhood children. He enjoyed sports a bit, but he usually preferred indoor pursuits. He liked to read and draw, and he even liked to cook. He was good about doing his chores, and he was also a good student, although he did get into a few fights. Anna didn't mind because she knew he was defending what was right. He went to USC to become a lawyer, specializing in divorce law. He met his wife Theresa through his work, and they had three children, two boys and a girl. And the older boy, Mike, named after his grandfather, had given Anna a most amazing gift - her first great-grandchild. It filled her with pride to think of all she and her children had achieved, to think that they were now a fourth-generation American family. Her husband would have been proud, too.

And now another branch of the family tree had touched down in America. Anna's great niece, the daughter of her sister Olga's daughter, had arrived a few months ago. Danika was nineteen, just two years older than Anna had been when she immigrated back to the United States after growing up in Czechoslovakia, and she saw a lot of herself in her great niece. She saw the apprehension when she first arrived, knowing little English, missing her loved ones, becoming familiar with new, gregarious extended family members. But she also saw the indomitable spirit of adventure, the thrill of making a dream come true, or at least completing the first part of it. Feeling her feet walking on new ground. There was something about the immigrant experience that made one feel stronger than one ever believed possible. Anna knew that Danika felt it too. It connected them and it connected the thousands of others who had trod in their footsteps.

Anna had always wanted to crochet an all-white blanket. She wanted it to be of the softest, most pliable yarn so that the blanket could sink into every crevice of her body as she curled up in her favorite rocking chair. It was old, a high-backed mahogany giant that Michael had made during her first pregnancy. It was shipped from New York to California when they relocated in the late forties. She had rocked her three children, her five grandchildren, and now her great-grandchild in it, but her old bones needed some new padding. And white was pure, simple, beautiful, like snow. She hadn't seen snow in a long time, with her own eyes. She didn't miss the cold, but she did miss the ethereal grace of the snow, God's blanket for the earth. She remembered five-year-old Anya, arms outstretched, twirling around in the gently falling snow one morning when they lived in New York.

Anna heard a car pull up the driveway, then a knock at the door, and got up to let her daughter in. Anya had not been looking well these days; Anna suspected it was because she was not getting enough protein. Anya refused to eat most of the traditional fare that they had been raised on – sausage, cabbage, eggs, cheese, and bread – stating that it would be murder on her cholesterol, not to mention her diet. But Anya had lost a bit of weight recently, so the diet must have worked. *Maybe too well*, Anna thought, eyeing her daughter's thin frame as she stepped through the doorway.

"You need to stop diet, Anya," she told her as she embraced her.

"Hi, Ma. I'm off *the* diet now." Anya constantly corrected her whenever Anna didn't attach an article to her nouns. But that was how she was taught to speak English, she tried to tell her daughter, and it became a habit she was never able to kick. Anna would occasionally remember to use an article, but then she would revert to the old structure that had been second nature to her for so long. Michael had spoken the same way. It was how they were taught, they always told Anya.

She came in with brown paper grocery bags in her arms and walked over to the kitchen to deposit them on the counter. Her shoulder length silver-streaked hair did not move as she walked. Anna noticed that she was wearing jeans and tennis shoes, not her usual dressier work clothes with pumps. "Made any chocolate chip cookies lately?"

"Yes, have some." Anna padded along, following her daughter into the kitchen. "They're right here. What is all this in bags? I have food."

"I figured you might need some fresh produce, Ma. I don't know how often you get to the grocery store these days." She tucked a lock of stiff hair behind her angular face as she began unpacking the lettuce, tomatoes, carrots, broccoli, apples, and pears she had brought. "I also brought some chicken; I thought I'd make dinner for us tonight."

"What about Tom?" Anna asked. She had always liked her tall, strapping son-in-law who made sure to greet her with a smile and helped her with yard work.

"He's fine; he and James are going out for pizza tonight." Anya finished putting the food away, folded the bags, and put them under the sink. She bit into one of the chocolate chip cookies. "Oh, Ma, these are the best! I'll make us some tea to go with them."

"You have as many as you want," Anna said, heading over to the couch. "See what I started on?" She held up the beginnings of her blanket. "I always wanted white one for myself."

"That's going to be beautiful, Ma."

"You showed me how, remember? When you were going to have babies and you got so big, doctor said you had to stay off your feet? And you were so bored that you told me to come over so you could teach me to crochet. You said if you didn't have something to do you would go crazy!" *And that was when I told you that soon you would know how consuming it is to love your children.*

"I remember, Ma," Anya said wistfully. "Then they were born and I felt like I was going crazy anyway!"

They talked for a few minutes about what the twins were like as babies, how James was a lot like his Uncle Peter and how Claire was so much like her Aunt Marya. Anna asked how they were doing lately, and if she had heard from Marya, who didn't come to visit as often as they all would have liked.

"I talked to Claire last week, and she said that both she and Marya are going to be coming for Easter next month, so that will be good." She picked up two white porcelain saucers with matching tea cups and headed back to the living room. Her hands shook a little as she placed the steaming cups on the wooden coffee table in front of her mother and sat down next to her.

"Ma, I have something to tell you that will be hard to… accept," Anya began, and took a deep breath. "I found out that I have ovarian cancer, and it's not treatable. It spread too much. I…there's nothing they can do, Ma."

Anna's eyes widened and she felt her heart skip a beat. She tried to sound nonchalant. "No, no, you're just sick. You can get better. Just get back to healthy weight -" *Not my Anya! Not my good girl!*

"Ma, it's cancer. I'm sorry to put it so bluntly, but…I'm not going to get better. It's not just a matter of gaining my weight back."

Anna persisted. "But we don't have cancer in our family. You remember a few years ago when I had that lump, and it was – what's the word?"

"Benign."

"Yes."

"But mine isn't benign, Ma. It's called malignant. It's in an advanced stage." Anya seemed so calm. Anna figured that she must have known about it a while.

"But you're too young! You're only fifty-three!"

"Age has nothing to do with it. Even children can have cancer."

"Why didn't you tell me sooner?" Anna's eyes watered and she felt her throat constrict. The reality suddenly hit her and she turned away, unable to look at her daughter. *Why didn't I feel this? Why not me?*

"I just found out a few weeks ago, Ma. We weren't sure at first; they were doing tests...ovarian cancer is not as easily detectable as other cancers. When they discovered what it was, it was too late for surgery. It had spread to the lymph nodes...They tell me I have three to six months to live," Anya said quietly.

Anna felt it then. She felt a throbbing ache in the region of her ovaries, a hard pulling sensation. She winced, crying. Ever since she was a young child, whenever she was near anyone who was in pain, she could feel it. Her mother had told her it was a gift, but it always felt like more of a curse, this physical empathy, this pain-filled connection she shared with others. Whenever she heard a child cry out in pain, especially one of her own, a stabbing jolt hit her. It was as if she were trying to take away the pain, lighten the load, partake of the suffering. Her connection with her daughter was so strong that it surprised Anna that her ovaries did not begin this pain-sharing sooner, even before Anya knew.

"Ma," Anya whispered. She put her arms around Anna as they sat on the couch. "I know this is hard. I'm sorry...I've stopped teaching. Tom and the kids and I are going to take a trip to Ireland in two weeks, and Tom's taking the next term off. I want to spend a lot of time with you, too. Maybe we can crochet something together." Anya pulled away and looked at her then, her brown eyes filled with tears.

Anna's mouth quivered and her breath was shallow. She could not contain herself any longer and embraced her daughter as she cried - hard, rasping sobs that raked one's soul. *Anya! My sweet little* dievca, *my girl. My beautiful white snow, washed away by the pouring rain.*

*

Theresa could hear the rain drumming on the roof above the kitchen, could see it drizzling down the top of the slanted skylight above her head as she put the flour and sugar back in the pantry.

She had been making a blueberry pie for dessert and felt good about getting back to baking, her main creative outlet. She loved the precision of baking, the almost guaranteed formula. She loved the fact that if you followed the recipe exactly, you could produce something that tasted so good and brought pleasure to those you love.

And she did. Theresa baked everyone's desserts for their birthdays, including Heather's. She loved her daughter-in-law (although it felt strange to say that she had one, when her son was only nineteen) and in some ways identified with her, realized that with all the times she screwed up taking the pill in college, it was a wonder she hadn't wound up pregnant at that age. And Heather was quiet and respectful, as Theresa had been, and she appreciated that. But the similarities ended there. They looked nothing alike, for one thing. Heather's brown hair was cut shorter than Mike's, which he seemed to be growing out. She was also considerably shorter in height than Theresa, and had an annoying, breathless laugh that always sounded gratuitous. She did plan to go to college eventually but wanted to major in "business and marketing," which sounded like a vague, unoriginal cop-out to Theresa. Half of the teens she came in contact with – Mike's and Kat's friends - said that's what they wanted to major in. But Heather graciously helped with chores and cooking, which Theresa found invaluable. She decided she could look beyond the irritating laugh and vapid life plans.

Theresa wiped down the counters where she had assembled the pie. She realized that baking gave her a sense of purpose. Not that taking care of her grandchild and children wasn't purposeful, she just felt that she wanted to be doing something additionally, after all this time. Baking contributed something tangible. Baking was creative. And it tasted divine.

Well, only if it was from scratch. She recalled the time when she was in college that she and her then-roommate Mandy (whom she really needed to get back in touch with) had bought cake mix at three in the morning after leaving the bars one night. A just-baked chocolate cake sounded like an ideal way to top off the evening, and fortunately there had been a 24-hour supermarket within walking distance. They also thought it best to stock up on a bottle of tequila and another bottle of wine while there, congratulating themselves for thinking ahead. Surprisingly, the cake had not been burned, but not surprisingly, at least in retrospect, it tasted like brown margarine on a brown sponge. She never made cake from a mix again.

In fact, she thought about starting a bakery but realized that she didn't want to get up that early. Of course that wasn't much of an issue in college, when she seemed to have more energy than she knew what to do with. Why couldn't she be that way now? Obviously, she was twenty-five years older. But still. She would give anything to feel that fire within herself again, that aliveness, that focus and drive. She really needed to go back to work, but the thought alone was daunting. So much had changed in the legal system! She couldn't possibly just jump back in.

Theresa stuck her head out of the kitchen in the direction of the living room to listen for Leif, who was taking a nap there. It had taken her about forty-five minutes to prepare the dough for the crust, roll it out, combine the ingredients for the filling, and make the crumb topping. Leif's naps usually ran about an hour to an hour and a half at this age, so she figured she had about thirty minutes left. She loaded the mixing bowl and other utensils in the dishwasher, along with the breakfast dishes. She groaned as she wrestled with the top rack of the thirteen-year-old 'Harvest Gold' appliance, which matched the refrigerator, stovetop, and oven. They all looked so dated and were showing signs of wear. And the dark, drab oak cabinets? The fake brick linoleum? The fluorescent tube lighting? Talk about depressing. She vowed that the next room she updated would be this one.

Maybe the kids could vote on it. Kat would immediately agree, and Mike would too, but Joseph probably wouldn't have an opinion, at least from an aesthetic standpoint. He was nothing like Theresa's father, whom he was named after. Joseph wasn't temperamental and gregarious; he was introspective and, for a nine-year-old, pleasantly consistent. He was his own self. Mike was very much like Theresa's brother, Mark, who was steadfast yet open-minded, compassionate yet diplomatic. Nothing like Kat, who was like Bridget in so many ways. The competitiveness, the self-centeredness, the superficiality. She hated to think these things about her own daughter, but she couldn't deny that the traits were there. Kat was the middle child just like Theresa; why weren't they more alike? Maybe because Kat wasn't content to take the back seat, and Theresa accepted it.

She and Bridget hardly talked, still, twenty-four years since it happened, since she slept with her sister's fiancé. Theresa had lost count of how many times she'd apologized over the years, but it seemed that no amount of apologies could get through to Bridget how deeply she regretted what she'd done. Finally, about ten years ago, they just settled into a routine of acknowledging each other's presence on the occasions that they saw each other. They even air-hugged, as if the other were sick, contagious. (Perhaps Bridget thought Theresa was.) Even with these pretenses for everyone else's benefit, Theresa still could not look Bridget in the eye. When she spoke to her, she looked elsewhere – her chin, her forehead. Theresa felt that she did not have that right; she still felt twenty-four years of shame and regret. She would have felt like an imposter if she looked into Bridget's eyes, like someone worthy of communicating with her sister on a level she hadn't experienced since childhood: a level of trust, of camaraderie, a level of understanding, and love. She had forfeited all of that twenty-four years ago.

But Theresa couldn't allow herself to dwell on it or she would go to an unbearable place of self-flagellation and sadness. And she had been there too many times before. To distract herself, she finished cleaning the kitchen and walked through the family room/eating area adjacent to it and around the corner into the "formal" dining room. It was small by dining room standards; they'd had to remove both leaves to fit the large, ornately carved oak dining table in the room and still have walking space. And of course they rarely used it. They could only fit six of the matching carved, cane-backed chairs - with the gold velveteen cushioned seats - around the table. With the leaves in place it would seat twelve, and the rest of the chairs were stacked in the storage area under the stairs.

Theresa bent down and opened a door of the six-foot long matching buffet cabinet to find the cardboard box of Easter decorations.

There were two and a half weeks until Easter, and, though it wasn't as much of a production as decorating for Christmas, she still enjoyed it. She loved pulling out the fake straw baskets that she had bought for each of her children when they were babies, filling them with the scrunchy green paper grass, and setting them on top of the buffet. She pulled out one for Leif and Heather. Then she pulled out the crystal basket and filled it with white paper grass. Peter had bought it at Robinson's department store for their first Easter together and filled it with his mother's hand-decorated pysanky eggs. Theresa loved the bold red, yellow, black, and green geometric designs that Anna was so skilled at making. Some years she had tried different types of designs, so their collection was varied, and each egg unique. They were stunningly beautiful, and Theresa was as proud as Peter to display them.

There were the construction paper bunnies that the kids had made when they were younger, the yellow daffodils made out of cut-up, painted egg cartons, the poem about "spring-time eyes" and "rainbow-colored eggs" that Mike had written in school and put in a painted popsicle-stick frame. Theresa walked out to the living room and began to place the homemade decorations on the walls, noticing that Leif was beginning to stir.

Suddenly a sonic boom filled the house, a crashing explosion that made her jump and shake. She gasped, Leif began shrieking, and she dropped the stack of decorations onto the stereo cabinet. It had come from the kitchen, and she started to run in that direction, but stopped herself when she realized she should pick up Leif so that in his state of hysteria he wouldn't fall down the stairs. She grabbed him and held him close, told him he was okay, and walked back to the kitchen, her heart clanging in her chest, her limbs shaking uncontrollably. Leif hiccupped sobs into her shoulder.

Theresa peered around the corner and saw little cubes of broken tempered glass everywhere: the fake brick floor, the Harvest Gold tile counters, the lidless fruit bins, the desk area by the phone, the gold-orange carpet in the family room/eating area, as well as the fake oak table where they usually ate. Everything was covered in broken glass. The oven door had exploded, her pie was inedible, and she couldn't feed the hungry, upset toddler in her charge because she couldn't get anywhere near the kitchen. She felt herself going to that dark and hopeless place she'd tried to avoid and wanted to sob along with him.

CHAPTER FOUR

Peter held Theresa's coat for her as she slid her arms into the sleeves. He kissed her neck and smelled Chanel No. 5, her signature fragrance. She had probably worn it when he met her twenty-three years ago. It was the easy gift for birthdays or anniversaries; she didn't seem to mind her annual bottle. Peter, an if-it-ain't-broke kind of guy, liked it on her, even after twenty-three years. And this year, for her forty-seventh birthday, he really didn't know what else to get her, in addition to the new kitchen appliances, which he knew were *not* birthday gifts.

She'd had various interests over the years, including baking, gardening, reading true-crime novels, and even golf, for a while. They seemed to be distractions rather than hobbies, since nothing really stuck (except baking). But Peter encouraged her to try new activities, anything to relieve the doldrums that hung overhead at certain times over the years. Theresa would throw herself into her new obsession with exuberance, and during those times she would be upbeat, engaging, and happy. And then her interest waned, or her energy lapsed, or something happened that caused her to drop the interest like a summer crush and return to her melancholic, unmotivated frame of mind. The cycle was disruptive and exhausting, affecting the entire household. They'd nixed the annual family ski trip two months ago because of it. Everyone seemed so distant from each other. They hardly talked around the dinner table, if they even ate at it. *It's not supposed to be this way,* Peter thought.

But she seemed positive tonight, enjoying the spotlight of her birthday dinner at a local seafood restaurant. It had been a rough week, what with the exploding stove, and Peter wasn't sure what to expect with her. He wasn't even sure if she'd be willing to go out at all, since she hadn't wanted to go to Disneyland with them a couple of weeks ago. He told her then, as he slipped her camel hair coat over her shoulders, that he was glad she felt well enough to go out, that he enjoyed having dinner with her.

She turned to look at him, and he saw a slight glare. "I'm not *sick*, Peter. I'm just tired sometimes."

Peter didn't feel like reminding her of all the things she'd missed in the last couple of months because of her being "tired." It would not have been worth a spoiled evening. And it *had* been a good evening - a good day, in fact. It was Saturday, so Peter worked in the yard. He fertilized the lawn and finished pruning the rose bushes, which he disliked. The leaves had brown spots, and the roses looked more like dying red carnations. They were leftover from Theresa's gardening phase, but he figured that taking care of them was easier than taking them out. He tried to get Joseph to play catch with him in the backyard, on the small patch of lumpy grass adjacent to the wooden deck, but that lasted all of ten minutes.

"Dad, you know I'm not a sports guy."

Peter coughed. "Well, I'm not really either, I just thought it would be something fun for us to do on a Saturday afternoon, just a father-son thing," Peter responded, putting his arm around Joe's shoulders.

"Well, how about playing chess?"

"Okay, Joe," he said as they walked back inside. At least Joe wanted to do something with him. Mike was too busy between work (he was a shift manager at a fast-food taco place), school, and having a two-year-old to take care of. At least he was under the same roof and Peter could see him occasionally. He wanted to spend more time with all of his children, but that seemed to be harder and harder to accomplish. Kat seemed to view him as the most embarrassing father to walk the planet, and now that she had her driver's license, she rarely needed him for anything anymore. Peter happily taught her to do her tax return last weekend because it was tangible time that he could spend with her, although of course she was less than thrilled. He looked forward to spring when she would have track meets that he could attend, if she didn't think he would embarrass her. He was reaching for anything. His little girl was almost grown up! He loved to remember her wispy blond toddler hair, so soft between his fingers. He would run them through her hair every night when he tucked her in. Now he considered himself lucky if she yelled out "Night, Dad!" before shutting her bedroom door and putting on her headphones.

Dinner went fairly well, although Theresa had not been as conversational as Peter had hoped. Any other observant husband might have thought that his wife was being cold and quiet in a passive-aggressive way, but Peter knew that sometimes Theresa was just that way, and it had nothing to do with him.

He handed Theresa her purse and they headed out to the parking lot. The heels of her knee-high leather boots scraped and clacked on the wet pavement, and she held onto his arm. He loved that. He loved moments when he felt like a protector; he took pride in that. Since he wasn't a "man's man," a fishing-hunting-camping-football-playing guy, he always felt like he had to prove himself, like he was lacking. He hoped that he didn't project that onto his sons, even though he made sure to let them know that he valued them no matter what. He always tried to teach them that the pen is mightier than the sword, and if a guy's smart enough, he can figure out a solution to anything.

This line of thinking was something that he ascribed to early on, an indirect result of his verbally abusive grandmother. When his older sister Anya had been a baby, their paternal grandmother came to stay with them in New York. Their parents were both working at the Endicott-Johnson shoe factory. It was a far better living than mining coal, and their parents were glad to have the work. They planned to save up money so that they could start their own construction company, and they paid for his mother to come to America and watch Anya during the day while they both worked. She was not a loving, nurturing grandmother. She was a bitter woman who never wanted to leave Czechoslovakia in the first place and resented watching the children, verbalizing this to them on a daily basis. One of Peter's oldest memories was when he was three years old and Anya, seven, dropped a bowl of batter for the pieroghies she was going to make for dinner. It splattered to the floor, and Baba smacked Anya's head, causing her to lose her balance and fall into the mess. "Stupid girl!" she yelled in Slovak. Peter, sitting at the table, started to cry, and Baba turned to him. "You stop crying or I'll give you something to cry about. And you better be smarter than your sister and your mother or you'll be *no good*, just like them." Her shrill voice still resonated in his memory. Every time he heard Slovak words it reminded him of her.

He and Theresa got in their old blue station wagon, which they both hoped to replace sometime soon, and began the drizzly drive home in silence. The windshield wipers beat rhythmically across the window, almost hypnotically. He wished he could read Theresa's mind, even just for a day. It might help him to understand what was going on with her, to figure out a way to help her. He thought it might be manic-depression; her symptoms and patterns pointed to that, from what he'd read about it. But she wouldn't admit that she needed help, so he didn't know what to do. He really wished that she would start working again, even just part-time. It's not that they needed the money; he took pride in supporting his family, sexist as it might sound. It made him feel valued, needed. But he knew that Theresa was not thriving, that she would benefit from some outside interaction, from reclaiming her identity. She could do something in the mornings and then be home in the afternoons for when Joseph got home from school. They could find a babysitter for Leif. He wondered if Theresa was trying to be the grandmother that Peter should have had, that in some roundabout way she was trying to undo the damage that was done to Peter by taking care of Leif. They'd never talked about it, but Peter wouldn't be surprised if that had something to do with it. And as much as they loved their grandson and wanted to help out their son and daughter-in-law by opening their home and being supportive, it was an emotional strain, especially for Theresa, who watched Leif every day. But Mike and Heather were nowhere near ready to get a place of their own. Mike had at least three years left to finish his history degree, and Heather, who was also nineteen, worked at a clothing store in the mall. She was a sweet girl, loved Mike and was a good mother to Leif, but she wasn't the brightest. Not exactly college-bound, Peter had to admit. At any rate, Theresa felt as strongly as he did about helping out their son, being supportive on all levels, so that was good. At least she didn't openly resent their presence. But, Peter had to admit, it was taking its toll on his wife and their marriage.

On the positive side, he was glad to have a night out with her, just the two of them, glad that she was receptive and gracious and, yes, still beautiful. He would do anything for her. To Peter, loyalty was more important than love - because love wasn't perfect. Of course, he still loved Theresa, doldrums and all, and so he vowed to make the best of what he had. She hadn't turned into a recluse, she still took care of herself and their children and the house, she could still talk politics and tell courtroom stories and make a good impression when she needed to. And they even still had sex a few times a month.

But Peter wanted her to be better. He missed her vibrancy. He missed the woman who loved to plan international trips with him that they'd probably never take, and laughed together about that. He missed the way they would see a movie in the theater and laugh at the same lines. He missed her smile most of all.

He stared at the road ahead of him, the wipers still going. Theresa didn't like listening to the radio anymore, so all they could hear was the sound of the road beneath them. Then, out of the corner of his eye, Peter saw something that made his heart jump, almost as much as when Leif had been lost at Disneyland. It looked like a man lying by the side of the road, and he wasn't moving. Theresa saw it too.

"Peter! Stop! There's a man there!"

"I see him!" He hit the brakes, being careful not to lock them or start hydroplaning, and he stopped about a hundred yards beyond the man.

"What should we do?" Theresa cried. "We have to do something!"

"I wish we had a car phone so we could just call the police. I don't know what to do, Theresa! We can't put him in the car! We'll have to just get to the nearest phone and call the police and describe to them where he is."

"Well, what if he's alive? We should check! We can't just leave him here if he's alive!"

"All right! I'll go check. You stay here," Peter said, reaching in the back seat for the umbrella. Then he began walking back to where they saw the man.

God help me, see if he's still alive. The man is dead, Theresa. He was probably drunk or high on crack and wandered out on the road and got hit. How would I know if he's dead or not? I'm not a doctor, for crying out loud. I certainly don't want to touch the guy.

Jesus Christ.

He's dead, all right.

The man's head appeared to have been bludgeoned. He was face-down on the wet, muddy ground by the side of the road, wearing blue jeans, once-white tennis shoes, and a quilted plaid flannel shirt. Peter could not determine the man's age or his ethnicity. In shock, his heart racing, Peter said a quick prayer for the man's family and jogged back to the car.

"He's dead, honey," he said, shoving the umbrella in the back seat.

"How do you know?"

Peter described what he saw as they proceeded toward a gas station up ahead. Theresa cried and stayed in the car while he ran up to the window that housed the night attendant at the self-service station.

"Hey, you need to call the police. There's a dead body by the side of the road back there," Peter said, pointing.

"I can't dial out," the twenty-something guy said without looking up. His baseball cap covered his eyes.

"Call 911! This is an emergency!"

"What should I tell them?"

"Tell them what I said! Tell them there's a body on Colima Road about a quarter mile south of this cross street! I think the guy's been murdered; his head was bashed in."

The attendant made the call and then told Peter that he was supposed to wait for the police to arrive. He went back to the car and was glad to see that Theresa was no longer crying.

"Oh, Peter, it's so horrible. I can't stop thinking about it. What if he had a family?" Her eyes were red and she started wringing her hands in her lap.

"Honey, calm down. We're doing all we can. The police should be here soon, we'll tell them what we saw, and then we'll go home and have a cup of tea and you can take a bath. How does that sound?"

Theresa breathed in sharply. "I've never seen a dead person before. I mean, aside from my grandmother when she was in a casket. Not someone who had been killed like that."

"It was definitely unnerving," Peter said, not mentioning that at the age of seven he had sat with his dead grandmother for two hours because he thought she was sleeping on the kitchen floor. She had had a massive stroke, but he had no way of knowing that. He found her there on the floor when he got home from school and stayed with her until his parents got home.

Peter was glad that Theresa had stayed in the car and not seen the condition the man was in. She reached across to him then, her arms outstretched, and he held her. At least she still turned to him for comfort, and it was good to feel her, smell her hair. He lightly ran his fingers through it, just because he couldn't help himself.

*

It was Saturday, Danika's day off, and Ben and Lisa had dropped her off at the newly restored Pier while they did some shopping with the kids in Santa Monica. It was cloudy and cool, but not raining as it had been most of the week, and she couldn't wait to get out of the house. She also couldn't wait to see Eddie.

They had made up immediately, passionately. He had called her back within minutes, apologizing, readily taking the blame. She cried and he soothed her, told her he knew it was not her fault, her illegal status, told her he knew what it was like, how awful it felt, like you're always looking over your shoulder, like someone's coming after you in a scary movie, like something-something. And she told him, *Slow down, I can't understand you.* And the next day he came to the house and brought her pink carnations from the store. And they kissed in the rain and Danika thought, *Yes. He really does love me.*

Everyone fights. My parents always fight, and they still love each other. It doesn't mean you're not right for each other.

She had thought before that someone loved her, but now she realized it was probably just romantic friendship or temporary infatuation. She had grown up with Damek Nagajda, a soft-spoken guy with a stocky build. They had started school together at the age of five and ended at eighteen. He was her boyfriend for a year when they were

sixteen and when she began studying English and indi-
cated a desire to go to America, they began to drift apart.
Damek thought that he might like to travel someday and
see America, but he planned to go to school to become a
dentist and work and live in Czechoslovakia. They stayed
friends after breaking up, and when Brian Leech from
Australia attended their school as an exchange student
their last year of secondary school, Damek seemed to understand and even tolerate Danika's fascination with him,
since he was from another country and spoke English.
Damek graciously stepped out of the picture.

Danika dated Brian for about eight months; they spent
the last few months of the school year as a couple, and
then they toured Europe together. She fell in love
quickly, practically love at first sight, and fell hard. Brian,
tall with sandy blond hair and a fetching smile, was her
ticket to making her dreams come true, if not in America,
then in Australia. He was witty, charismatic, and loved to
travel. Absolutely perfect, Danika thought. And Brian
told her that he was just as crazy about her as she was
about him. They toured German castles and had fun in
Amsterdam, and under the Eiffel Tower he asked her to
marry him. They spent the next week deliriously happy,
talking about having their wedding in Australia and hon-
eymooning in Hong Kong.

Then that summer came to an end, and Danika went
back to waiting tables at Reagan's Café, named after
Ronald Reagan and full of American memorabilia. She
was saving money to move to Australia, but first she
wanted to visit relatives in America on the way there, as

a stopover. She saved up enough to get to Los Angeles via New York, and her parents helped her pay for the Australian leg of the ticket. She applied for a three-month U.S. visa, even though she only planned to stay one month, and excitedly packed her bags. She would see Yosemite, the Grand Canyon, Venice Beach, Disneyland, and her Aunt Anna.

In retrospect, she realized that Brian probably thought that she wouldn't really make it. She had called him the night before she left Czechoslovakia, and he sounded stunned, which she took to be excitement. He told her that he couldn't wait to see her (in a hesitant voice, she thought in retrospect), and she boarded that plane with a sense of elation like nothing she'd ever experienced. She was doing it! She was going to America and then getting married and going to Hong Kong and then going back to live in the different country and she would own her own business - a travel agency – and then she would be living her dream. And she *might* have children. She wasn't sure about that one yet.

She arrived at the airport in New York early in the morning and had a two-hour layover until her flight to Los Angeles. Customs was exciting for her; she thought about how different it was from going through Ellis Island in the early part of the century, needing shots and a shower. Here, she just waited in line, walked up to the window at the green booth, handed the official her passport and visa papers, and was finished in five minutes. She walked over to the gate for her flight to Los Angeles, checked in, and went to go find a pay phone to call Brian.

It took him a while to answer, since she forgot that it was the middle of the night over there. "Bugger off, who is it?" came his angry voice.

"It's Danika."

"It's three o'clock in the morning!"

"Sorry, I do not know the time in Australia. I am in New York!"

There was a pause on the phone, and then Brian said, "New York? Well...Danika, actually I think you should stay in America. It's just...I don't think you should come to Australia, see? I uh...I feel differently now, I'm really not wanting to get married. I'm sorry. You're a great girl and all, and I had a really great time with you last summer, but things have...changed. It's time to move on, you know? I'm sure you'll meet lots of cool American guys, being the sweet girl that you are. Okay?"

Tears sprang to Danika's eyes and a wave of panic nearly knocked her to her knees. "You do not want to marry me?" she stammered.

"Aw, Danika, I'm sorry. But I just can't...I gotta go," Brian said, yawning. "I hope you have a great time in America! Good on ya!" And he hung up the phone.

A deep sob became stuck in Danika's throat. How could he do this? After all their plans! She went to the bathroom and sat in one of the stalls for twenty minutes and cried. She didn't know which was worse – the rejection or the feelings of failure. What would she do now? How could she tell her parents? She walked through the airport in a daze, trying to find her gate, trying to figure out what on earth to do, trying not to feel betrayed.

But then she was warmly welcomed in Los Angeles and tried to forget about Brian Leech. She spent the first two weeks sightseeing and visiting relatives. Then she found her live-in nanny job, and soon after, she found Eddie, who made her feel like a goddess, even though sometimes he showed off by talking too fast in English. But she knew she could trust him, that when he said he loved her he meant it. She felt sure that what happened with Brian happened so that she would meet Eddie. *Everything happens for a reason,* she told herself, proud that she had learned another American phrase.

Danika, wearing jeans, a turquoise and purple flowered top that Theresa had bought for her, and a black twill jacket, stood in front of the burger place where Eddie had told her to meet him, and just as she started to wonder where he was, he came up behind her and said, "Hi, beautiful." She turned around and their lips fused. She breathed deeply and tasted his minty tongue as it explored her mouth. Then he gently pulled away, smiled, and gestured with his head. "You hungry?"

Danika smiled back and told him "a little bit," so Eddie, still in his restaurant work clothes, bought some fries in a paper bag and they began to walk together. He held the fries in one hand and put his other around her shoulder, and she alternated putting fries into both of their mouths. They commented on the construction of the amusement park and how fun it would be when it was finished – the roller coaster and Ferris wheel, maybe other things. It would be a few more years until completion, Eddie said, but maybe they could both be there for the grand opening?

Danika felt her stomach flip with excitement – not about the amusement park, but because he wanted her to be with him years from now. Maybe before then they'd be married; she would no longer have to hide her status. She smiled broadly and told him yes, and Eddie smiled and kissed her. They finished the fries, threw away the bag, and walked holding hands, commenting on the seagulls perched on the pier.

"Let's walk on the beach," Eddie said. "What time do Ben and Lisa pick you up?"

Danika looked at her watch. "In an hour."

Eddie commented that they had plenty of time and steered her onto the sand. They walked slowly, their tennis shoes (his black, hers white) sinking into the cool sand. Danika looked out at the choppy, dark waves and realized that she had not yet seen a California beach looking how she expected it to look! But she had arrived in November, and it was late March. Eddie mentioned that someday he would love to show her the beach in Mexico; it was much warmer and more beautiful. He had explained previously that he was from Mexico but he was half-Mexican; his father was from Spain and met his mother while on a business trip in Mexico City, where she was the concierge of the hotel he stayed at. Eddie was seven years old when they immigrated to the United States, but he remembered how it felt to learn a new language, to be in school where everyone around you is speaking it. To feel lost and vulnerable.

A few other people milled about on the beach, walking or reading a book on the sand. Eddie said he wanted to show her something and they moved toward one of the empty lifeguard stands. As they approached it, Danika noticed pieces of white copy paper had been taped together to create a sign with letters drawn with multi-colored markers, saying, *Will you marry me?*

She gasped twice, looked at Eddie's expectant face with his thick, raised eyebrows, his full lips turning up into a hopeful smile, and proclaimed *yes, yes, yes, yes, yes* as she threw her arms around him and backed him up against the lifeguard stand for an exuberant kiss. The seagulls squawked overhead, but Danika tuned them out. She would be okay. She didn't have to worry about being deported and having to face her parents. She focused on the fact that now her dream could be salvaged, and in the back of her mind wondered what level of certainty was necessary for true love.

CHAPTER FIVE

Anna rolled up the sleeves of her robe and started boiling the second batch of eggs. Anya had told her not to; she might burn herself, the pot would be too heavy, she might boil them too long. How silly! After all these years, one thing I know I can still do is boil eggs. She may have taught me to crochet, but I taught her how to make pysanky.

Because that is what a mother teaches her daughter. That and so much more. Sometimes, a mother teaches her daughter what not to do.

Anna was about ten when she began to realize that her mother was a mousy, quiet sort of woman. The other women in the village did not respect her, sometimes to her face, and she said nothing to defend herself. She just looked away, acting like she didn't hear, or laughed with them when she couldn't look away. One or two of the women started having Anna's mother do their laundry because they offered to make halupki, a cabbage-wrapped meat dish, for Anna's father, claiming that her mother's halupki was no good. So she would do their laundry while they talked about her behind her back. Anna recalled the time she had to go inside for more lye and overheard two women behind the house. One of them said that a good man like Michael Petrovich was wasted on a woman like Mary Surdulla. Anna's eyes stung with tears and she vowed that she would never be passive like her mother. She swore that when she was a grown woman she would command respect.

But her petite mother did teach her several useful things, among them how to grind wheat, bake pascha (bread), churn butter and make hrudka (cheese), and how to make pysanky. Mary Surdulla's pysanky was exceptionally beautiful. That was probably why the other women in the village hated her – they were jealous. A woman's pysanky was her crowning glory and, traditionally, when she became of marrying age, the best pysanka was given to the boy that she hoped to marry. That was how Mary Surdulla got Michael Petrovich, or so the rumor went. It was her pysanka. Anna knew that and it made her proud, but it confounded her. She couldn't understand why her mother would let the other women walk all over her and take advantage of her.

Anna turned to her handsome father, short of stature but taller than most Rusyns, their growth stunted by a diet high in carbohydrates, to learn whatever else she needed to know in life. He taught her about horse breeding, bee husbandry, local politics, and America. Her mother never spoke of America after they returned to Czechoslovakia, so Anna would go to her father as he was cleaning their beehive out behind the house, and he would answer her questions about what it was like in the coal mines, where they lived, and if they would ever go back. He told her he wouldn't, but someday she could.

In America, no one hit a man for making the sign of the cross in front of a wagon. No one forced a man to leave his family to fight for the side that turned around and persecuted them, turned them into little better than slaves. Serfs working the communal land, no longer their own farms. But that was after the war. That was after the Hungarian police took her father one way and then took her mother, brother, sister, and her the other way. They were forced to leave their home and their village to march through snow-covered mountains to go to a holding camp. A policeman carried Anna while her pregnant mother carried her three-year-old sister. Her brother John, seven years old, was forced to walk wearing nothing but burlap slippers. Anna cried as she witnessed her brother's suffering, felt his pain searing through her own little legs. His feet became frostbitten and he caught whooping cough. She remembered his final days, still in the holding camp two months later, when she sat with him as his violent coughing racked his small frame, and she felt his pain reverberate through her. She sang songs to him and sang stories to him about brave men like their father, who would come to take them home. Their mother sang with them. Everybody sang, as if they could sing away the pain.

Their father did survive the war, even though John did not. After three months, the families were allowed to return to their villages. Anna's village was among those not burned; others were less fortunate. After the family had been told that he was dead, her father returned home six months after that, his already weakened lungs further violated by tuberculosis, although they didn't know it at the time. After the devastating news of her father's supposed death, Anna's younger brother had been born prematurely, shortly after they returned to the village. He only lived three anxious weeks, throwing Anna's mother into a debilitating depression. Most of the traditionally female chores fell to six-year-old Anna, and whatever she could teach to four-year-old Marya. The horses were gone, but to Anna, most things were the same. They had a cow, a pig, chickens, and bees again. After his return, her father slowly regained his strength and her mother ventured back into her role. The village seemed to slowly come back to life, even though many of its members were no longer with them.

But life went on in the Rusyn village. They eased back into their seasonal patterns of a life that centered around the religious holidays of Byzantine Catholicism. Christmas came first after her father's return, a six-week long celebration that began on December 6th, the feast of St. Nicholas. They would receive stockings with hazelnuts and homemade candy and cookies. Christmas Day, per the Gregorian calendar, was on January 7, and the Epiphany, Christ's baptism, was held on January 19. The whole village went to church and then went out the creek to bless the water. There would be a church procession with the priests in elaborate vestments, ankle-length linen robes and Phelonion, a type of cape with embroidered edges, and an Epitrachelion, a long stole-like garment wrapped around the backs of their necks with the front ends, embroidered with crosses, hanging nearly to the hem of the robe. Altar boys, dressed similarly but without

Phelonions and Epitrachelions, carried wooden crosses and icons. That year that Anna was six, the wind was frosty, but not the ground. The tradition was for the priest, as soon as everyone had crossed the creek, to break the ice at a thin area, bless the water, and then all the villagers would take some and anoint themselves with the blessed water. The significance was cleanliness before a holy supper - the Christmas feast. As the procession crossed the creek, followed by the villagers, the ice cracked and everyone fell in. The freezing water came up to Anna's shoulders! She could still feel it, how it seemed that her heart stopped from the cold. They all remembered it as "the year the whole village was baptized." The villagers, unfazed, quickly returned home to dry out and warm up and prepare their traditional feast. The Christmas Feast was a twelve-course meal without meat or dairy products. They ate nuts, vegetables, pieroghy (a hearty potato-filled pastry), garlic in honey, etc. Her father dipped his finger in honey and put a cross on everyone's forehead, so that they would be loved and protected. Then he tied a rope around the kitchen table, signifying that the family would always stay together. When Anna left for America, she tearfully told her father that she was sorry to break the rope. He looked her in the eye and said, "We are always together in our hearts."

Easter was always the biggest holiday. It was preceded by a strict forty-day fast during which they could not eat any eggs, meat, or dairy products. This forty-day fast was difficult for the farm people. When they could at last have eggs, they wanted to show their appreciation by decorating them as beautifully as they could. Each year they added to their beloved heirloom pysanky collection. In preparation for Easter, they also made kielbasa sausage and pascha, big round loaves of bread, some as big as a washtub. They made bacon seasoned with paprika, chunks of butter carved into the shape of sitting lambs, horseradish, hrudka, and halupki. They put all this wonderful food into hand-woven baskets covered with elaborately embroidered coverlets, and then they would carry all of it to the church to be blessed by the priest. Anna remembered how her father carried their heavy basket in front of him and balanced the big pascha on his back. It looked funny on his short, stocky frame, and she giggled, carrying a candle behind him. All the villagers slowly made their way up the slippery, muddy hill to the church. One man ahead of them dropped his basket with all their food in it, and all the beautiful pysanky rolled down the hill, past the other villagers, who tried their best to get out of the way. Right behind the pysanky came the man's big pascha, bouncing and rolling like a loosened bicycle wheel. Everyone was afraid to laugh; the family's Easter feast had just rolled into the mud, and they felt bad for them. But then the man who had dropped his basket called out, "Well, I'm not surprised those little devils went, but the big devil went too!" And they all laughed, and after church and the blessing of the baskets, everyone shared their food with the family who'd lost theirs.

Anna smiled at the memory while she extracted the eggs from the hot water. She held each one individually on a slotted spoon as she ran it under cold water and then deposited it on a kitchen towel that was spread out on the counter. These days, her pysanky was far less elaborate than when she was younger. Just as her mother had wooed Anna's father with the intricate designs of her pysanky, so had Anna wooed a boy as well. His name was John Nagajda, and he was the most handsome boy in her village, with beautiful blue eyes, a smooth, round face, and a strong build. He was also friendly, helpful, and smart. All the girls in the village felt the same way, and for Easter one year, he received seven pysanky. But he told Anna that he would have picked her even if she hadn't made the best-looking pysanka. And then she started to fall in love.

Anya knocked and walked through the front door then, followed by Danika, who had come to help with the preparations for Easter dinner. Anna figured it might be the last year that she would host it. She didn't want to think about the fact that it might be the last year that Anya attended.

"Ma! What are you doing? I told you not to start the eggs alone," Anya said, setting a bag of groceries on the kitchen table. Danika set another bag down beside it.

"I know how to boil eggs, Anya!" Her daughter, looking weaker but in good spirits, came over to embrace her, as did Danika. "But I don't know if I can do fancy designs anymore. Not as good, anyway. Where's Claire and Marya?"

"Well, we'll just dye them then. That'll save a lot of time," Anya said as she turned back to the groceries.

"Claire and Marya are right behind us. They'll be here soon. And Danika has some exciting news!"

Anna turned to her great niece. "What is your news?"

Danika smiled and blushed. "I am…engaged! My boyfriend Eddie asked to marry with me!"

"Congratulations!" Anna said, and went to her to kiss her cheeks the European way, first right, then left. "I am so happy for you. And is he citizen?"

"Yes, but I want to marry with him also if he is not a citizen, because I love him." Danika still smiled, but Anna recognized something in her face, ever so brief. But it was there.

She's settling, Anna thought. Her visa expires in two months and she doesn't want to leave. Well, why would she? My mother was sad to leave the opportunities that this country offered us, and I would be too. Danika is adventurous, like me, and also smart. Surely this Eddie is also an opportunity to her, but a big one at that. If Danika's not sure he's 'the one,' so what? Love can grow from opportunity more easily than opportunity can grow from love. I know how that is.

"Well, bring him to Easter dinner tomorrow!" Anna said.

"Thank you, Teta Anna, to invite him, but he has to work."

"Where does he work?"

"Ma!" Anya said. "Enough with the third degree!"

Danika smiled nervously, probably not knowing what the third degree was, and said, "On weekends he works at a restaurant, but he is a car mechanic, and he wants to have his own mechanic shop in the future."

"That's good. Owning a business is best way to get ahead. That's what Michael and I did with the shoe store and then construction business when we came here from New York. Eddie is smart guy, I think!"

"Yes, he teaches me to speak English better, too!"

"Dobre," Anna said quietly, the Slovak word for good. Danika smiled and Anna continued, "Now, will you help me make halupki?"

Danika assured her that her grandmother, Anna's youngest sister Olga, had taught her well. She reached for the cabbage and began preparing it, and Anna told her where the pan was to cook the ground beef that would be rolled inside. Anya announced that she would get started on the pascha, and Anna began making her special prune butter crescent roll cookies, a recipe like so many others that she had memorized from years of experience. She mixed the dough and rolled it out flat while reminding Danika of the steps for making halupki. Fifteen minutes later, Anna was nearly finished spreading the prune butter onto the triangular-cut pieces of dough when Marya and Claire arrived.

Anya may have been her good girl, but Marya was her lost lamb that Anna always hoped to bring back to the flock. And she loved them both equally. But Marya was harder to love, with her defiance while growing up and her emotional distance as an adult. But somehow, Anna saw more of herself in Marya than she did in Anya. She saw the fire in her that made her go after her goals, and she saw her self-respect. Marya would never tolerate anyone talking behind her back – or even to her face – as Anna's mother had done. And Marya had a lot to be proud of, having become the editor of a large city newspaper two years ago at the age of forty-three. Anna was very proud of all of her children; she loved to tell people that she was the mother of a professor, a lawyer, and an editor. She even stopped asking Marya when she was going to get married.

Marya boisterously entered in her typical extroverted way. Her short brown hair had spiky edges, and she wore jeans, a black leather jacket, and black boots. Anna wondered what she would wear to the church service tomorrow, or if she would even go. Well, at least she was here.

"Hi, Ma, you look good," Marya said as she set her luggage down and hugged Anna.

She always says that, even when I'm in my robe and my hair is under a babushka. Sweet girl.

Anna kissed Marya and held her own hands out to the side to avoid touching her. "Sorry but my hands have prune butter on them."

"Let me go take off my jacket and I'll help you," Marya said as she walked back to the living room.

Claire walked up and hugged her grandmother. "Hi, Baba. It's good to see you." Claire, a gorgeous blend of Eastern and Western European lineage, smiled broadly and pushed some of her chin-length auburn hair behind her ear. She was taller than Marya, but the two shared a similar energy that seemed necessary for success in the field of journalism.

Claire briefly greeted her mother and cousin, since she had already spent the morning with them. She gestured to the triangle cookies on the kitchen table. "Would you like help rolling those up?" she asked, pushing up her sleeves.

"Yes, sweet girl. And I will get everything ready to do the pysanky," Anna said. *Oh, I love Easter.*

*

Danika placed the last rolled halupki in the rectangular glass pan and spooned a tomato sauce mixture over the top of them, noticing that they looked like little burritos from Eddie's work. Then she covered the entire pan with plastic wrap and found room for it on a shelf in the refrigerator. She hadn't made halupki in over six months (since she had been working so much before she left for America), and it made her feel homesick for a moment. Not because she wanted to be back home, but because she missed the familiarity of it. It was difficult being around new people and food and a different language for a sustained period of time. She missed not having to think every minute, to not have to constantly wonder if she was doing or saying something correctly. But the trade-off of making her dream come true was worth it. She had no regrets.

"Teta Anna? What bowl for the pysanky for the...for the colors?"

"We can use coffee mugs up in that cupboard," Anna said, pointing to the cabinet above the dishwasher.

Danika reached up and pulled down five white ceramic mugs with dark blue around the rims. She set them on the counter where she had made the halupki.

"Let's do it on the table, so we can sit while we make the designs," Anna directed.

"You're not making pysanky, are you?" Anya called out to her mother. "I thought we were just going to dye them this time."

"No," Anna said, "I decided we are making pysanky. Don't argue about it."

"I'm not arguing! I'm just saying we don't have to make pysanky. And anyway the eggs are hardboiled; you didn't empty them."

"So we'll eat them; I don't care. Or we can keep them until the whites dry. I have some old ones like that. They don't stink." Anna's face looked sad as she brought the boiled eggs over to the table. Danika realized that it would be Anya's last Easter, unless a miracle happened. She knew that was why Anna wanted to do the pysanky anyway. Danika avoided her great aunt's eyes and poured water into each of the mugs.

Anna handed Danika a bottle of white vinegar with a spoon and quietly said, "Put a spoonful into each cup while I prepare the kistkas." Danika poured vinegar into a small bowl to make it easier to measure out spoonfuls for the mugs. Anna pulled some beeswax out of a plastic bag on the table and broke off small chunks to put in the brass receptacle on the end of the kistka, the tool used to draw the wax lines on the eggs. She prepared three kistkas this way and set them aside. Then she picked up the box of food dye and handed the red and yellow droppers to Danika. "Let's do ten drops each."

When the dyes were ready, Anna lit two votive candles that were in glass holders on the table, sat down, and picked up a kistka. She looked at Danika, seated to her right. "You've done this with your baba, right?"

"Yes, Teta, she showed me, but she always said that your pysanky was better," Danika said, smiling and picking up a kistka.

"Oh, that is sweet of her to say. Really it was our mother who had the best pysanky." Anna called over her shoulder, "Claire? Sweet girl, come and make some pysanky. Marya, Anya, you too." She set the kistka back down and picked up a paintbrush instead.

As the other women made their way to the table, Danika said, "My baba also said that your other sister made black pysanky. How did that happen?"

Anna closed her eyes for a moment. "Yes, that was our sister Marya. That was who I named this Marya after," she said, gesturing to her daughter at the end of the table. "She was about thirteen, and she had made pysanky year before, but she wasn't paying attention and left her egg in the black dye too long. Dye seeped under the wax and made whole egg black! Everyone in village heard about it."

Danika smiled and said, "It's good we don't have black!" She held her kistka in the flame of one of the candles to melt the wax.

"Sounds like something *I'd* do," Marya said with a laugh as she reached for an egg.

"You do remind me of her," Anna said, smiling. She picked up a paintbrush and an egg.

"Ma, let's not do the intricate Ukrainian style, okay? That takes too long and as Danika pointed out, we don't have black -"

"All right, all right, Anya. Everyone, let's just do one or two colors using traditional Rusyn style with flowers or sunrays or curved lines. There are also some paintbrushes if you want to use thicker wax. I like to do that for the sunrays; that's what my matka used to do," Anna said.

Danika noticed a faraway look in her great aunt's eyes and wondered if she ever got homesick too, even after all this time. "Teta, how many years since you left home?"

"Sixty-two," Anna answered in English and repeated it in Slovak.

"Very many years," Danika said, gently setting her egg in the purple dye.

"Yes." Anna dipped her paintbrush in the candle wax and continued with her sunray design on each end of the egg. "Claire, sweetheart, make one egg. I know you know how."

"Yes, Baba." Claire leaned forward, picked up an egg and paintbrush, and sat back down. Danika didn't think it really seemed like Claire wanted to participate. But maybe it was because the thought of this being her mother's last Easter saddened her.

Anna broke the silence by saying, "I should have told you before you started, but you have to work your way backwards with pysanky. You think of how you want it to look, and then you figure out steps you need to take make it to look like that." She reached over to dab her paintbrush in the wax again. "I think maybe you can do that with life, too. Yeah? Especially you younger girls. You think of what you want to achieve in your life, and think what are steps that you need to get there. You look at your life backwards and then you can figure it out."

"I will try to do that, Teta," Danika said.

"Yeah, that pearl of wisdom might have saved me some time and trouble," Marya said, dipping her egg in the yellow dye.

"Except that you don't always know where you're going to end up," Anya pointed out, moving her kistka around without looking up from her egg.

"Yes, Anya. There are many things in life that we don't know will happen. We don't plan for cancer and car accidents and strokes. But if you don't have plan, you won't achieve goals. That is my point. Doing pysanky reminded me of that."

"I know, Ma. It's okay," Anya said gently.

Claire stood up and put her egg in the blue dye and announced that she needed to go to the bathroom. Anya asked if she was okay, and Claire said that she was fine. As soon as she was out of earshot, in a low voice Anya asked Marya how Claire had been doing, and Marya said that Claire had been going out a bit but that she seemed fine.

Danika thought about how she would feel if she learned that one of her parents was dying. How she would do whatever she could to get back to see them. Because even though they accused her of being flighty and foolish for becoming engaged so quickly in America, even though she'd always felt like she had to prove herself to them, even though they couldn't even be happy for her that she had found love again after being betrayed, she still loved her parents and would make it a priority to spend time with them before they died.

She had called her parents the night of her engagement to Eddie, breathless and wide-eyed with excitement, and was sorely disappointed that they did not share her enthusiasm. Why did they always have to be so critical of her? Well, they would see. She would do what Teta Anna suggested and look backwards on her life of owning a travel agency and figure out what steps she would need to take in order to achieve her goal. As soon as she and Eddie got married, she would find a new job, maybe in a clothing store. Then, after she had some retail experience, she would work in a travel agency so that she could learn how to manage one.

Danika leaned across the table to dip her egg in the blue dye and, as she leaned back to her seat, placed her hand in the bowl of vinegar she had poured earlier. It immediately spilled and splashed the lower half of her pink shirt and the table.

"Sorry, Teta Anna!" she gasped.

Marya got up to grab a towel and handed it to her, and Anna said, "Don't worry, Danika, it won't harm anything."

Danika looked at her soaked shirt. "Teta Anna, please

I can wear one of your shirts until my shirt dries?"

"Yes, of course. There are some t-shirts in the dresser in the spare bedroom. Go ahead," Anna said, gesturing toward the hallway.

Danika walked down the hallway and around the corner to reach the back bedroom. The door was shut, but thinking that Claire was still in the bathroom, she walked in. She saw Claire bending over the waist-high wooden dresser as she finished snorting a line of cocaine. Danika jumped when the realization hit her.

"Sorry, Claire, I thought -"

Claire immediately stood up and entreated, "Danika, Danika, please, please don't say anything." Her eyes were wide and she rubbed her nose. "Sometimes I need this to help me cope, you know? Do you understand?"

She didn't, but Danika nodded. "I need to find a shirt," she said, holding the hem of hers out to show the spill.

"Okay, well, I better go check on my egg," Claire said as she scooped up the paraphernalia and put it in her brown leather shoulder bag. She left Danika standing in front of the dresser, somehow faintly reminded of being in that bathroom at the airport in New York, shocked, confused, and not knowing what to do next.

CHAPTER SIX

The matriarch in her element, Peter mused as he watched his mother, wearing a faded floral print apron over her blue crepe church dress, direct traffic in her kitchen, telling everyone where to sit at the adjacent dining room table. *Sometimes she's so on top of things, and then other times...*

It was time for their annual family Easter dinner, and this year all of them were in attendance. Usually the guest list consisted of Peter, Theresa, their three children, and now their daughter-in-law and grandson, and Anya and her husband and their children, and sometimes Marya. There had been Easters in the past when Marya had brought along a "friend," always female, often referred to as a roommate, but not this year. Peter knew that she had ended a three-year relationship last year, with a woman he liked and thought was good for his sister, and he felt for Marya. He knew that it had been a difficult break-up. It was good that their niece Claire had moved to Tucson eight months ago to live with her, to distract her. Even though everyone but Anna knew that Marya was a lesbian, it was still not discussed, especially at Easter dinner. Everyone figured that their mother couldn't handle it, wouldn't accept it. Marya tried not to be resentful about living a lie, but Peter knew that it weighed on her.

Danika, of course, was new this Easter. She wore a floral print skirt and blue knit shirt and had her hair up in a bun, accentuating her Eastern European features. She cheerfully helped bring dishes out to the table, bowls of small pascha rolls, sautéed green beans, and decorated eggs and the big plate of halupki. She picked up Leif and hugged him tight and admonished him not to run off again, thinking the two-year-old boy would remember what had happened over a month ago.

Kat and Joseph sat on the couch in the living room, waiting to be called to the table. Kat had her Walkman player on, as she usually did when she wasn't jumping hurdles, swimming, or eating (sometimes). Peter wished she would interact more with everyone, but she resisted his efforts, and he couldn't rely on Theresa for support. He felt like it was up to him alone to steer his daughter into emotionally stable adulthood. Joseph, meanwhile, quietly flipped through an old issue of TV Guide. He looked uncomfortable in his belted dress pants and white oxford cloth shirt, but it was Easter, and they dressed up for Easter. Kat, much to Peter's surprise, wore a pink knit skirt and matching top, which looked appropriate for the occasion. And at least his children weren't bickering, he realized with relief as they got up to walk over to the table and take their seats.

Peter thought of Easters past, when his father sat at the head of the table, leading the family in the singing of "Christos Voskres" – "Christ Is Risen" - before they began eating, and the toasts of "Na zdravie!" as Peter did now. He wondered how his mother felt, remembering, if she stopped to think about it. Maybe she welcomed the distraction of all the people bustling about, clanking glasses and scraping dishes, talking and gesturing, taking pictures. Peter remembered how his father had been the last Easter he was alive - sometimes looking like he didn't remember where he was, who all the people were, how much time had passed. Mike, then eleven, was the same height as his grandfather, his namesake, yet as soon as he would greet him with a hug and a kiss, Peter's father would look at his grandson and ask him, "You go to school yet?" In his mind, his grandson was still four years old, which was the year that he'd had his first stroke and his mind started to go. And he would say that to Mike every time he saw him, from the age of four to eleven. Peter always looked away and choked back tears, but Mike handled it well. He just smiled and said, "Yes, Djido," and told him what grade he was in. "Oh, good boy," Djido – a Rusyn nickname for Grandfather – would say in his high-pitched, scratchy, post-stroke voice, patting Mike's shoulder. "You're a good boy."

Peter looked at Mike now – almost six feet, thin but healthy, with short brown hair and his mother's green eyes. Mike picked up his son and put him in a high chair between himself and Heather. His wife! Peter's nineteen-year-old son had a wife! And a son of his own! Peter was still reeling from that; it had been disappointing, but he was supportive. It floored him to be a grandfather at forty-seven, but, he told himself, at least that way he had the energy to actually play with his grandson. And Heather was a sweet girl, quiet and respectful. Peter would never have pushed them to get married, but they insisted, as soon as they turned eighteen. He could see that they felt they had something to prove, wanted people to see that they were mature. And in some ways they were, but they were still just kids. Peter couldn't understand people who would disown their children or kick them out because of a teen pregnancy. All the more reason to *help* your children! When they need it the most! But it – a teen pregnancy – was still a bit of a blow, especially for a family mediation counselor.

Truth be told, he really wanted to get out of divorce law and focus on counseling. He couldn't stand the constant parade of predictable grievances from stubborn, greedy husbands and shallow, materialistic wives. And the deception! It was demoralizing to hear about so many extramarital affairs on a weekly basis. If his clientele's behavior was any indication of the state of current society's integrity, they were all screwed. If these people had so little respect for the one person who's supposed to mean the most to them, it would be easy for them to be disreputable in their dealings with anyone else they would come in contact with who meant less to them. The thought sickened Peter. The concepts of loyalty and fidelity were dear to him; he wanted to focus more on mediation so that he could convey those values to others, and possibly do something to reduce the abominable divorce rate instead of profiting from it.

His mother would hear none of it - he was a *lawyer*, her son was a *lawyer* – her claim to fame. Admittedly, he had his profession to thank for the opportunity to meet his wife. Theresa had been a legal secretary for the opposing side. Peter, at twenty-six, was representing a man in his fifties whose wife of eight years, his third, had claimed that she'd had an affair due to the emotional stress of being married to a workaholic, therefore she was entitled to half his annual salary for alimony. Peter and Theresa met for drinks that night, vowing that they would never be like that if they ever married someone and had to get a divorce. Peter had been about to say that after all he'd seen, he never wanted to get married at all, but he didn't want to blow his chances with Theresa.

He glanced at her then, sitting across from him, next to Joe. She'd only had one bad day that week, and she bounced back from it. She was doing all right at the dinner, gracious, conversational, not sullen. Their nephew James was seated on the other side of her, and she asked him how things were going in his last term. James, unlike his father, was soft-spoken and subdued, a little overweight, but pleasant. He was probably the most introverted out of the extended family. Accounting seemed to be a good field for him, and he briefly talked about his plans post-graduation, which was in two months. He'd been offered a permanent position in the firm with which he'd done his internship. Theresa commended him for his hard work and wished him well in his endeavors. She ate a few more bites and then told Anna and Anya and Danika how good all the food was. She laughed politely at Anya's husband's joke about President Reagan. Tom, a Republican economics professor, was a convivial, barrel-chested man – the type that students would remember years later as their favorite professor. He and Anya had been married for twenty-six years, and although everything always seemed well for them, Peter couldn't help but wonder what sort of marital problems they'd faced over the years. If they had, they kept them to themselves. Of course they had problems! One thing Peter knew from his work was that no marriage was immune to them. He glanced at Theresa then, talking with Marya now about how her work was going, and he couldn't believe that this was the same woman who, just four days ago, could not, would not, get out of bed. Or who fell in a crying heap on the kitchen floor because someone in their household of seven had eaten the last of the tuna salad, and she had wanted it for her lunch. He was starting to think that some medical testing might be in order, in addition to counseling.

They were telling stories now, his mother and Danika, about Czechoslovakia, and relatives they knew. They spoke half in English, half Slovak, sometimes laughing breathlessly. They talked about an endless array of cousins, uncles, strenas (aunts who were not actually related), in-laws, and everyone's children. One uncle was a colonel in the army. A cousin was a security guard at an apartment complex. Someone's brother-in-law had bad teeth. Little Thomashka, another cousin's ten-year-old son, had two black eyes last Easter. Then Anna retold the story of the pysanky and pascha rolling down the hill on Easter morning back in the village in Czechoslovakia. Marya, smiling, stood up, straightened her green silk shirt and beige slacks, reached behind her for the camera that she'd set on the side table, and began videotaping everyone around the table.

Anna held up her etched crystal water glass and toasted Danika's engagement, prompting more exclamations of "Na zdravie!" and glass clinking, with the nostalgic sound of reverberating crystal. Claire asked Danika if she was going to get an engagement ring.

Anna, sensing some sort of embarrassment on Danika's part, interrupted before Danika could answer and said, "That's just silly tradition. It doesn't mean someone loves you less if you don't have it. I never had engagement ring, and Michael and I were married fifty-eight years!"

Anya spoke up then, exasperated. "Ma, why must you persist in dropping your articles? Till the day I *die,* you'll drop your articles."

All motion around the table stopped. Peter's jaw dropped, due more to shock than planning to insert the fork that had halted right in front of his mouth. Marya, still filming, pulled her wide-eyed face away from the camera to glance around the table. No one could think of a response to Anya's sobering prediction that would most certainly come true, and all too quickly.

It was then that Mike could no longer stifle the laugh that ultimately lightened the room. "I'm sorry, Aunt Anya, the way you said that just sounded kind of funny!"

Peter, mortified, glared at his son and drew in his breath as he readied himself to somehow smooth everything over, to make Anya realize that her imminent death was not something they were all going to laugh about.

But then Anya smiled, and the rest of the table breathed a collective, almost audible sigh, laughed lightly, and resumed eating, scraping plates and picking back up with their broken-off conversations. Their relief was palpable. Peter wondered if his mother even knew what articles were.

He chuckled, thinking of similar tense situations, glad that Mike's outburst had not upset Anya or their mother. He remembered an Easter about ten years ago when Claire had been doing a family heritage project at school and interviewed her grandparents. His parents were talking about relatives, trying to remember names, and at one point his mother asked his father, "Who was that uncle from Svednik who was a drunkard?" His father retorted, "Well, he was from Svednik, but he wasn't a drunkard." His mother waved him away and said, "Okay, let's forget it." They fought a lot while Peter was growing up, he could not deny that, but their usual banter was harmless. Peter found that he missed it. And as his parents got older, they learned to pick their battles and drop things that weren't worth arguing about. Peter remembered when Marya had been a toddler and learning to talk their mother was afraid that her first words would be "Son of a bitch!" because their father would come home from the shoe factory cursing about something every night. Or because their mother would yell at him and tell him to go down to the basement to cool off. But she was right – one night, Marya yelled "Son of a bitch!" in her baby voice and threw their father's hat across the room, just like he did. One of his favorite curses was an old

Rusyn saying that translated to "God strike you dead with lightning!" A few Easters ago, Anna had told the story about how afraid she was that three-year-old Anya would go up to one of the old women at church and say that.

This year, this Easter, no one wanted to talk about Anya. They all tried to pretend that she looked as vibrant as ever, that she didn't have untreatable ovarian cancer, that it wasn't killing her. They all talked to her, of course, asked about her family's recent trip to Ireland, told her how wonderful the food was - the broiled chicken with her special tangy sauce that she'd made, probably for the last time. No one wanted to break open the beautiful pysanky she'd made and spoil the intricate designs, destroying something by which to remember her. Peter felt helpless and awkward. How could he not know what to say to his own sister? His sister he'd grown up with, played with, learned from, idolized. His sister who'd sat in the back of the car with him for over three thousand miles when their family moved from New York to Los Angeles on Route 66, when he was ten. She was fourteen and talked to him like an equal, not a pesky little brother. They both tried to occupy six-year-old Marya with yo-yos and I-Spy games and singing. Their parents argued over the map and Anya would roll her eyes and Peter would try to distract them from fighting by telling them that they were being too hard on themselves and needed to take a break. So then they stopped fighting and tried to find an ice cream parlor. Anya would turn to him in the back seat with a smirk on her face and wink. He would miss her wit, her wisdom, her strength, and her love.

He looked at her then, seated next to Kat, leaning over and whispering something in her ear and the two of them smiling. Was it in response to something someone had said at the table? Was it a quote from Oscar Wilde that fit the situation? He hoped that somehow the essence of his lovely sister would transmit to his daughter, be absorbed by her young heart and mind, and stay with her. Kat was strong-willed and determined, set up for success, but she lacked the one characteristic that would truly enrich her life - compassion. And Anya was the most compassionate soul he knew.

*

Theresa placed the rectangular glass pan of lasagna in the new oven in her kitchen and shut the door. She had used it every day in the past week – first a replacement blueberry pie, then baked potatoes, chocolate chip cookies, and now tonight's dinner. It was therapeutic really, and it motivated her to stay out of bed and helped her to feel purposeful. She set the timer for forty minutes.

"It was uncomfortable and morbid," she said into the cordless phone, which was wedged into her shoulder as she cleaned up the kitchen. "Danika, Peter's cousin who emigrated from Czechoslovakia, and who knows how to speak plenty of English, hardly talked at all unless Peter's mother spoke to her in Slovak. And everyone was uncomfortable because of Anya."

"How much time does she have left?" asked Mark Cassidy, Theresa's brother. Four years younger than Theresa, he was the baby of the family, and the only boy. He'd been a mediocre high school football player, but their parents were proud nonetheless and had attended many games, which they presumably would have had time to do since Theresa and Bridget were away at college. And unlike them, Mark stayed home and went to Cal State L.A. He got his degree in computer science and pursued a good career with Hewlett-Packard, whereupon he moved to the northern half of the state. From then on he was not-so-jokingly referred to as the Prodigal Son, although he – and his wife and three children – were always dearly loved no matter where they were geographically.

"The doctors told her three to six months, and that was two months ago. She looks gaunt; she doesn't look good. I feel so sorry for all of them," Theresa said as she stacked dirty bowls and utensils in the kitchen sink.

"They have two kids, right?"

"Yeah. I can't imagine if Mom died when we were in college. And Peter is losing his sister."

"I would feel horrible if something happened to you or Bridget."

"I miss her," Theresa said quietly, as if not wanting to admit it because she didn't deserve to miss her. She had never talked with Mark about what she had done, but Theresa figured someone else in the family must have.

And she was right. Mark then told her that Bridget had told him why she avoided speaking to Theresa. Theresa told him that she'd apologized many times, including before Bridget's marriage to her second fiancé, the replacement for the one that Theresa had slept with. Theresa foolishly hoped that Bridget would have been more receptive, perhaps in a forgiving mood, since she had found love again within two years and was seemingly happier than she had been in a long time, not to mention preoccupied with wedding plans.

Mark's tone was gentle. "Why did you do that, Theresa?"

She paused and rubbed her inner brow. "I don't think I was in my right mind, Mark. I think I have a disorder that affected my behavior. I'm going to see a doctor about it."

"What disorder could cause you to do what you did?"

Theresa exhaled and sat down at the kitchen table. "I think it's manic-depression, which is now being called bipolar disorder. I exhibit symptoms of both depression and the manic state. One of the symptoms of mania is heightened sexuality, and I exhibited that periodically in my early to mid-twenties. I've felt it since then, and it causes me to dress provocatively and act flirtatiously, although I *never cheated on Peter*." She held her breath waiting for some word of understanding from her brother.

Mark seemed to consider that for a moment, as if remembering some birthday party or event in which she had acted questionably. Then he said, "You may be right, and I've noticed at certain points over the years that you've been depressed."

"Just a few days before Easter it was so bad I couldn't get out of bed!" Theresa quickly interjected. She willed him to understand, to not judge her. To concede that it wasn't some grievous character flaw that caused her to wrong their sister.

"I'm sorry you've been depressed, Theresa. I hope you're able to get some help. And...I wanted to let you know that Bridget is moving to Boston as soon as their house sells. I thought you might want to see her before she goes."

"Boston! What's that about?"

"Bill got a good promotion." Bill Amoruso, the pinch hitter second fiancé, was a marketing executive for Proctor and Gamble, and provided an ample income for his once-jilted wife (Theresa was sure Bridget had filled him in, as she had Mark and, no doubt, their parents) and their two daughters, who attended private colleges on the East coast, which was where Bill was from anyway (New York). He had lived and worked in Los Angeles for twenty-three years and was likely looking forward to returning to his massive *familia*, and being much closer to his daughters, Stephanie and Isabella.

Yes, Theresa told Mark, she would like to see Bridget before she left. And Mark hoped that it was positive and said he would see her soon, and Theresa said thank you and hung up the phone and sat there at the table, twisting her hands and staring at the fake brick linoleum. And Leif woke up from his nap crying as usual and Theresa wondered why she should bother trying to apologize to Bridget again. Why should things be any different? They never were. They never would be.

CHAPTER SEVEN

Anna was proud of the fact that she still had all her own teeth. How many other almost eighty-year-olds could say that? She had strong teeth, strong bones (never broke one), a strong immune system (was never vaccinated and never had any major childhood illnesses), and a strong spirit. She'd always been independent, self-reliant, viewed herself as someone who'd climbed to the top and stumbled a little along the way. All her life she'd been striving to reach some unmarked ideal, like all she *did* accomplish was never enough.

And she stumbled now as she came in from the backyard after watering her bed of petunias. She caught herself before she fell, amazed that her dulled reflexes worked in time, but she noticed that ever since the break-in her right leg always seemed to be popping out of joint and giving her trouble. It was a constant reminder of her vulnerability, this jarring memory of being assaulted in her own home. Peter had hired someone to put bars on her windows, but now she just felt like a prisoner. Like she was the one being punished after her belongings had been stolen. Peter agreed with her, said it was "adding insult to injury," but he said that he would feel better knowing that no one could get inside through the windows anymore. What bothered Anna the most was the loss of her heirlooms. All of them were irreplaceable. Her ruby choker necklace and earrings from the fifties, some old gold rings, her gold watch, her strand of pearls, and her mink stole. She mourned the loss of all of them. She knew that made her seem a bit materialistic, but she felt that with all of her hard work and Michael's, they'd earned it. And everything that had been taken had more senti-mental value for her than monetary. It's not like she would ever sell them or, God forbid, take them to a pawn shop. They had been lovingly worn on special occasions for decades, and now they had been hocked for drugs. It pained her to think that she'd never wear any of them again.

But the missing of her finery paled in comparison to the mourning for her daughter, preparing herself for the inevitable. Anya's impending death made her think al-most constantly of her own mortality, the thought that she might not be able to care for herself alone much longer. Would she need to go to a nursing home? These thoughts weighed on her, and then she berated herself for making it all about her, forgetting that Anya was leaving behind a loving husband and children. That Anya would soon be gone from this world and so would her sweet-ness, her compassion, and her love. Anna remembered the day that Anya graduated from college back in 1956, how proud she was of her daughter. She was the first on both sides of the family to go to college, and then she got her master's degree and became an English professor. Anna wrote letters to her sister back in Czechoslovakia beaming about Anya's achievements.

But each time Anna saw her, she looked paler and thinner, strained, even though she tried to keep a smile on her ailing face. Anya would not want her family to suffer as well, watching her waste away. She laughed and told jokes on Easter and seemed in good spirits even though she moved more slowly and looked like a shell of herself.

Parents shouldn't have to bury their children! I should die first! That's how it's supposed to be! I'm old – not Anya! Life is just one robbery after another. You never know what's going to be taken from you next.

She sat on her couch and cried then, missing her husband, her daughter, the old things she held dear. If you don't remember the past, how will you see how far you've come? Anna looked at her wrinkled hands.

All I am is the past. Used up. What more can I do? Anya has so much more that she could do. So much more life to live.

It would be easy to feel sorry for herself, especially since now everything was so much more difficult. Gardening, crocheting, and even household chores all posed problems. Yes, she had strong bones, but they were compromised now, not broken, but stiff and unreliable. Her fingers dropped things, they were no longer precise, and coupled with her strained vision, she didn't know how she was going to get her white blanket made. Who was she kidding that she thought she could produce a finely crocheted afghan? She would be lucky if she could still knit a pair of slippers with her arthritis. She'd drop her lunch plate on the floor because it just fell out of her hands, and she couldn't even open a sealed bag of cookies without needing to use scissors. She discovered last week, to her chagrin and dismay, that she no longer had the dexterity to make the intricate pysanky designs that she'd been known for.

She remembered the design she'd made for John Na-gajda, almost seventy years ago in Czechoslovakia. Her mother had told her that it looked more Ukranian, but the detailed diamonds and cross-hatching appealed to her, and to John. Anna had done her research. She helped John's mother with her laundry one day and caught a glimpse of her style of pysanky. Anna figured that if she produced something like what John's mother made, that he would prefer hers over other village girls' eggs. And so, Anna inherited her mother's talent for making the pysanky but came up with her own design, influenced by what she had seen by Mrs. Nagajdova, who feminized her husband's last name by adding –ova to the end, as was the custom. Anna hoped that she would be the next Mrs. Na-gajdova. The Easter she was fifteen, she crafted several stunningly beautiful pysanky using red, yellow, and black dyes mixed in with the little bits of exposed white of the eggshell. Her designs featured stars, triangles, and other geometric shapes separated by bands of cross-hatching and dots.

Anna couldn't help but wonder if there was some sort of curse on her family. Her father had been taken from them and forced to fight for the Hungarians in the war. Her older brother had died in the holding camp when they were run out of their village. Her pregnant mother had marched to the holding camp carrying a three-year-old the entire way, watched her beloved first-born son die in the holding camp, been told that her husband had died in the war, returned to their village still pregnant, and gave birth to another son only to have him die six weeks later. Anna's father survived the war only to come home to two dead sons. Less than a year later, her mother gave birth to twins – a live girl, Olga, and a still-born boy, Andrej. Marya's death occurred the year before Anna went to America, and their father's death the year after she left. He'd contracted tuberculosis in the war.

What, Anna wondered, had happened to John Nagajda? Had he, like so many uncles and cousins, fought and died in World War II? Had he married one of her pysanky rivals in their village and had five children? She knew he hadn't followed her to America. No, not John Nagajda. He was too good for America.

John was sixteen when he chose Anna's pysanka, from the seven he had received that Easter, and Anna smiled at the memory of being John's girlfriend. He would carry her laundry up from the creek, help her churn her butter and tend her bees and milk the cow. He even built a wo-ven-branch fence with her father. When no one was looking, John would take Anna's hand and they would sneak behind the barn and kiss. And oh, was John a good kisser! His full lips would press down on hers with such urgency as he held her to him and ran his fingers through her hair at the back of her head, under her babushka. Their hearts would race with excitement and they couldn't wait to get married.

You never forget your first love! Anna thought, feeling

warm there on her old floral print couch.

One day, as plans for their wedding neared after a year of courtship, they went inside the Nagajdas' dark barn, no longer content with just kissing. Anna did not want to have intercourse because she did not want to get pregnant yet. They rolled around in the hay, half-dressed, caressing each other, and Anna told John that they should wait until they got jobs in America before they had children.

"America?!" John asked. "We're not going to America! We're getting married and staying here." He propped himself up on his elbow and gave her a look that could almost be called stern.

The hair stood up on the back of Anna's neck. "I want to go to America. We can have a better life there. We can raise a family there. I have relatives there who can help us."

"We can have a good life here. Besides, your parents only lasted five years there and then they had to come back because they lost their jobs. I don't want to end up like *that*," John said, rolling his eyes.

Anna bristled. *How dare he? What does he know?* "That was not their fault. Back then that was the only kind of job available. Now there are other jobs and more opportunities. You want to be a farmer your whole life?"

"Yes, I do," John said with defiance. "My father was a farmer, and his father was a farmer, and they've lived good lives and so will I. And so will my family. I don't need to go to America to live a good life. I don't want to shovel coal all day long! If you think I want to leave this village and my family, cross an ocean for a week, go to a country where I don't speak the language, all so I can be underground in a coal mine all day long, you're crazy!" He stood up then and began straightening his clothes in a huff.

Anna tried one more tactic. "But I do speak the language. My father's been teaching me English at night, and I'll keep learning more. That way I can get us a house and jobs. And you won't have to work in a coal mine – there are steel mills and shoe factories now."

John took a deep breath and put his hands on her shoulders and looked into her eyes. "Anna. Stop this crazy talk. We're not going to America. We're getting married, and we're staying in our village with our families. This is where we belong, not America. We'll have a good life here. You'll see." Then he smiled and kissed her lips for the last time.

All Anna could think of, after promising herself that she wouldn't be like her mother, was that a woman should be true to herself. "John, it's always been my dream to go to America, where I was born. I know that's what I need to do, that it would be right for me. I had hoped – dreamed – that we would go together, but…I see now that…that you would rather stay here. And I have to go, John. I have to follow my dream."

John stepped away from her, shaking his head. "I can't believe you're going to do this. I can't believe you're going to throw everything away."

"I can't believe you don't want to go! That you want to be a farmer all your life! You think I want to milk cows, churn butter, bake bread, wash clothes in a creek, collect eggs, and tend bees every day for the rest of my life? America is an opportunity for something better!" She stared at him, wild-eyed, holding her breath.

"Maybe better for you, but not better for me. I love you, Anna, but I'm not going to America. And I can't marry you either, since you don't want to stay here and be a farmer's wife." He turned and walked out of the barn.

Anna remembered the strange combination of heartache and determination that she felt at that moment. It seemed like she had felt that way for most of her life.

The phone rang then, jarring her away from her memories. She hoisted herself up off the couch and padded over to the phone in the kitchen. It was Peter.

After assuring him that she was fine, that the doors were all locked and she had remembered to eat lunch, she asked, on a whim, how Theresa was doing. And it was like she could hear the wheels turning in her son's head. Why shouldn't she ask about her daughter-in-law? She could tell that they had been having problems, just by the way they interacted, and the fact that Peter never volunteered any information. Anna didn't necessarily want all the grim details, but she did wonder what was going on.

"She's fine, Ma, she's fine. She's been um, a little stressed lately. I think it's just hard for her to have seven people in the house, and having to watch Leif every day is wearing on her. In a few months he'll be in daycare, and then Theresa can maybe go back to work part-time, and then she'll feel better."

Anna figured she wouldn't get much more than that

out of him. Maybe Anya or Marya knew what was really going on. "That sounds like a good idea," she said, trying to sound supportive.

"So, Ma, the reason I'm calling is that I have some good news for you!"

Anna's heart jumped. She hoped it was something good about Anya, some breakthrough or turnaround. A miracle. *Please, God, please.*

"The police contacted me and let me know that your mink stole has been found. Isn't that great, Ma?"

Anna swallowed back tears of disappointment and tried to sound pleased. "Yes, that is good news. Where did they find it?"

"In a pawn shop in Riverside," Peter said.

A pawn shop. The ultimate degradation. Anna fought the emotions welling up in her. "Will I be able to have it back?"

"Yes, yes. I'm going to go pick it up tomorrow on my lunch break and then I'll bring it to you, okay?"

"Okay, I'll see you tomorrow."

Anna hung up the receiver of her old black telephone and shuffled back to the couch and eased herself onto it. She wasn't sure if she was crying because her stole had been found or because her daughter wasn't cured or because she had broken her own heart so long ago and never forgiven herself. She had never let go of John and the what-ifs, the abandonment of true love, and the disappointment of never finding it again.

*

It was as if Theresa's own iron curtain had been lifted. The sun seemed brighter, she breathed more deeply, she finally felt happy again. She and Kat were out shopping at the local mall on a Saturday, and Theresa felt infinitely better. She was glad she hadn't made a doctor appointment yet since now there was no need. She got better on her own! And she was so glad the depression was gone. Theresa loved how she felt – alive, alert, human. The sun seeped into her pores, energizing her.

Theresa's legs were bare and she felt the cool spring air swirl around them beneath her skirt as she and Kat walked up to the white pillars and dark blue sign of the Robinson's entrance. Her clean, blow-dried hair swished across her shoulders and she straightened her beige linen blouse, which was tucked into a denim skirt. Her lime green kitten heels clacked on the tile floor as she and her daughter walked through the department store.

At least Kat liked to shop. Theresa had never really been interested in sports, so she didn't share that wiring with her daughter. She had no knowledge of camaraderie, how it felt to be on a team (other than a legal team), to high-five and cheer and cool down in the locker room. At least, that's what Theresa thought it was about. There was more, of course: the training of athletic skill, the dedication, the pushing oneself, the exhaustion. She'd done a little cross country in early high school; it didn't stick. But Kat was in her element with sports, and although Theresa was as supportive as she could be, she preferred their little shopping excursions.

Kat, in her bleached Levis and blue and white striped t-shirt, told Theresa that she was going to check out a store she liked called Extras that sold various accessories – jewelry, hats, belts, purses. Theresa said she would be at the fragrance counter and to meet her there in ten minutes because they had to get to the clothing stores. She was hoping she would have time later in the afternoon to spend with Peter.

When she left him, he was settling into a sunny spot where his big papasan chair happened to be, *National Geographic* in hand. He could be out enjoying the day! They could have gone for a walk in the park! They could have gone to the horse races at Santa Anita. Not that they ever did that, but it might be fun to try sometime. Theresa just wanted to go out and do things. She finally felt fully awake, and there was so much to do, so much to see, so much life to experience. Rubbing her wrists together, she tried a new fragrance by Estee Lauder.

Theresa hoped by now that Peter was at least spending some time with Joseph, designing Lego bridges with him or something. Peter did say he was going to finally teach him to swim this spring, saying that he needed to spend more time bonding with the kids. And while this was true, teaching Joe to swim was something he *needed* to do; it wasn't like Peter went out of his way to think of something that Joe would *enjoy* doing that he could do with him. Their younger son loved to play chess; she had taught him about a year ago when he was home sick from school, and he would play games against himself as a way to practice and learn strategy. If Peter had played with him yet, she hadn't heard about it.

Her children were so different – Kat with her athletic nature, Joe with his eye for design (he'd inherited that from her father), and Mike with his love of history. She supposed it was no different from her family, and wondered if her parents ever mused about their children's different interests: Theresa with her baking and law, Mark with computers, and Bridget with her books. Bridget with her grudge-holding. Why did she have to be like that? After all these years, all Theresa's apologies? She wanted to see Bridget before she moved, but she had no idea how to approach her after the previous failures. Maybe things would go better now that she was out of the depression. Theresa could definitely communicate more effectively when she wasn't locked in its fog.

She became aware of a voice over the store sound system calling her name. "Theresa Sopko, please come to the customer service desk," and she put down the perfume bottle she had picked up and headed toward the middle of the store, adrenaline coursing through her. She knew something had to be wrong with Kat.

At the customer service desk a woman with short curly brown hair and glasses told her that she was being paged at Extras, that there was a problem with her daughter. She didn't have that far to go as that store was in the Robinson's wing of the mall, but Theresa's heart raced, wondering if Kat had fainted or had a seizure or was injured. Eyes wide, she ran in the store up to the counter and announced herself.

"What's wrong with my daughter?" she breathlessly

demanded.

"I'm sorry, but your daughter was caught shoplifting," a black-haired, accessory-clad, gum-chewing young woman told her. Her nametag read "Amber, Assistant Manager."

"What?" Theresa crowed. "That's impossible! Where is she?"

Amber came out from behind the counter. "Right this way," she said, walking to the back of the store. Theresa followed, and her fear transformed to anger. How could she have done this? She had no reason to!

Amber opened the door for Theresa to enter, and she saw Kat sitting in a chair near a table stacked with packing material. Kat, whose head had been down, looked up when Theresa came in, and a sob emitted from her chest. Her eyes were swollen from crying. A big-boned mall security guard stood off to the left, and a woman whom Theresa presumed to be the store manager stood next to him, arms folded across her chest. She wore a silk floral print dress with purple pumps, and her permed, immobile hair grazed her shoulders as she turned to Theresa, disdain on her face.

"Because your daughter is under eighteen, I will not press charges. But she is, of course, banned from this store."

"And if she ever shoplifts again, she will be arrested," the clean-shaven security guard said, turning his head in Kat's direction, in case she hadn't been paying attention.

Theresa, seething and embarrassed, muttered an apology, said *Come on* in a threatening tone to Kat, and stormed out. She walked quickly out through the store, avoiding eye contact with anyone, and when they were out in the mall area she became aware of Kat blubbering an apology as she tried to keep up. Theresa kept walking, not wanting to make more of a scene than they already had. They got out to the parking lot and Kat insisted with her attempt to justify and downplay what she had done, since the apologies had not been acknowledged.

Finally, they got in the station wagon and Theresa fired it up. She wrenched it out of the space and began driving. Her daughter was a thief, and their shopping day was ruined. In a voice near yelling she said, "What possessed you to do such a thing?"

Kat began crying again. "I said I was sorry! I just needed some headbands and I didn't want to have to ask you for money."

"Don't make this about not wanting to inconvenience me! You made the decision to steal! And you made a huge mistake!"

Kat cry-whined, "Yes, I made a mistake and I said I was sorry! I'll never do it again!"

"You're damn right you won't do it again!" They were nearing the end of the parking lot, and Theresa drove over the last speed bump. Suddenly, her mind flashed with the bump, and for an instant she was driving on a dark night, and she hit a man who had been standing by the side of the road. It was a memory, one she had shoved down, way down. It flashed, briefly reminding her what she was capable of, and then it was gone again.

CHAPTER EIGHT

"Big fat zero," Peter said into the phone. He was seated at his desk in his office, flipping a ballpoint pen as he talked to one of his more obstinate clients. "I'm sorry, Steve, but if you try to go after her inheritance, that's what you'll get." He paused, listening. "You were only married three years! You have to be realistic."

"I know that her affair caused you stress and trauma. You're not suing an insurance company here. No judge is going to award you any of her inheritance for damages." Peter rolled his eyes. *What a waste of my time,* he thought. "Steve, I've got somebody coming in right now. We'll have to go over this later."

Peter hung up and glanced at his watch, then stretched. In truth, he was free for almost forty-five minutes, but he couldn't stand to continue that conversation. Men could be gold-diggers too - freeloading, sue-happy bastards. Peter's family mediation counseling service hadn't really taken off enough for him to do only that. Most of the couples he spoke to in mediation were clients that he was able to steer in that direction, so he wasn't getting much new clientele. And he found that most of them were motivated more by trying to save what they stood to lose financially as a reason to try to save their marriages. Not to mention lawyer's fees, even though Peter usually rolled them over into mediation counseling fees. He wished more people went that route, just because divorce was usually so messy and painful, so negative. He certainly wouldn't want to go through with one, after all he'd seen.

And he also still loved his wife, depressive episodes and all. Although lately she seemed to be in more of a manic state, which in some ways was better, except for the not sleeping and the spending money part. She was spending like crazy, redecorating the house, buying new wardrobes. The kids loved it, of course, especially Kat. Peter was mortified that she had shoplifted and faulted himself for not spending enough time with her. He vowed to change that.

But during Theresa's manic episodes, shopping trips were an almost daily occurrence, to the mall and to furniture stores. Peter came home from work one day the previous week looking forward to some decompression time on the couch only to find that Theresa had bought a new one – tan leather. And she had on a new outfit every day – tight designer jeans and slinky animal-print or striped tops. Peter had to admit it was good to see her smiling, and dressed, although she had a wild look in her eyes. She would run over to him as he came through the front door of their tri-level hillside home and throw her arms around him with even more exuberance than when they were first married. He warned her that she should ease up on the shopping a little or else they wouldn't be able to afford that trip to Greece they'd been talking about.

Yes, part of him tolerated her manic state, but the other part dreaded it because she would often drink too much. He recalled their tenth anniversary, when they couldn't get a babysitter, so the kids accompanied them out to dinner at Polynesian Paradise. Mike was nine, Kat was six, Joe wasn't born yet. Peter noticed as they neared the end of their meal that Theresa was getting embarrassingly drunk, slurring her words and spilling things. The kids had finished eating so he sent them to the waiting area in the front of the restaurant, where they played with the cigarette machines and looked at the lobster tank and aquariums. Theresa was a disaster. She was singing, laughing her cackling-witch laugh. Then she sneered at him and accused him of having an affair.

"Don't be ridiculous," he sneered back, insulted. "Of course I'm not having an affair." And then a flash hit him that maybe *she* was the one having the affair; he'd read that some people did that – had an affair and then started acting suspicious of the other person. But no, Theresa wasn't suspicious, she was just drunk. She started crying then, apologizing for making a scene, and he wiped her face and picked up her purse and they staggered out, kids in tow.

Was he being co-dependent? An enabler? He was just trying to keep his family together, to keep his marriage above water. He could put up with occasional drinking bouts, spending sprees, and depressed days in bed. No one ever said that love was perfect. She was sometimes difficult, but she wasn't abusive or psychotic. And if they could make some changes in their household regarding their grandson being put in daycare, Peter was sure that it would help Theresa since she could go back to work, at least part-time, and she would feel better. In his mind, it had all started when Mike was born and she quit work. Perhaps it was post-partum depression that never went away? There'd been complications at the end of her pregnancy with Mike – her blood pressure was high, his heart rate was low – and she'd ended up needing an emergency cesarean delivery. Peter was frantic thinking that he might lose them both. And a week later, when they'd been released from the hospital, Theresa was so weak that she decided not to go back to work at all, even after her six-week leave. Staying home - three children later, four if you counted Leif - had stifled Theresa's intellectual needs. Peter missed their lengthy discussions about law principles and Greek philosophy.

That was long ago. It was decades since Theresa had given him the Aristotlean plaque that still hung on the wall of his office: "Man perfected by society is the best of all animals; he is the most terrible of all when he lives without law, and without justice." It was flanked by the more modern, but equally important: "To err is human, to forgive – divine." Peter faintly hoped that his clients would at least glance at them when contemplating what type of a divorce they wanted to have, or if they should go through with it at all. He tried to decorate his office in as soothing a manner as possible – leafy plants in the corners, soft blue upholstered chairs, inspirational quotes on the wall. In the end, maybe it only helped him to deal with his own stress, and not very well at that.

He never really set out to be a lawyer; he never said, "I want to be a lawyer" when he was a kid and people asked him what he wanted to be when he grew up. He liked baseball and was usually the umpire when there were enough players out of the neighborhood kids. But he hadn't really wanted to be a baseball player. He worked in his mother's shoe store after school in his teens and knew that he had no interest in pursuing that as a career. But then he got on the debate team and realized that he was good at it. And he did like it. He liked reasoning, finding flaws in it, shaping an argument to his viewpoint. His teacher got him interested in law, steered him that way, and since he had always cared about people and helping them find solutions to problems, he decided to specialize in divorce law. For the most part, it had served him well, afforded him and his family a good life, gave his parents an excuse to brag. Well, he took some pride in that. He had worked hard, after all.

The firm's secretary, a quiet, professional, librarian-looking type of woman, poked her head in his office. She had worked for the firm even longer than he had. "Peter, I've been trying to buzz you, but -"

"Oh, sorry, Nancy, I had turned the ringer off after the last call. What is it?"

"There's a young woman on the phone for you, says she's your cousin. I couldn't quite make out the name. She sounds upset."

"Thank you, I'll take it."

"She's on line two," Nancy said as she turned to go back down the hall.

What could this be about? "Danika?"

"Peter, I'm so glad you're there! I need help; I need help!" came Danika's frantic, accented voice.

"Calm down, Danika. What's wrong? Are you hurt?"

"No, I'm not hurt, but Jacob, the little boy I am nanny for, he -" Danika's voice broke off into splintered sobs. She cried unreservedly and spoke in Slovak.

"Danika, honey, I can't understand you. If Jacob's hurt, you need to call 9-1-1!" Adrenaline began coursing through Peter's body.

"I did – I did call 9-1-1. They came and took him to hospital. He – we walked in the neighborhood, and the baby in stroller dropped her bottle, so I picked it up, and Jacob ran in the street, and – a CAR -" she began gasping again.

Oh, my God! "He was hit by a car?"

"Ye-e-s," Danika said between sobs.

Peter's heart raced. "Danika – Danika – where are you now?"

More sobbing. "I – I – am at – *police building!*"

"Okay, I will come to get you. What city is it? Do you know? Can you ask someone?"

"Brentwood," Danika said, her sobs subsiding.

"Okay, I will be there as soon as I can. I'm leaving right now. Don't worry, Danika. You'll be okay."

Peter flew out his door, calling out, "Nancy! What's the address of the Brentwood Police Station, please?"

She had it within ten seconds, and Peter was out the door, yelling that he would explain later and to notify his three o'clock that he would have to reschedule. He ran to his car parked in the lot behind the building, got into his silver BMW sedan and pulled onto the street. Brentwood was about twenty-five minutes from Pasadena, barring any traffic. He entered the 110 Freeway. Fortunately there was not too much traffic at 2:30 in the afternoon.

He tried to steady his breathing and his speed, going as quickly as he legally could. He didn't even know if the little boy was alive or not, but regardless, Danika was vulnerable and needed legal representation. What a horrible thing to happen! He weaved in between cars, realizing that he was driving on auto-pilot. He would arrive there and not remember having driven.

The thought was not lost on him that Danika felt like a daughter to him. He wanted to protect her and help her, do for her what he wished he could do for Kat, if she would only let him in. He realized that his daughter was probably thinking that her dad was an embarrassing clown. Why else would she not want to have anything to do with him? Roll her eyes every time he asked her a question? Peter told himself it was just a phase. He wanted to be the "cool dad," but still be her father. He had to come up with some way to regain her esteem without seeming orchestrated.

As he exited the freeway, Peter wondered if they would try to deport Danika, and if her engagement to Eddie would have any bearing on that. He needed to do some research into immigration law and wished he had more knowledge of it going in. Well, he would do his best for the time being.

He parked out front, jogged into the building, and

stated his business at the front desk. In a moment, an officer named Kyle Banks came and spoke to him, assuring him that Danika was not being charged in the accident with the little boy who had been in her care, and that he was alive but in critical condition.

"Mr. Sopko, is it?" the tall, balding, forty-ish man asked as he fingered his navy blue tie. Peter nodded. "Before we continue, I'd like to know the nature of your relationship with Ms. Zarachnak. You say you're her *cousin?*" he said with a bit of a disbelieving squint.

"Yes – I *am* her cousin," Peter stated vehemently, wondering – and then it hit him. They thought Danika was his 'kept woman' or something, his international lover, perhaps. He continued, "She is my second cousin, that's why I'm older than she is. Danika's mother is my first cousin. My mother is Danika's great-aunt. Danika's mother is *my* mother's niece. Does that make sense?"

"Thank you, Mr. Sopko, I understand. And now, the reason why we're holding Danika is because her visa has expired. She's here illegally. Were you aware of that?"

"It can't have expired! She was issued a six-month visa and she's been here less than five months! There must be some mistake," Peter said.

"Mr. Sopko, I've obtained a copy of her visa, and it clearly states three months," the officer said, unrolling a piece of thermal fax paper and holding it out for Peter to see. Peter leaned over and noted with dismay that the officer was correct.

"Officer Banks, I can assure you that no one in our family knew that it was only a three-month visa. I don't believe that *Danika* knew she had a three-month visa. She must not have applied for the one she thought she was applying for, or else she was given the wrong one by mistake and didn't realize it because her English is limited. And she's engaged to be married! Her boyfriend proposed to her three weeks ago! How does that figure in?"

"Yes, she did mention that. We hear that a lot, you understand. We would need proof of legitimacy."

"What sort of proof? All her relatives here all knew about it and will confirm it. And you can talk to her boyfriend."

"Oh, we *will* be talking to her boyfriend. Her employers swear that she told them she had a six-month visa, and under the circumstances, they won't be held accountable."

"She told them she had a six-month visa because that's what she believed she *had*! We *all* thought she had a six-month visa!"

"But no one checked."

"Why would we have thought there was a need to check?" Peter asked, exasperated. He took a breath, not wanting to seem uncooperative. "Okay. So what happens now?"

"I'm sorry, Mr. Sopko, but she's going to be fined and deported."

"But she's going to be married. Here in the United States, to a U.S. citizen. I'm an attorney, and I will represent her in court."

"Mr. Sopko, I don't know how familiar you are with immigration law -"

Peter cut him off. He tried to sound as authoritative as he could. "I know marriage law. And I know enough to know that you can't deport someone who's engaged to a U.S. citizen." He wasn't sure if that was true, but he made it sound like it was.

"All right, Mr. Sopko. Then this matter will need to be decided in court. I'll get you a copy of her deportation order, since that's what you will be contesting," the officer said, holding out his hands as if surrendering.

"Thank you, Officer Banks. When all the paperwork is in order, I'd like to see her and have her come home with me."

"Are you posting her bail?"

"*Bail?* Good God, bail *and* a fine?" Peter asked, eyebrows raised.

"Mr. Sopko, please appreciate the fact that she's an illegal alien. I'll get the paperwork and you can take care of the bail at the front," Officer Banks said, turning and walking away.

Shit, I wonder how much this is going to be, Peter thought as he walked back to the front desk. It turned out to be a manageable amount for him, nothing for which he would have to take out a second mortgage, in fact probably less than Theresa had spent in the past two weeks.

After some time, Danika was released and brought out to him. Her entire face was swollen and blotchy from crying, her hair messy and her pink T-shirt and jeans smudged with sweat and dirt. She threw her arms around Peter and thanked him repeatedly, with quivering lips and fresh tears forming in her eyes.

*

Danika couldn't stop crying. Just when she thought she might be able to, her eyes welled up again and a sob caught in her chest. She couldn't believe this was happening.

How could she have let Eli run into the street? Why didn't she keep him close? She was such a terrible nanny! What if he died?

Peter walked her out to his car, a protective, sympathetic arm around her back. He kept telling her it was going to be okay, but how could it possibly be okay? After they got in the car and Peter began driving, he told her that he was taking her to his house for a few days, and she could borrow clothing from Kat until they could get back to the Davidson's house to get her things.

Peter merged onto the freeway. "Danika, I'm sorry to ask, but what happened?"

Danika's eyes watered again and she hid her face. "I took the children for a walk around the neighborhood, same as many days. After some time, the baby dropped her blanket, and it was stuck in the wheels of the stroller. I go down to fix it, and Eli ran into the street when I was looking at the blanket." Danika took her breath in sharply and continued. "A car came, and I heard the screech of the brakes and the sound when it hit Eli," she sobbed. "A sound so horrible I will never forget!"

The driver of the white Cadillac, a short, older man in a pinstriped suit got out of the car and yelled, "He ran right in front of me! Why didn't you stop him?"

Danika, barely able to register what happened, began to cry in panic. "I was helping the baby!"

A retired neighbor lady came running out of her house, her floral print housecoat flapping around her. "I called an ambulance!" She came and stood by Danika, which helped her to keep semi-calm, even though she wanted to scream.

Baby Brittany started to cry and Danika, crying herself, picked her up and tried to comfort her. The man kept saying, "You should have been watching him!" and the neighbor lady countered with, "It was an accident!" Danika kept crying, kept looking at little Eli, motionless on the street, kept praying for him to be okay. But how could he be okay? He had been hit by a car and wasn't moving.

Finally the ambulance arrived, and the police. While the two male EMTs readied Eli to be moved into the ambulance, the police, a male and a female officer, talked to Danika, the driver, and the neighbor. The driver went on the defensive again, blaming Danika, but the neighbor confirmed that she did see Danika bending down trying to fix the stroller wheel when Eli ran into the street. Then she heard the screech of the brakes, saw that the little boy had been hit, and called 911. Danika, through broken sobs, tried to make her statement to Officer Bryant, the sympathetic, black female officer, while Officer Green, the short male officer in sunglasses, obtained and recorded the driver's information. The ambulance took off, the driver was released, and after the officers held a short conference a few feet away from Danika and the neighbor, they came back and Officer Bryant told Danika they would need to see her identification.

Just when she thought she couldn't feel any worse than she already did, Danika was faced with submitting an expired visa. She said that she didn't have it with her, and explained that the house was just around the corner. The neighbor lady offered to come with her to hold the baby, and she and Danika walked with Officer Bryant while Officer Green moved the police car.

Once inside the house, Officer Green called the parents and told them what happened and which hospital to go to. Danika handed Brittany to the neighbor and went upstairs to get her papers. She kept wanting to scream, to make this all go away. They would be just getting back from their walk now, and she would start preparing lunch for her little charges: scrambled eggs and apple, cut into little skinless cubes. And they would drink milk. Then they would watch the Disney Channel and Danika would call Eddie.

Eddie! She had to talk to him! He could help her, he would know what to do. Oh, this was horrible. What if she was deported? What if Eli died and she was held responsible? What then? She couldn't bear to think of it.

She trudged slowly down the stairs with her purse and visa papers and decided to say that she thought it was for six months. How could she explain to them about what happened with Brian Leech? That she hadn't planned on being here that long? That she hadn't even planned to stay long enough to need a job? She didn't even know if she could say all that in correct English.

She walked into the kitchen and everyone looked expectantly at her. After she handed the papers to Officer Green, who was closer, he asked, "So you're from Czechoslovakia?"

"Yes," she said. The neighbor jostled a whimpering Brittany, and Danika said, "It's time for her lunch. We should give her some food."

The neighbor put Brittany in her high chair at the table while the police officers conferred. Danika began cutting an apple and poured milk into a yellow plastic cup with a lid. She felt like she was moving in slow motion in a dream. A bad dream.

Officer Green asked, "Ms. Zarachnak, were you aware that your visa expired?"

"No! I got a six-month visa!" Danika said, chopping the apple.

"Well, it clearly says here that it's a three-month visa. We're going to have to arrest you."

Danika unsuccessfully fought back her tears. Officer Bryant gently said, "We know that what happened with the little boy was an accident, but because your status is now illegal, we have to arrest you. Do you understand?"

Danika tried not to sob. "The baby . . . is hungry," she said, putting the apple on a plastic plate that matched the cup.

Officer Bryant turned to the neighbor and asked if she was a friend of the family. "Oh, yes, I see them all the time. I come to all the birthday parties and holiday parties."

"Are you able to stay with this child until the parents return?"

"Yes, absolutely."

Danika brought the food over to the high chair and set it down. Then she kissed the top of Brittany's head and said quietly, "She likes also scrambled eggs, cut in pieces."

The neighbor nodded. "Don't worry, I'll take good care of her."

"Okay, Ms. Zarachnak, we need to have you come with us," Officer Bryant said, gently taking her arm.

Danika, there in Peter's car, began crying again as she told him about how scared she was to ride in the police car and how sick she was about Eli. "I'm sorry, Peter, very sorry."

"Danika, it wasn't your fault. It was an accident," Peter said, switching lanes.

"It was horrible to sit in the jail. I was very scared."

"They should never have done that. I'm going to bring that up in court."

Danika knew she should feel better knowing that her cousin was a lawyer and could help her, but all she could do was focus on the overwhelming anxiety, the desperation, the unrelenting fear, the heavy shame. She was an illegal alien, and due to her negligence, a child in her care might die. It couldn't get any worse than that.

CHAPTER NINE

Anna turned off the TV that afternoon and continued crocheting her blanket in silence. She had always liked to watch *Jeopardy* so that she could learn things. Of course most of them were useless things, but it was knowledge nonetheless. She remembered that Danika had told her last week that she watched TV to learn English. Anna asked her which shows she watched, and she said, "*Family Ties* and MTV." How could she learn English from rock stars? Anna had learned from the radio. She and her cousin, the one whose clothes she had shared, would listen together in the evenings after they had cleaned the dinner dishes.

She thought about Danika's situation and the accident yesterday, the fact that now her young niece might have to leave. Things were so different now. Seventy years ago, they had been welcomed, recruited even. Representatives from coal and steel companies had gone to Eastern Europe to entice emigrants with stories of American riches. The companies even loaned the emigrants the money to leave their countries, along with the opportunity to pay it off through their work, taking it out of their wages. And they worked their way to becoming citizens. Now America only issued visas for a limited time, and then you had to leave. There were no overseas recruiters, no wage-loans for passage. Just permission to visit. She remembered the night before she left to come to America, and her father had talked about the message on the Statue of Liberty. "Give me your tired, your poor, your huddled masses yearning to breathe free, the wretched refuse of your teeming shore. Send these, the homeless, tempest-tossed, to me: I lift my lamp beside the golden door." And Anna wrote down those words in Slovak and read them again, after being on a ship for five days, as she passed the Statue for the second time in her life. *There are so many. Just on this boat alone. So many tired, poor, huddled, homeless, tempest-tossed. I hope the golden door is wide. I hope there is room for everyone.*

But most of them no longer came by boat (except the Cubans, she was told). And even those that did would not pass the Statue, the Lady. Perhaps they didn't know about her promise. They would come for the opportunities they had heard of, whether or not they knew of the message portrayed by Lady Liberty. Some would come on foot, or by air, as Danika had. Whether they knew of the Statue's message or not, it did not matter. They could come, but they could not stay. The golden door had closed.

Anna felt confident that her lawyer son would know what to do to allow Danika to stay and marry her fiancé. What it would involve, Anna did not know, but she was certain that Peter would figure it out and save the day. Anya was very smart, being a professor, but Peter was smart *and* practical. And Marya was smart too, of course, but she was so...*difficult*. Anna loved her younger daughter as much as her other children, but she considered her to be the black sheep of the family. Not surprisingly, she was also the one who lived the farthest away.

Anna thought for a minute and realized that *she* was the black sheep of her own family of origin. After all, she was the only one who left. Well, Marya (her sister) had died young, but she probably wouldn't have left. And Olga, the youngest, stayed in the very same village. She was a farmer's wife with three children. She seemed happy, though. She and Anna wrote letters to each other and sent photographs every year. One of Olga's daughters was Magda, Danika's mother. Olga had written to Anna about how quiet it was after she left. And a year later their father died, leaving Olga and their mother alone. Olga was eleven. She and her mother worked the small farm together, and then Olga married at seventeen and her husband took over the duties of the farm. They built a new house in front of the old one for Olga's new family, and their mother lived in the old house on the property for twelve more years. She died of pneumonia one winter and was buried next to their father, three blocks away in the village cemetery, next to the old church. Olga wrote to her, describing the new tombstones poking out of the hillside cemetery. But their mother was the last one buried in the church lot. Everyone else got put on the hillside after that. Anna wondered if that was where Olga would be buried. And how many tombstones would fill the hillside then?

Peter called. Anna, frustrated, set down her blanket on

the couch beside her and heaved herself up off the couch. She hadn't even completed two rows! Well, it was nearly finished. She wanted to add another six inches or so, and then a little bit of a fringe. Anna was pleased with how it looked and felt – soft, luxurious – just as she'd envisioned.

"Ma, I'm coming to pick you up. Anya is in the hospital, and she's – she's very weak. I want to take you to see her. Okay? I'll be there in fifteen minutes."

Anna could hardly speak. "Okay, Peter," she croaked, hanging up. She breathed in sharply. She felt the weight of all of her family's tragedies, but this one worst of all.

Anya! "Oh, Anya," she whispered, crying. She felt the sobs come up involuntarily and tried to suppress them.

Anna tried to put the grief out of her mind and focus on getting her shoes on, her blue Keds that Anya had bought for her when they had gone shopping a few months ago. They were the slip-on style, since she never knew when her arthritis would act up. Fortunately Anna had changed out of her nightgown earlier because her cleaning lady had come by. Peter had hired Lourdes to help her around the house and check to see if she needed anything. The middle-aged Mexican woman, also an immigrant, came once a week. Anna liked her and looked forward to Wednesdays. It helped to break up the week.

Soon she heard Peter's car pull up, and a moment later he came through the door, in his gray tweed suit, having come from work. His face was drawn, his lips tight.

"Do you need help with anything, Ma?" he asked quietly.

She shook her head. "I want to take this," she said,

holding her white blanket. "I want to show it to Anya."

"Okay, do you want a bag for it so it doesn't get dirty?"

"Yes, I have one under that table," Anna said, gesturing to the lamp table next to the couch. Peter reached in and pulled out a blue canvas bag with a white Disneyland logo printed across the front. He carefully inserted the folded-up crocheted blanket.

"Okay, let's go," he said, guiding her out the front door. The afternoon sun hit her sensitive eyes and she almost tripped on the threshold, even with Peter holding her hand. She shuffled to the car and gingerly stepped in, clutching the Disneyland bag. Peter shut her door, got in, and backed down the driveway in silence. Only when he had turned onto the boulevard did he speak again.

"Ma, I just want to prepare you. She's – very weak. She's conscious, and she can talk a little, but James told me that the doctors say that – that she doesn't have much longer." Peter choked on his words.

It was so hard to hear. It was so soon. Anna had hoped that they were wrong, but the doctors had been right about the time they gave Anya. She thought that surely Anya, active, outdoorsy Anya, was strong enough to fight it off. Anna didn't realize that Anya never even had a chance to fight. It was too late before she even knew about it. She had experienced some symptoms – pain in her abdominal area, mostly – in the months before her diagnosis, but she'd written it off as menopausal side effects and ignored it until she could ignore it no longer. It had spread to her uterus and into her lymph nodes, and now her liver. Even a full hysterectomy could not help stage four ovarian cancer.

Tears began rolling down Anna's cheeks. She didn't know what to say. Down Sepulveda Boulevard, kids walked home from school, stoplights changed, buses pulled over, cars signaled and turned like nothing was different.

After a moment, Peter asked, "Ma? You okay?"

"Yes. I'm just so sad." Anna touched the blanket inside the bag and breathed in sharply.

"Me too, Ma. I wish this wasn't happening." He reached over and put his hand on hers as he drove.

But it is, Peter. This is life happening. Births and deaths, with a few weddings in between. A few graduations. Many Easters. Sometimes, the deaths happen the same day as the births. It is happening today.

They arrived at St. Joseph's hospital in Burbank, where Anya's children had been born, and Peter's first child. It was a stately building, seven stories tall, a large cross on the side of it. The sunny spring day betrayed their somber feelings, mocked them. Peter put his arm around Anna as they walked inside, asked about Anya's room, and then stepped into an elevator.

It was so quiet. Anna heard her heart beating in her ears. What would make Anya's heart stop beating? Wasn't her heart still strong?

As they exited the elevator, they saw Claire standing out in the fluorescent-lit hallway, leaning against the wall, covering her face, her hair falling softly around her shoulders. Anna could not stand the sight of her grand-daughter's pain. It filled her, seized her, and Anna quickly sat in a chair that was out in the hallway. Her heart felt so heavy with Claire's pain, and her own.

Peter went over to Claire and held her. "Uncle Peter," she gasped, and cried into his chest.

"Claire, honey, I'm so sorry," Peter said, tears running out of his eyes. "Is your dad here?"

Claire pulled away and took a deep breath. "Yes, he's in the room with my mom. And James is, too. She's resting now, I think, but you can see her." She went over to Anna where she sat in the chair and reached down to hug her. "Hi, Baba. Can I get anything for you?"

"My sweet girl. Just a tissue, please," Anna said with a little smile.

Claire smiled too through red, puffy eyes and said, "I'll be right back."

Peter walked over and asked if she would like to go in the room. He had blotted his tears with the backs of his hands.

"In a minute, after Claire comes back with some tissues. You go ahead, Peter." *Say goodbye to your sister.*

She watched him walk down the hall, feeling his sadness. He and Anya had been so close all their lives. She had felt that way, that sadness, when her older brother John had died during the war, and she remembered what it was like to sit at his deathbed, even though she had been so young. But she was old enough to understand death. Old enough to miss someone she loved.

Claire returned then, holding out a long box of hospital tissues, and Anna smiled and pulled one out to dab her face. Just then the elevator dinged, and through the doors came Theresa with Danika, Mike, Kat, and Joseph. They exchanged hugs with Claire and Anna and waited in the hallway, unsure of what to do. Anya's husband Tom came out of the room then, followed by James, and exchanged the same anxious greeting ritual. Tom said that he thought Peter might want some time alone with Anya, and then the rest of them could go in in a few minutes.

They migrated out into a waiting area with more chairs and tables and a vending machine filled with cookies and chips. Tom came and asked Anna if she'd like to move out there with them, mentioning that there was a nice window to look out of, a welcome change from the bare, flickering, claustrophobic walls of the hallway. She let him help her out of the chair and walk her over to a blue fake velvet upholstered chair. She did like the window, and the view out of it. Down below was a pretty garden area. She stared at it, the lush greenery, and at the pale blue sky. The smog wasn't bad that day. Anna became aware of how quiet it was in the room; no one was talking. Tom sat on one couch with his arms around his children, Claire with her face buried in his chest, and James staring ahead, red-eyed. Theresa sat with Kat and Joseph on the couch across from them, and Mike and Danika had separate chairs like Anna's. Heather had stayed home with Leif.

No one brought flowers that day; Peter told Anna that they had brought some when Anya was admitted a week earlier. No balloons, no cards. Did they make cards for the dying these days? Anna wondered. Because it seemed that there were cards now for every other occasion.

Graduating from preschool, losing a job, getting a driver's license, getting braces taken off. There were probably cards for immigrants now. *Sorry to hear about your deportation order. Congratulations on your fake marriage! Happy Green Card Day!* But cards for the dying? *Sorry to hear about your cancer. You'll be at peace soon. We'll miss you.*

Anna tried to think of anything but Anya, anything. When thoughts of Anya crept back to her, she waved them away like a bothersome fly. She knew that if she gave in to them that she would start crying and wouldn't be able to stop.

Peter came out of the room then. He put his hand over his mouth, but she could see the anguish on his face. He came out into the waiting area and walked over to the couch where his family was seated. They rose and greeted him, and it was decided that they would go in to see Anya, who was awake. Peter motioned for Danika and Mike to accompany them, and James rose and walked over to Anna, then sat in the chair next to her. He took her hand and asked if she needed anything.

"James," she said to him, needing to clear her throat. "You are such a good boy. I'm so proud of you, my first grandchild." Their tear-filled eyes met, and James embraced her.

"I love you, Baba," he said, and continued holding her hand.

"I think I could use a little water," she said.

"Sure, I'll get you some."

Claire lifted up her head. "You okay, Baba?"

Anna nodded. "Yes, sweet girl."

*

About ten minutes later, Anna found herself seated next to her dying daughter. Anya looked gray, almost twenty years older, and had an IV in her arm. She could barely hold her eyes open. Even though the pain was masked by morphine, Anna still recognized the feeling, just as she had so long ago when her brother died in his hospital bed. It was the feeling of imminent death. And it permeated the room.

"Ma," Anya croaked. "I feel like... I'm on display."

"Don't think like that, sweet girl. Your family loves you." Anna tried to look at her without really seeing her, the sunken eyes, the protruding cheekbones.

"I don't want...to be remembered this way," Anya whispered through her labored breathing.

"I'll remember you as my loving daughter. A sweet girl grown into a remarkable woman. When people think of you, they'll remember you throughout your life, not like this," Anna said, stroking her daughter's arm.

"I know, but...I told Tom and the kids and Peter that... I don't want an open casket. Okay, Ma? Please?" Anya coughed and winced.

Anna could no longer contain her sorrow. She grimaced as she began to cry. "Anya...my Anya..." She could only think of her as a little girl, always smiling, willing to help. She did not see the shriveled shell before her. Only her little girl. Her little girl who was dying.

"Ma, it's okay... I'm weak, but I'm not in pain, really. I'm ready to go." She talked a little about Marya, and how she wished she was there, but that she was on the way. Maybe she would make it. Then she was quiet for a while, resting.

Anna dabbed her face with a tissue and then pulled the white crocheted blanket out of the bag. "It's almost finished," she said. "Here, feel it." Anna put Anya's hand on top of the blanket and pushed a fold between her fingers.

Anya whispered through closed eyes, "Oh, Ma, it's beautiful. It's so soft...like what you wanted."

They sat there a moment, scrunching the white blanket between their fingers, as if the blanket were a conduit of love, of hope. Then Anya spoke again. "Ma. All these years, you've never gone to see your sister and her family. You've never seen your parents' graves." Anya coughed a little before continuing. "You need to go back to Czechoslovakia to visit them. Before it's too late, Ma. Peter or Marya could go with you. But I know you need to, and they need to see you too." She stopped talking then and sucked in a breath.

Czechoslovakia, Anna thought. *Yes, I should go, see Olga, our old house, the hillside cemetery. Maybe John Nagajda, too.* "I will, Anya. You're right, I'll go soon."

"Ma? I need to rest now."

"Yes, sweet girl," Anna said. She looked at her and saw everything then – from the IV poking out of her skeletal arm all the way back to the first time Anna held her in her arms. From her high school graduation to the birth of the twins, and everything in between. Anna saw it all.

"Don't forget your blanket," Anya whispered, her dark eyelids fluttering, trying to open. "It's so beautiful."

"Not as beautiful as you."

"Ma… I love you."

"I love you with all my heart, Anychka. I love you," Anna said again, and leaned over to kiss her daughter.

*

It had been a hell of a week. First Kat shoplifting, then remembering hitting someone with the car - or maybe it had been a premonition of what happened to the little boy Danika watched – then Danika coming to stay with them, and now Anya dying. Theresa felt like she was ready to burst from the stress.

She hardly recognized Anya there in the hospital bed, looking infinitely worse than she had at Easter, when she was already sunken and gaunt. Now, her abdomen was swollen with ascites, since the cancer had spread to her liver two months ago. The rest of her, covered with blankets, was skeletal. Theresa sat in a chair by the window of Anya's sterile room, punctuated by a congregation of well-meaning bouquets on the opposite side of it. She watched as her children gathered around their aunt and noticed Kat's eyes watering and her mouth quivering, causing her own emotions to well.

Is this how it is? Why? Why can't we remember the happy times right now? The Easters, the Christmases, the Mother's Day picnics at Laguna Beach? Why does it all come down to the loss and the sadness?

Each of Theresa's children told Anya they loved her, and she told them they were good kids, but it became obvious to Theresa that Anya could barely speak, that it was an effort to whisper, to form words, to even think of the words, perhaps. For an English professor, how desolate must that feel? Theresa, notoriously uncomfortable around death, rocked ever so slightly in her seat.

Mike, Kat, and Joseph stepped back from the bed as Danika, who had been standing in the other corner of the room with Peter, came up to say goodbye.

"Anya, I wish I could have spent more time with you," Danika said, and Theresa realized that she had no idea what she was going to say to her sister-in-law. What can you say? "I've always admired you" sounded trite – an afterthought, a go-with-everything handbag. But she *had* always admired Anya - her poise, her intellect, her grace.

"Thank you for being so kind to me," Danika said, kissing Anya's cheek. Danika, already emotional because of the car-and-arrest incident, apparently could not stop her tears from flowing and turned away quickly. She stood up and reached for a tissue and then stood next to Kat.

And then Theresa got up out of the chair and went over to try to embrace her sister-in-law. She thought of Bridget, how even though she loved her, she had been closer to Anya for over twenty years. "You've always treated me as a sister," she ended up saying, "and I hope you felt that I have done the same for you, because that's how much you meant to me all these years."

"Thank you," Anya croaked. She was no longer able to

smile.

Then Peter asked Anya if she would like to see their mother now, and Anya whispered yes, and he kissed her and told her he loved her, and they all filed out to the waiting area, going through the motions, like somehow they knew what to do when a loved one was dying in a hospital bed. It felt surreal, like they were all performers in a play, rehearsing their lines and their blocking. It wasn't real death. It wasn't real life.

Theresa walked over and greeted Ma, sitting in one of the upholstered chairs. She embraced her and told her how sorry she was. What else do you say to someone losing his or her child? Theresa hoped she would never know that pain. Then she went to say goodbye to Tom, James, and Claire, which was infinitely harder than saying goodbye to Anya. Peter joined her quickly, thank God, and offered Tom assistance, getting food, anything. Tom graciously declined, said they had more than they knew what to do with, that their colleagues at the university had been more than generous, that they turned out to be an even better community than their church. And then Tom broke down, although he fought it, and then Peter broke down, and so did James and Claire. And Theresa put her face in her hand; it was just too sad.

After they had all embraced and handed out tissues, Peter told her, "I'll see you at home after taking Ma back to her house, and Kat said she wants to come with us."

"Okay, so I'll take Danika and the boys," Theresa said, digging around in her purse for her keys.

"Thanks, honey," Peter said, kissing her quickly. "I

love you."

"Love you too." Theresa rounded up her sons and a wet-eyed Danika and headed to the elevator and then out of the building. She felt terrible about Anya, but she could barely stand to be there another minute, surrounded by such sorrow. She worried that it might throw her back into a depression.

Walking toward the car, Danika tried to make conversation. "It is so sad."

Theresa wondered if she just meant Anya's death or life in general or the accident with the little boy. Such a horrible thing! How do you get on with your life after something like that? Especially since there would be permanent damage, in addition to the fact that she would probably be deported. She had heard Danika crying more than once in the two days since she had been staying at their house after the accident. They had her sleep in Kat's room, which wasn't very big, but Danika didn't have any of her stuff, so it worked for a few days. Peter would be taking her to pick up her stuff at her former employers' home the day after tomorrow, so they just had two more nights. Then she would be staying at Anna's house until the court date, which would be good for both of them. Well, for everyone. Theresa really liked Danika, she was a sweet girl, but there certainly was not room for one more person in their house. It was crazy! She and Peter, Mike, Kat, and Joseph, Heather, Leif, and now Danika. Just what was she supposed to make for dinner tonight? They had already had lasagna again. Burgers? *That might work.*

They were leaving the parking lot now, and as Theresa went over a speed bump she had the flashback again, jogged loose by the thump, following the braking too hard because she hadn't seen it until the last second. It was a dark, quick, jagged memory – she was certain she had hit a person while driving. But when? Where? What could she do? She had to talk to Peter, but now would be the worst time. How could she have done such a thing and then forgotten? What the hell was wrong with her?

CHAPTER TEN

If I make it through this week, Peter thought as he switched lanes on the 210 Freeway, it will be an act of God. He was on his way home after having taken Danika from his house, where she had been staying since the accident just three days ago, over to her previous employers' house, where she had been living for four months, so that she could pick up her belongings. Then he had dropped her off at his mother's home so she could stay there until the court hearing in three weeks.

His mother expected him to solve every legal issue their family encountered. Not that there were many, but still. He always vowed to do what he could, but in this case it wouldn't be much.

I'm not an immigration lawyer, and when all is said and done, she's still an illegal alien.

The mood at the employers' home had been grim. The little boy had stabilized, but his back was broken, and it appeared that he might have sustained some brain damage. Danika sobbed at the news and threw herself at the mother's feet, apologizing. The mother, Lisa, a petite woman in her thirties with shoulder-length chestnut hair, graciously picked Danika up and, crying herself, told Danika that it wasn't her fault, that it was a horrible accident. The two women held each other as they cried. Peter, already emotional from his sister's death just one day ago, walked around the corner for a moment to steady himself. He saw family portraits in the living room of the spacious, well-to-do home, and thought about the fragility of life, that the only thing we can be sure of is the time we have now. That not a moment should be wasted when we have loved ones who might not be with us tomorrow.

Anya, his brother-in-law told him, had experienced a horrible last night on earth. They were watching a TV show there in her hospital room - *Jeopardy*, of all things - and when it was almost over she began retching and vomiting and continued to do so every fifteen minutes. A nurse gave her a suppository that was supposed to stop the vomiting, but it didn't work until four o'clock in the morning. Her ragged breaths caused her chest to rattle, but somehow she finally slept. Tom went to the bathroom, and when he came back he returned to his post by her side. James and Claire tried to sleep in the beige vinyl-upholstered hospital room chairs near the foot of their mother's bed.

"I love you, my darling," Tom said, stifling a gasp. As he sat down, Anya turned her head toward him, and her jaundiced eyes gazed into his for the last time. Then she turned her head toward the ceiling, looked at it for a moment, closed her eyes, and exhaled her last breath.

Peter walked back into the kitchen to suggest to Danika that he start carrying her things out to the car. She was blowing her nose in the bathroom. He walked over to Lisa and gently put his hand on her shoulder. "I'm sorry for what you're going through. I wish I could be of more help, but my sister died yesterday, and I'm afraid I'm not at my best."

"Oh, I'm so sorry for your loss. This is such a terrible week. My husband and I have been taking turns spending time at the hospital. Eli was conscious for a few minutes yesterday, which was wonderful. The doctors are hopeful, and of course we are too, but oh, this is so hard. I hope your family's okay?" Lisa said, looking at him with wet, red eyes.

"I think we're managing. She had cancer, so we had a little time to prepare ourselves, but it's never easy."

Danika appeared, hiccupping, and said that she would go upstairs to pack her things. She turned and walked out of the room.

"That's awful about Danika's visa. Is she still going to be able to get married?" Lisa asked.

"I'm going to do all I can to help her," Peter said. "I'm a lawyer, but I don't know much about immigration law, so I need to do some research."

"I'm so glad that Danika has someone to help her. We really love her and will miss her. She was so good with the kids," Lisa said, catching her breath in a sob. "I'm sorry. I'm really emotional. This is all just horrible."

"Of course. I understand completely," Peter said. He put his hand on her arm. "I'm going to see if I can help Danika, if that's okay."

"Oh, go right ahead. I'm going to check on my daughter. She's taking a nap."

They both began walking up the split staircase, and Peter eyed the Tiffany-styled lamp hanging in the landing. "You have a lovely home."

"Thank you," Lisa said. They reached the top and she pointed to a door at the end of the hall. "That's Danika's room."

Peter thanked her and headed in that direction.

Danika was nearly finished, so Peter helped carry her bags down to the entryway. After a tearful goodbye with Lisa, Danika climbed back in Peter's car, and they got on the freeway to go to Anna's house in Van Nuys, about eight miles away. Mid-day traffic was good, so at least that did not add to Peter's stress level. He thought about what everyone must be feeling: Danika, berating herself for what happened to the little boy; Tom, his brother-in-law, making funeral arrangements, consumed by grief; Claire and James, missing their mother; his mother, missing her daughter.

Marya had arrived, so that was good. She was staying with their mother until a day after the funeral, which would be in two days. Danika would be staying with Anna for at least a month, depending on the outcome of the hearing, and that relieved Peter. He was starting to worry about his mother's ability to care for herself, even with Lourdes coming once a week to clean and check up on her. Now that Anya was gone, Peter would need to stop by more often. And he was fine with that in princi-ple, but his schedule was already so full. For one thing, he had signed up as a parent coach for Kat's softball team as a way to be more involved with her. Four days a week of practice and Saturday games would start in two weeks, and Peter wasn't sure he knew what he was getting into. Kat didn't seemed too pleased at the prospect ("You don't have to do this, Dad"), but he hoped she'd come around at some point. He had to try.

Marya, shrouded in grief, embraced Peter and Danika, and Anna walked with Danika to her room.

"How are you?" Marya asked Peter. He'd never seen her look so sad, worse than when their father died. They'd had a decent relationship, but neither she nor Anya had ever been Daddy's little girl. They were not spoiled by any means.

"Sad. Stressed. I'm okay, though. Holding down the fort. You? How was your trip?" He didn't want to draw attention to the fact that, according to Tom, by the time Marya arrived at the hospital that evening, Anya could no longer speak. But at least Marya got to say goodbye.

"It was fine. Rushed, of course." Her eyes watered and her mouth quivered. "She didn't even look like herself. It just ravaged her body so fast."

Peter didn't say anything, just nodded and took a breath. Then he said, "I was just remembering how we used to all go to Laguna Beach on Mother's Day. Remember Anya's sand castles? They were like forts. She and James and Mike built them together, digging deep moats. And then the tide would come in, first filling up the moat, and then finally washing away the castle completely. The boys would groan and Anya would say something like, 'Nothing lasts forever!' and then splash them or something," he stopped, his voice catching.

Tears streamed down Marya's face. "I hadn't seen her since Easter. Fuck! Why didn't I just drive out every weekend? It's only eight hours!"

Peter held her to him and noticed that their mother had entered the room. Her face began to contort. "Ma, Ma, it's okay," he said.

Marya turned around and blotted her own face with her sleeve. She walked over to their mother and guided her to sit down on the couch. "Let me make us some tea, okay, Ma?"

"I'm going to say goodbye to Danika," Peter said. He walked down the hallway to the bedroom and saw Danika sitting on his old bed, writing in a journal. He sat down next to her.

"This is a really comfortable bed," he said. "At least, it was. I'm not sure how it is now." He tried smiling a little. It felt odd.

"It's good," Danika said softly. "I like it."

"I have to go now, Danika. Do you need anything?"

"No, I'm fine. Thank you, Peter. Thank you for driving to Brentwood to get my things."

"Of course. And don't worry. I'll find out about immigration law and do all I can so you can still marry Eddie."

Danika, tearful, reached over and hugged him. Peter said goodbye then, and walked back out to the kitchen. Marya asked if he would like some tea.

"I would, but I've got to get going. Thanks, though."

"Okay, I'll see you soon. I'm going to bring some food over to Tom tonight."

"That's good. I'll call you tomorrow," Peter said. He kissed his mother and went out the door, very glad that she was not alone.

*

Peter was relieved to be home, knowing that he didn't have to drive any more for at least twelve hours, unless it was to pick up something at the grocery store. He always looked forward to taking off his suit upon arriving home, and his shoes, checking the mail, decompressing for a few minutes. That day he had not worked, so he was not in a suit, but he still enjoyed walking through the front door of what he felt was his sanctuary. He was never quite sure what sort of a mood or situation he would walk into, but whatever it was, he could handle it. It was better than L.A. traffic.

Theresa was in bed. *Damn.* The manic rush had ended abruptly, probably brought on by Anya's death. Joe was watching cartoons in the living room; Kat was in her room talking on the phone. Heather was downstairs with Leif, and Mike was at class. All was semi-well. Peter found the mail on the kitchen counter and sifted through it, finding nothing of interest. He walked out the living room and flopped on the couch next to Joe. The Transformers cartoon was on the TV.

"Hi, Dad," Joe said.

"Hi, Joe. How was your day?"

"Fine. Mom was in bed, though."

"Yes, I see that. I'll go talk to her in a minute. Everything go okay here?" Peter asked.

"Yeah. Am I staying home from school again tomorrow?"

Peter told him he could if he wanted to.

"No," Joe said. "I'm okay. I mean, I'm sad about Aunt Anya, but I think I'm okay to go to school."

"Okay, Son," Peter said, remarking inwardly at his son's maturity. He also figured that Joe probably didn't want to stay home again to listen to his mother crying all day. "I'm going to go see Mom now."

He walked back through the hallway and across the stair landing over to the master bedroom and opened the door. There she was, in bed, either pretending to be asleep or really asleep. Peter wasn't sure. Usually, when he came home and found her in bed, he would go around to her side and sit down and wait for her to "wake up" before she would talk to him. He decided to try a different tactic this time. He went around to his side of the bed and climbed in next to her, still in his clothes. She bolted upright.

"Peter! You scared me!"

"Theresa, you knew it was me," he stated.

She huffed and lay back down. At least now he knew for sure that she was awake. They lay there for a few minutes, Peter quiet and motionless, Theresa turning over every fifteen seconds or so. She seemed unnerved by his presence in the bed.

"Peter, I have to talk to you about something."

His blood went cold, not knowing what to expect. It could be anything. But it would most assuredly not be good. "What is it?" he said, still lying on his side facing her.

"The day that we went to see Anya at the hospital, I remembered something. I had blocked it out, I guess, because it was - so upsetting. I'm scared, Peter, I don't know what to think, what to do." She turned to face him.

"What?" he prodded. *What in God's name did she do?*

Theresa sighed. "I think it happened a couple of months ago, one night when I was driving home from visiting my mother on her birthday, and...I think I hit someone with my car, Peter. This memory just flashed into my mind of driving on the dark road after I left her house, and I heard a loud thud and felt a jolt from hitting something."

"How do you know it was a person? It could have been an animal. I think you're just remembering the night that we found the body by the side of the road. That was upsetting. I think you're remembering that and being influenced by what happened to the little boy that Danika was a nanny for. Really, honey, if you had hit a person, you would have known it."

Theresa sat up and covered her mouth. Her eyes watered. "But it was. I really believe that it was a person I hit. Peter, I have to do something! I could be responsible for someone's death! I couldn't live with myself!"

And then Peter realized – she was not in a typical depressive episode. According to what he'd read, it sounded like she was in a mixed state – depressed but also manic. Either she really was delusional enough to make herself believe that she had hit someone with her car, or – and Peter didn't know which was worse – she actually had. *My sister dies and the next day my wife has to put the focus back on herself. We haven't even buried her yet, for God's sake. Ohhh...she really does need help. This is the last straw. She has got to start seeing a therapist, but I can't suggest it now. I have to just get through the next few days. I'll deal with this after Anya's funeral.*

Peter took a deep breath, and then he knew what to say. "Honey, we'll get through this together. If you believe that's what happened, I believe you. We'll have to talk more about this, but don't worry. I'll help you. You can count on me. But right now, I've got to get dinner ready for the kids, and us. You need to eat, honey. Everything will be all right."

"Oh, Peter, I'm so scared," Theresa said, clutching him. "What's going to happen?"

"Nothing right now, sweetheart. We'll look into it right after Anya's funeral. I'll start making some inquiries - I know who to call. We'll get this sorted out. Just give me a little time, okay?" The fake words rang in Peter's head, sounding far away and foreign. He wanted to yell at her, It's not about you! *Oh, she has lost it. Something is terribly wrong. It's like she doesn't even remember that Anya died.*

As if reading his mind, Theresa said, "I know you're upset about Anya, but I'm glad that you realize how serious this is. I'm really scared and I'm glad you believe me."

"Of course I believe you," Peter said, looking into her troubled eyes. "I'm going to go start dinner now, okay, honey? You keep resting if you want." He kissed her forehead and got out of bed, discreetly clenching his fists. *My sister died a horrible death yesterday. Yesterday!*

"I'll be all right. Just a few more minutes and then I'll be out," Theresa said, lying back down.

Peter shut the door and walked into the kitchen feeling as if he were in a trance. *What am I going to do? She needs medication soon. But I can't do anything yet. I have to get through this weekend. Anya's funeral is on Monday, and then first thing Tuesday, I'll take Theresa to the doctor. Tomorrow's Friday. I'll call tomorrow to make an appointment for Tuesday. But Theresa can't know. Oh, my God, I think she's lost her mind. I have to let her think that I believe her. I have to placate her. Is this enabling? No. This is survival. This is calculated survival.*

*

Eddie came over to Anna's house to see Danika for lunch the next day, since he was off work from the mechanic shop and would be working the evening shift at the restaurant. He brought her yellow carnations and she wrapped her arms around him, not wanting to let go, wishing he could take her away, and all of this would have never happened.

"Hey, hey," Eddie said soothingly as he pulled out of the hug and looked at her distraught face. He wore his work uniform – black pants and white button-up shirt – so that he could go straight there from visiting her. "It's okay. You're okay, you're not in jail, and Eli didn't die, and if you get deported, we'll deal with it."

"My parents won't 'deal with it.' I have to tell them tonight, and I'm so afraid! I'm ashamed that I made a mess of my life."

Eddie suggested they go sit down and talk in her room. They walked back through the hallway, went past all the family portraits (both black and white and color), and into the room that Danika was staying in. She had made the bed, a double size with an orange twill bedspread from the 1970s, and put her suitcase on the floor next to the small wooden desk, which had a chair from the dining set pulled up to it. On the wall was a calendar of horses, a foot-long three-barred metal cross, and a poster of Yosemite Valley. Danika hadn't been there yet.

They sat down on the edge of the bed, and Eddie turned to her and took her hand in his. "Two years ago, when I finished high school, my parents wanted me to go to college. They had saved up five thousand dollars for the first two years. And I told them that I really wanted to start my own business, that this was America, and it was time for me to do go after my own dream. After all, I was young when I came here, but I am an immigrant too!" Danika nodded and smiled, and Eddie continued, "So I told them I wanted to invest in a company that was already established, so I could be part owner. And I wanted to do that with the mechanic shop. But I needed ten thousand dollars, and I thought, all I have to do is double what I have. And so I gambled on sports games. And I lost all of my parents' money that they saved for me. I was so ashamed. I was afraid to tell them, just like you. And they were upset when I told them, but then I said I would work two jobs to earn back the money and repay them, and that's what I'm doing. Danika, your parents love you, or they wouldn't have helped you in the first place. And I love you too, but I have to go to work now, okay? I'll see you soon." He took her face in his hands, kissed her, and left.

Danika lay back on the bed, remembering what she'd said to Theresa when she stayed at their house: "I guess I'm not very good with kids," and started crying, remembering the horrifying screech and thud. How could she tell her parents? How? And Anya was dead, and everyone was so sad. Maybe that's why Claire was doing drugs, to deal with the pain of losing her mother. So very sad.

She cried quietly, not wanting to disturb Anna, who was taking a nap in her bedroom down the hall. But she had momentarily forgotten about Marya, who was staying in the third bedroom, which had been turned into an office.

A minute later, Marya, in jeans and a dark blue long-sleeved t-shirt, stood at the door, saying she heard her crying and asking if she was okay. Danika apologized and said she needed a tissue, and Marya ducked into the adjacent bathroom to grab one and handed it to her. Danika blew her nose.

"I feel so guilty about the accident and my visa, and I don't know how I'm going to tell my parents!"

"Maybe if you tell them, afterward, it will help you to feel better. You know, like a confession?" Marya said, getting on her knees briefly and putting her hands together to mime the word.

"Yes, maybe you're right," Danika said, dabbing her eyes. "And, I have another…confession."

"What's that?"

"The day before Easter, when we make the pysanky, I went to the bedroom and saw Claire putting drugs in her nose. She asked me not to tell, but I am worry about her."

Marya covered her mouth with her hand and tears welled in her eyes. Danika knew it wasn't for the first time that day. "That's my fault. Claire's been living with me, and I should have seen it, I should have noticed something. I should have talked with her more. She's just a kid," Marya said and gasped. "Thank you for telling me, Danika. I'm going to do everything I can to help Claire."

"That's good. I hope she will be okay."

"She will be."

Danika said that she needed to call her parents and not wait any longer, and Marya reached down to hug her before closing the door behind her. Danika fished through her purse for her international calling card and dialed out on the standard beige push-button phone.

Her mother answered. It was around 10:00PM there, and Danika hoped that she would be rested, watching television before bed. At first she sounded irritated that someone would be calling then, but when Danika said it was her, she sounded more pleasant.

Danika thought it best to begin with a neutral topic and talked about Anya's death. Her mother offered condolences to Anna and all of the family members, saying how sad they must be.

"I'll tell them, Matka. And there is some other sad news I must tell you," Danika began. She got up, swallowed, and paced the small bedroom as she described the events of the accident and her arrest.

Her mother's reactions vacillated between horrified shock ("He was hit by a car?") and disappointed anger ("How could you have continued to stay there illegally?").

Danika began crying again, and her mother's emotions turned to abusive rage. It was then that Danika realized there might have been a subconscious reason why she always wanted to get away.

"Crying isn't going to help anything! You think crying is going to make me feel sorry for you? You made a mess of things and shamed your family! You wanted to chase your dreams but didn't bother to make a contingency plan. Meanwhile you wasted your parents' money and ruined another family's life! You better pray that you are not deported because I don't want to see your face again!"

CHAPTER ELEVEN

Anya's funeral was held at St. Mark's Roman Catholic Church, which was also the same church Theresa's parents had attended for at least fifty years. They had been married there, and Theresa and her brother and sister had all been baptized there. She remembered that Anya and Tom had been married there too, twenty-five years ago. They made it to twenty-five years only to be wrenched apart, Theresa thought. The church had changed so little but the people so much.

Theresa wore a black knit, knee-length wrap dress with three-quarter-length sleeves. It had a deep V neckline, but she never wore the type of bras to create cleavage, so she felt it was not in poor taste. It was just her style, and she felt comfortable in it. She figured people had enough to think about at funerals.

She looked around the church and stared at the sun beaming through the stained glass windows onto the heads of the parishioners on the other side of the aisle. Dust particles swirled above them as they always had on a sunny day. Perhaps that happened on cloudy days as well, but no one could see it.

The church was full, and more people stood in the back. Theresa suspected that most of them were from the college where Tom and Anya were professors. Theresa felt terrible for Tom, entering retirement without his love, the woman who got to that point with him. She could see him crying as Tom's sister sang "Ave Maria." And she felt so sad for their kids, losing their mom just as they were beginning adulthood. Peter then gave the eulogy, although later the priest did another one. Peter's voice broke a few times while he spoke, and Theresa felt sad for him and Marya, losing their beloved sister.

She thought about Bridget moving and remembered the last time they saw each other, briefly (in passing) on Christmas at their parents' house. She remembered the obligatory, for-their-sake hug that passed between them. Bridget could not even look at her face, let alone her eyes, after twenty-four years! Theresa had to call her, had to see her before she moved to Boston. Her only sister!

Theresa's brain was churning. She hadn't been sleeping much at all the last few days; her brain wouldn't shut off. Lying in bed, even when she had cleared her mind of any thoughts – things she had to do the next day, things the kids needed, things that happened years ago, things that hadn't happened yet, things that never would happen – someone else's thoughts invaded her brain. Random, racing thoughts – words, phrases, images – that had no continuity, made no sense. One night she heard basketball statistics from an unrecognizable male voice in her head, saying things she would never have heard and wouldn't have known. Where did that come from? Her brain kept whirring all night. Even when the rest of her body attempted to sleep, her brain did not. She awoke tired from two hours of "sleep," dragged herself through the day, yet still could not sleep the next night. Or the next. But it wasn't insomnia – at least with insomnia it was her own thoughts that kept her up, not those of a phantom basketball coach. She could barely sit still there in the church pew, constantly feeling the urge to get up or rock herself to ease the churning.

When the service finally ended, she hurried outside with Leif, using him as an excuse to make her quick exit. She walked around holding his hand through the gardens around the back of the church, looking at the terra cotta fountain inlaid with glazed turquoise tiles. The addition worked well with the mission-themed church, and Leif enjoyed a little splashing until it was time to get into the cars and drive to the cemetery. Theresa was glad she had avoided standing in the reception line outside of the church, greeting everyone and exchanging condolences while the coffin was brought out. She couldn't handle the bleakness of it all.

When they arrived at the cemetery, Heather took Leif to a different area during the burial, and Theresa wished she could have been the one to do it, but she knew she needed to be with Peter. She sat next to him on the left side of the front row.

The coffin had been lowered into the ground already, and Theresa stared at it, remembering her grandmother's funeral when she was seven years old. Everyone was supposed to go up and toss a handful of dirt on top of the coffin, which seemed to her to be in a cavernous realm, the underworld. She watched Bridget go up and do it, and then it was her turn. As she stood at the edge of the abyss and put her hand out to toss the dirt, she felt as if she were being pulled, and she screamed as she fell in. Her father quickly climbed in and lifted her out and held her as she cried and gasped into his chest. All of her life since then she was plagued by nightmares about falling into darkness, into the depths of some kind of madness.

Theresa began rocking slightly in her seat, agitation filling her again. The sound of the priest reciting passages seemed to fade. Then she heard someone crunching tortilla chips, loudly. Alarmed, she looked around as the priest kept reading verses. The crunching sound got louder, and she jerked around in her seat searching frantically for the source.

"What's the matter?" Peter hissed at her.

"Who's making that crunching noise?" she said. "Don't you hear it?"

"There's no crunching noise," Peter hissed again.

Theresa kept hearing it, not like it was in her head, but like it was right in front of her face, an invisible tormenter with a bag of chips. She put her hands over her ears and yelled, "Stop it!"

The priest looked at her and asked, "Is something wrong?" at the same moment that Peter demanded, "What's *wrong* with you?!" and Claire started wailing. Theresa put her head down and began rocking in her seat. The crunching sound was abating, but there was no denying that something was, indeed, very wrong.

*

"Danika, could you help me to open this?" Anna called from the kitchen. Her arthritis was flaring up; it was difficult even to operate an electric can opener. She couldn't seem to get it aligned properly.

Danika came in a moment and did it for her, then she poured the tomato soup into a pot on the stove. Anna thanked her and asked her if she would like some for lunch. She and Danika had been cooking dinner together for the past week since Danika had moved in, but Danika didn't usually eat lunch. Anna could see her niece losing weight from the stress and not being able to eat, and she worried. She worried about herself, too. The combination of grief and worry was not good for anyone, especially when you have buried your child. She also wondered what had happened with Theresa; it was disturbing on several levels.

"Okay, I will have a little," Danika said. "Thank you."

"You need to eat more; you are getting too skinny. Too skinny is just as bad as too fat," Anna said, stirring the pot, trying not to think of Anya. "I am baking some rolls, too. You can have that with butter; it will be good for you."

Danika told her in Slovak that she had no appetite; she felt like she had to force herself to eat. She felt so anxious all the time, not knowing what was going to happen to her, worrying about the little boy. She said that she felt useless now that she wasn't working, that she was just biding her time. She said that she felt like a failure, that her time in America ended in shame. Her parents practically disowned her. Her one hope was Eddie, who called her every night and came to see her whenever he could.

"Don't worry, Danika. Peter will find a way for you to marry Eddie and stay in America," Anna told her. She knew how important it was for immigrants to feel that they succeeded. She knew the struggle, the frustration with not being able to communicate, the missing your family, the realization that nothing was going to be as easy as the recruiters said it would be, the longing for a lost love. So you find someone who you're attracted to and tell yourself you love that person, especially if they have something in common with you. But short courtships don't necessarily mean that two people aren't serious, or devoted, or don't really love each other.

She remembered meeting Michael, her husband. She had been in America for two years, living with her aunt. The memory made her feel like things had come full circle now that Danika was living with her. Anna's Aunt Mary was a big woman whose round face was always damp with sweat, and she had nine children. When Anna arrived, Mary's friends complained to her, saying, "Don't you have enough kids of your own – you have to take somebody else's kid?" They said that right in front of Anna, as if she couldn't hear, as if she didn't matter. But Aunt Mary spread her arms and said, "I'm like a chicken with big wings. I can cover them all." She had an answer for everything! Anna gladly pitched in and helped her with all the cooking, cleaning, and caring for the younger children, and Aunt Mary told her that she didn't know how she managed without her. Her oldest daughter had gotten married and had a baby of her own, and Ludmilla, the next oldest, worked as a seamstress and a cook to help support the rest of the family.

One autumn night, after she had lived in America for almost two years, Anna went to a dance with her cousin Ludmilla, who was only six days older than Anna. She had met other Rusyn and Slovak boys in America, but none who impressed her. Most of them worked in the coal mines, were uneducated, and did not have any prospects for the future. She knew from her family's experience that a man can only work so long in a mine and then his health suffers. She had learned six months earlier of her father's death and knew that the coal mines had begun his decline.

The dance was held at a local grange-type of hall, with people from nearby counties attending and socializing. It was 1929; Anna and Ludmilla wore long dresses with felt hats and smiled, giddy from the excitement of the night. While outside getting some air, Anna surveyed the crowd of people milling about and saw many good-looking young men, all dressed to impress. Then she saw a car pull up and park, and a short guy about her age, who reminded her of her father, got out of it and walked to the end of the entrance line at the dance. He had short blond hair and a hardy build under his button-up white shirt and tie. Anna kept her eye on him the whole time.

That's the kind of fella I'd like to meet. She had never seen a car until she came to America, and seeing a young man her age driving one certainly impressed her.

Anna pointed him out to Ludmilla and made her intentions clear. Ludmilla smiled and pointed to a boy she had her sights set on as well. "See you on the dance floor!" Anna called after her.

She ducked back inside and ran to get a beer to offer the young man as he came through the door, figuring that would get his attention. It did. She stood by the entrance, and after he came in, she handed him the glass and said, "You look like you could use a drink."

Surprised, he put his hand around the glass and smiled. "I must be in heaven because an angel is bringing me beer," he said, introducing himself.

Anna asked if he lived around there, and he told her that he was from a town about ten miles away. "You drove all this way for a dance?" she asked.

"Well," Michael said, smiling and winking, "I heard there were some pretty girls around here, so I had to see for myself. And it sure is true!" They discovered that they were from the same part of Czechoslovakia; their villages just a few miles apart, and Michael had also come to America at the age of seventeen. They marveled at their similar backgrounds and experiences. Soon, Michael finished his beer and danced with Anna for the remainder of the night, and then he gave her a ride home. He dropped her off with a kiss and a promise that he would stop by to see her in two days.

Michael kept his word. And he kept his word every other day for two weeks. By the third week, he was coming to see her every night. Anna was afraid that he would lose his important job as a machinist at the Endicott Johnson Shoe Factory. One night, sharing a beer at a tavern in Anna's town, their heads pressed together, Anna said, "It would be better, if you think the way I think, that we should go to the priest."

"That's what I was going to say," Michael said, kissing her.

They were married two weeks later in a small ceremony at Anna's church. The priest was the same one who had married Anna's parents twenty-three years earlier. He knew Anna, knew her feisty, independent ways, and he said to her the day before the wedding, "Don't forget – when you get married, the man wears the hat."

"Oh, I wear a hat, too!" Anna said, smiling coyly.

"You know what I mean," the old priest said.

"*J'aznat,*" she said. *I know.*

As with most ethnicities, Rusyns loved their weddings. During the liturgy, shiny, gold, jeweled crowns are placed on both the bride and groom to symbolize that they are now each other's king and queen of their own kingdom. They sing together, pray together, and receive communion together. The whole town has a party for the rest of the day, eating, drinking, and dancing. When Anna had been younger, there were weddings at least once a month. People married quickly and they married young.

And we stayed married, Anna thought. *We didn't divorce. It didn't matter how many times we fought or how many times I wondered what if I had married John Nagajda, I knew that Michael was the husband I chose. He kept his word and I kept mine.*

Immediately after the wedding they drove to Michael's town, Anna bringing only her suitcase of belongings and some wedding gifts, including two goose-down pillows from her Aunt Mary. They arrived late at night at the room and board where Michael lived, which was good, because they immediately went to his room and consummated their marriage. Their wedding night was full of young lust, but, she realized not too long afterward, not true passion. They were attracted to each other, but they both realized, in retrospect, that they had both married to get something – a partnership with fringe benefits.

They had no honeymoon; both wanted to move and get started at their new jobs, their new life. Anna got a job as a piece-worker and they rented a larger room, confident they had made a good decision as soon as they heard of the expansion plans. Endicott-Johnson built homes for their employees, and Anna and Michael wanted to buy one. Endicott-Johnson, or "E-J," as they called it, planned to build a whole community in fact – with stores, schools, restaurants, a post office, and a hospital. Anna knew that this was the life she wanted, not slaving away on what would become a Communist-owned farm in Czechoslovakia.

And the rest of the Endicott-Johnson community was built as promised, and thrived. The company produced nearly all of the shoes and footwear for the US Army during World War I and II and eventually had retail outlets in thirty states. There were plenty of jobs. Michael and Anna worked six days a week and saved their money. Some of it would be used to send back to Czechoslovakia for Michael's cousin John to come over, and the rest of it would be for them, and for their children. And their children's children. They were doing it – they had immigrated to America and were proudly living the American Dream. *Their* dream.

And Danika's might be cut short. *Her* dream. Anna felt Danika's frustration, her disappointment. She felt her fear of failure. It consumed her like fire.

"Is Eddie coming over tonight?" Anna asked as they ate their warm tomato soup on the rainy spring day.

"No, he has to work late," Danika said, not looking up.

"Car mechanics work late?"

Danika picked up her head. "He has two jobs to make more money. At night he washes dishes at a restaurant. Sometimes he is a waiter for the lunchtime. That is when I met him."

"Oh, that's good; he's hard worker. He's smart boy." Anna spoke in simplistic English for Danika's sake. She remembered how difficult it was to follow English the first year that she lived in America.

"Yes, I hope I can work again soon," Danika said, biting into a buttered roll.

"Peter will take care of that. He is smart boy, too!"

Danika smiled. "He is a good son to you. You are proud of him?"

Anna switched to Slovak to be able to speak at length and have Danika understand her without having to speak slowly or translate. "Yes, very proud. God was smiling the day he was born!"

"I hope someday that my son will be as good to me as Peter is to you. So helpful, and kind. And smart. But I feel so uncertain about my future! I'm so scared, Teta! My parents will be so angry if I have to go back. They paid for most of my plane ticket here, and...and to continue on to Australia."

"Australia?" Anna asked incredulously.

"Yes. I was supposed to stay here only a few weeks – a month at the most, visiting and sightseeing – and then continue to Australia. I – I had a boyfriend there. He was an exchange student in Czechoslovakia last spring, and we fell in love, and I was going to Australia to marry him. And then I called him when I landed in New York, because I was so excited to be here, and I wanted to tell him. So I called him from the airport, and he said that he changed his mind and he didn't want to marry me anymore," Danika's voice broke, but she continued. "He said that I should either stay in America or go back home. And I couldn't go back home. I wanted to work off the money that my parents had spent on the plane tickets!" Danika wiped her eyes with her white paper napkin.

"Oh, sweet girl," she said, shushing her. "You know that was not your fault. Your parents must realize that."

"They said that they never trusted him and that I was a silly girl for believing him!"

"Did you tell them what happened?"

"Yes. I told them that I wanted to work in America for a while to save up some money. I thought they would think that was a sensible thing to do," Danika said, taking a sip of water.

Anna's spine tingled. "Does Peter know about this?"

Danika's eyes watered again. "No...oh, Teta! I – I

didn't want him to know that I knew that my visa was only for three months, so I told him that I didn't know! When I applied for the visa I thought I was continuing to Australia, so I only got a three-month visa. It's all my fault! I made a mess of things! Now Peter won't be able to help me!" She covered her face and cried.

"Shh, it's okay, Danika. You have to tell Peter. He needs to know about it," Anna said quietly. She was glad that this information came to light before the court hearing. "I'll call him tonight and tell him, if you want me to explain it to him. Peter will figure out what to do."

Danika stopped crying. "Thank you," she said. Then, "Excuse me." She got up from the table and went to the bathroom.

Anna felt weary. It took a lot out of her to feel others' pain, and she was low on reserves – what "reserves" there could be for this sort of thing, her "gift," as her mother had called it - since Anya's very recent death. Anna remembered her mother telling her, as her brother lay dying of whooping cough long ago, "This energy makes you powerful; it is your protection that will transmute the pain of others. Breathe deeply, and let yourself feel the pain of the situation, knowing that your heart is big and strong enough to hold it. As you breathe, visualize healing light emanating from your heart and touching all that are suffering. You will help yourself as well as them." But Anna never felt that she helped anyone, especially herself. She got up to clear her place.

Danika returned and Anna said, "I'm feeling tired now. I'm going to take a nap. Will you be all right?"

"Yes, Teta Anna. Thank you for your help. I feel better," she said, giving Anna a hug. "I'll do the dishes."

"Okay. I'll see you in about an hour or so," Anna said, turning to walk down the hall.

She closed her bedroom door, closed the red drapes, and pulled back the embroidered bedspread on her queen-size bed. She had made the bedspread herself about thirty years ago, painstakingly embroidering the beautiful patterns of red, orange, yellow, and blue flowers with green leaves and stems swirling around on the beige muslin panels. Her walls were white, as were all the walls of her home. She liked the purity of white, the soothing property that it held. It was a potential for redemption, an opening of light. She wanted to surround herself with it.

Anna climbed into bed and turned on her right side, facing her three-foot-high, wide oak dresser with the big, oak-framed mirror above it. Her eyes flooded as she remembered Anya, in her prom dress, standing in front of the mirror, turning to admire the back of her lovely powder blue dress, the ribbons laced up the corset. She looked at her hair that Anna had piled up on the top of her head and pinned into place. But the most beautiful of all was her smile - Anya's radiant smile, infectious in its grandeur. Oh, how she missed her lovely girl. How she missed the light that she brought to the world.

Now I know, Anna thought. *Now I know why my mother was such a broken, quiet woman. It was because she grieved for her children. Her brave young son who had marched to his death, her infant son whose whole life had been taken away, and her daughter who had landed on her head in a fall. Oh! The pain of burying your children! Oh, Matka! I am so sorry! I can't tell you how sorry I am. I felt everyone's pain but yours!*

CHAPTER TWELVE

Next time, I'm taking her list and going by myself, Peter thought as he followed his mother around the grocery store while she pushed the cart. *She moves slowly enough without stopping every five feet to look at something, so help me God!*

But it was probably the first time she was out of the house since Anya's funeral, and she needed a change of scenery, Peter surmised. He let her take her time, tried to be patient. If anything, this lag time gave him a chance to mull over everything that had happened in the last two weeks, and try to make some sense out of it, or at least, to take a breath.

Getting through the weekend after Theresa's outburst was like walking through broken glass. Peter tried to discuss the incident with her and she refused. She actually did not lie in bed much, but she still seemed depressed. He didn't know what was going on with her, especially now that she was hearing things. Hallucinating! That seemed like a very bad sign. And believing she hit someone with a car! What if she did? But he supposed, if she had manic-depression, or bipolar, as the current psychology books that he'd leafed through had called the disorder, then she wouldn't have much control over her behavior, would she? Especially since she was unmedicated! Yes, he figured he had to just get through the weekend, get through his initial, raw grief, and take Theresa to her appointment on Tuesday that he had been fortunate enough to set up. It turned out that one of the partners in his firm had a brother who was a psychiatrist, so Peter called him. He didn't know how he could ever repay this man for seeing them on such short notice. He decided to tell Theresa after they got home from the wake.

Anya's funeral seemed to be more emotional than any Peter had ever attended. He knew that his sister had been a friendly, vibrant person, but he never realized the extent of her influence. She had touched so many lives. Many students attended her funeral, and of course university colleagues, but also dozens of friends and neighbors, even parents of her children's friends. It was truly remarkable how loved she was. The church was completely full; flower wreaths were piled all the way across the altar and covered her closed casket. Tom had asked Peter to give the eulogy, and he accepted.

With his courtroom experience, Peter felt comfortable speaking in front of people, but this was certainly more than he had ever spoken to before. And he had never felt this emotional before. When the time came, after Tom's sister sang a moving rendition of "Ave Maria," Peter stepped up to the sermon stand with his notes. He talked about how she had been as a child, recounted stories illustrating what a good big sister she was, and then what a wonderful wife and mother, daughter and aunt. He talked about her professional dedication and regaled the anecdote from Easter dinner, when she made the comment that their mother would drop her articles until the day she - Anya - died. He closed on as positive a note as he could come up with, saying how thankful he was for the time that he had with her, for enlivening the world while she was here. "For showing us that we're here for two reasons: to enjoy life and to take care of each other. Because that's how she lived, and I can't think of a better way to do it."

Tom came up after the service and hugged him. "Thank you for those words of love. It meant so much to me. Anya was blessed to have a brother like you."

Peter, choking up, could only say, "You're welcome. Wish I could do more."

The burial was surreal. It hit all of them hard, and Theresa's auditory hallucination didn't help. Their mother sobbed unreservedly; Peter and Marya sat on either side of her with tears streaming down their faces. And her frame of being, her immense sorrow, permeated the entire group in attendance. Tom, Claire, and James mourned, their arms around each other. Theresa cried quietly until she heard the alleged crunching. A ghost, perhaps?

The wake was held at Tom and Anya's stately home in Woodland Hills. The shaded, quiet street of their neighborhood offered a restorative serenity to everyone there, mostly extended family and close friends. But of course, Anya had many. Casseroles lined the kitchen counters and filled the refrigerator and freezer. Some were served at the wake so that they would not go to waste. Flowers filled the front part of the ranch style home and spilled out onto the front porch and lawn. Anya's favorite party game, croquet, was set up in the back yard, and a bunch of cousins played. Peter was glad to see that Kat was among them, participating. She was warming up to the idea of him co-coaching her softball team, actually joked with him about it, saying, "You better not play me too much, Dad. I mean, Coach! That wouldn't be fair to the team." Practice would start in two weeks, and he was relieved that both of them were looking forward to it.

At one point, when things seemed to be winding down and many people had gone, Peter walked through the spacious one-story home, trying to distract himself from the grief by stopping to look at the watercolor seascape paintings that Anya and Tom had collected over the years. He heard someone behind him and turned to see Marya, in her black pants and black button-up knit shirt, holding her arms out to embrace him. She stifled a sob as he held her.

"She had asked me to be Claire's mentor and I didn't pay enough attention to her. I treated her like a roommate instead of a niece who needed me to help her through the pain of knowing that her mother was going to die," Marya sobbed.

"Of *course* you helped her," Peter said, rubbing her back.

"She started doing coke, Peter." Marya pulled out of his embrace and looked at him with her wet, red eyes and tear-streaked face.

He put his hands on her upper arms. "That wasn't your fault."

"I should have been there for her!"

"You were… you were."

She took a deep breath. "I talked with her. I told her nothing's going to take away the pain, that alcohol or drugs will for a moment, but it's still there. I told her you have to make your way through it and just keep focusing on the love. That's all I could think of to say." Fresh tears spilled out of her eyes.

"That's good advice for all of us. I'm sure that helped Claire."

"I hope so. She seems to be allowing herself to feel instead of numbing herself. I think she stopped doing the coke."

"Good. She's a smart girl. And she's surrounded by people who love her, including you. Especially you. She's going to be okay."

Marya hugged him again and said that she was going to look for their mother. "I'll make sure she's eating."

Peter swallowed tears as he watched his little sister walk down the hallway. He closed his eyes and said a prayer for her, and his niece, as he walked into the library, his favorite room in the house. He noticed Anya's artistic touch in every room, but this one had its own look and feel. It was a meeting of the minds for two professors; Tom with all his economics and history books, and Anya with all her novels, short story and poetry anthologies, Shakespeare volumes, and a huge Oxford English Dictionary on its own four-foot-high wooden stand. The books were lined up on lovely, thick shelves made of varnished pine. A standing globe, flanked by two chairs upholstered in green velveteen, occupied one corner. Peter sat in one and looked at the books, thinking of Anya, wishing she could be there to ask her advice about how to talk to Theresa. Anya was always so level-headed and compassionate, she would know exactly how to present it. He visualized her standing in front of him, tried to channel her wisdom as he sat in her chair. What would she have suggested? Finally an idea came to him.

And so that night came, and the talk with Theresa. Peter felt so drained after his sister's funeral and now he had to deal with this "intervention" for his wife. And that's how he decided to treat the event, although of course that word would never be mentioned. He waited until Joseph was in bed and Kat was in her room for the night. Oddly, Theresa had been following Peter around the house all night. It surprised him at first, because she usually liked to have time to herself for a bath, or to talk to her mother or brother on the phone, or watch TV or look at catalogs. But when he thought about it, Peter realized that she had been waiting all weekend for this moment – to talk to him more about this idea of hers that she had hit someone with the car and what to do about it.

Peter went out into the living room and sat on the couch, and Theresa followed. He began with, "How are you feeling?"

"Oh, exhausted. This has been such a stressful week. First going to the hospital when Anya was dying. All that emotion just takes a lot out of me. Then the night that I remembered the accident, that was the worst. I have not been sleeping well at all. And just dealing with that all weekend, having it on my mind, not knowing what could be done about it. And the funeral." She held up her hands. "It's just been an awful week." Her voice was harried, and her eyes glazed.

"Yes, thank you for being so understanding, honey." Peter heard the words calmly come out of his mouth, but he wanted to yell at her, *I just buried my beloved sister today, and all you can think about is how it affected you!*

Theresa looked at him. Her eyes focused for a moment, and she threw her arms around him. "I'm so sorry about Anya!"

Peter's surprise was overruled by his grief. His eyes watered and a ragged breath escaped his throat. She really did care.

"And I'm sorry I made a scene at the funeral when I heard the crunching," Theresa said as she cried. "I think I need to see a doctor." She covered her mouth as she grimaced, about to cry.

Thank God! "Honey, I was noticing that things have been getting hard for you lately, and I already made an appointment. It's with a psychiatrist who deals with depression and other disorders. He's the brother of Frank, at the firm," Peter said, holding his breath.

"Oh, thank you, Peter. Thank you." Theresa hugged him again. "When's the appointment?"

"Tomorrow at ten." *This might work out okay after all.*

Dr. Robert Tucci was a handsome, large-boned, bearded extrovert who mirrored Theresa's mania in order to bond with her. Peter thought he was a genius. He had spoken with the doctor over the weekend to explain the situation and his thoughts about Theresa's condition and possible disorder. Dr. Tucci had agreed, after listening to Peter's description for a good twenty minutes, that Peter's assessment was probably correct. The "intervention appointment" went as hoped, and by that evening, Theresa had taken her first dose of medication for what the doctor confirmed was most assuredly bipolar disorder. And by the end of the next session with Dr. Tucci, Theresa had said that the doctor was probably right, and that finding the dead body by the side of the road that night when Peter was driving had been so traumatic for her that her subconscious mind created a memory of her being the one who had hit the person, a hallucinated memory. The doctor also said that auditory hallucinations can occur during manic episodes.

Peter was relieved that things went smoothly at the appointment, because by then he had Danika's court hearing to plan for. He was glad that the truth about Danika's knowledge of her three-month visa came to light, and that he knew about it, because he figured that they could actually use that to her advantage, as well as the fact that she had been taken to jail and interrogated when she was under extreme duress about the little boy, whom she loved, being hit. She only spoke broken English and had not had any legal representation throughout the process. Eddie was there to testify, along with Anna, who wanted to offer emotional support. Peter felt as prepared as possible, but still nervous. Danika's future depended on this.

The judge ruled, "According to current immigration

law, when a foreign resident is in the US but not eligible for adjustment of status (for violating terms of the visa by working, which Ms. Zarachnek did), the US citizen intended-spouse, in this case, Mr. Montoya, applies for the K-1 visa (a temporary visa for the fiancé of the US citizen) abroad at the US Consulate in their country of citizenship, in this case, Czechoslovakia. Ms. Zarachnek is allowed to receive the K-1 visa because she was not in the US illegally for more than 180 days. However, the law stipulates that the K-1 visa be issued for 90 days, and during that time, Ms. Zarachnek must stay in Czechoslovakia, and then she will be allowed to return to the US and marry Mr. Montoya. Ms. Zarachnek must also pay her own way back to Czechoslovakia or she will be deported and not allowed to return to the US for three years."

Peter was pleased with the outcome, although Danika was distressed, saying that she did not have the money to buy a plane ticket back to Czechoslovakia. Peter told her that of course he would help her with that expense. She threw her arms around him and kissed him on both cheeks. Eddie shook his hand vigorously, and Anna sat in her seat with a satisfied grin on her face.

At the time, Peter thought that his mother was just proud of her lawyer son again. But she turned to him now, in the grocery store, with a can of poppy seed pastry filler in her hand, and said, "Peter, when Danika goes back to Czechoslovakia, I want to go with her." She dumped the can in the cart and looked up at him.

He studied her face, really looked at the contours, the

lines, in a new, objective way. And those outer manifestations revealed her strength, her determination, and her spirit. There was a fire in her eyes that he hadn't seen before. "Why, Ma?"

"Because I have not seen my sister for almost seventy years. And that is far too long. And because I need to see my village again, where I came from. And because I need to see my parents' graves, and the rest of my family," his mother said, her eyes now watery and her mouth quivering. It lasted a few seconds, and she continued, "And also because Danika should have someone to go with her to talk to her parents. She is afraid to see them because she feels like she failed and they are disappointed in her. She needs the support of another immigrant, someone who can tell her parents what it's like, how hard it can be. I want to go with her."

"Okay, Ma, that sounds like a good idea. Danika has to stay for three months, but you don't have to. You can go over on the same flight, and then you can come back early. How long did you want to stay?"

"Maybe for three weeks. That should be long enough," Anna said. "When does Danika need to go?"

"They gave her thirty days before she was required to leave, which is four weeks from now. I was going to purchase her plane ticket in the next few days, so I'm glad you told me that you wanted to go with her before I bought her ticket. This way I can buy both of them at the same time, and you can sit together on the plane. Did you ever get a passport?"

"No, I don't have a passport," Anna said, a look of dismay on her face.

"It's okay, don't worry. We can apply for rushed processing, and we should have it within three weeks. It'll work out. It sounds like you really want to go, and I'll make that happen for you."

"Oh, thank you, Peter," Anna said, reaching up to embrace him. "I couldn't ask for a better son."

*

Theresa was driving, taking Leif to see his great-grandparents. He would be in daycare soon, and there wouldn't be these opportunities for much longer. "We're going to see G-G-ma and G-G-pa!" she'd told him as she buckled him in his booster seat. She had shown him pictures that morning and tried to get him to say their condensed names, since she figured "great-grandpa" was confusing and too much of a mouthful. Leif tried to reproduce "G-G-pa" and it came out something like "Djido," which was ironic because that's what Peter's father had always had the kids call him.

It was her second week on lithium. For the first time in her life, she felt grounded. She did not feel like crying for no reason or staying in bed all day. The periodic whirring in her brain that kept her up nights was gone. No hallucinations. Now when she thought of the possibility, the "memory," that she had hit someone with the car she realized there was no way it could have happened – there was no longer any "memory." She knew the memory did not exist because it didn't happen. Her brain in the manic state had culled the experience of seeing the body by the side of the road the night of her birthday with what had happened to the boy Danika took care of. Poor Danika. That was a real memory that would probably haunt her the rest of her life.

Theresa remembered the few days that Danika had stayed with them right after the accident, how shell shocked she was. Theresa made her cups of herbal tea and tried to console her. But in the end it was Danika who consoled *her*.

Theresa pointed out that Danika was so brave – "Do you know the word 'brave'?" – to emigrate from her home and her family. "I've never done anything like that," Theresa told her. "And to learn a foreign language so quickly – *that* is a success, not a failure. Look at me – all I've done for twenty years is stay home and take care of children."

Danika, tears in her eyes, looked at her and said, "Theresa, that *is* a success. That *is* brave. You are so important."

And Theresa realized that maybe she just needed to hear someone say it. Her value had always gone unspoken, unacknowledged. Uncelebrated. And it took a nineteen-year-old who'd done childcare for two months to tell her.

Her parents lived in Glendale, about fifteen minutes away in a '60s ranch-style home, shaded by magnolia trees. Theresa noticed that her father wasn't getting to the lawn as much, and there were some rogue, star-topped weeds that she remembered from childhood, and how he hated them, cursed them. Theresa parked the car in the driveway off to the right, and then she held Leif by the hand as they walked up the brick walkway toward the front door.

Her earliest memory occurred at the age of three, when she saw a black velvety spider with a fuzzy orange back climbing on a pile of bricks in the backyard. She was fascinated by the little hairs on its body and its jewel-like appearance in the sunlight. Its movements were jerky all over the brick surface, and it jerked itself into a crack between two bricks. Her father had been building the brick walkway, plus a brick patio in the back yard, on Saturdays in the summertime. It took him all summer to build them. During the winter, he would often go to the den to draw in the evenings – beautiful pencil sketches, usually portraits from photographs or newspaper clippings, sometimes of animals. They – she and Bridget - could watch for a minute, but then they had to leave the den. He kept his drawings in a large green footlocker in the den, and they were not allowed to open it. Decades later, when he was in the hospital recovering from a heart attack, she looked through the trunk one day, and among many other exquisite drawings, including the head of a prize-winning horse, their mother's high school graduation portrait, and President Eisenhower, she found a drawing of a black velvety spider sitting on a pile of bricks. He had seen it too, and marveled over it.

The door swung open and her father's full head of white hair looked up at her. She briefly noticed the deeper lines in his forehead, the fact that he hadn't shaved in three days, and how tired his black eyes looked. He wore a light blue button-up shirt tucked into belted kha-kis and slip-on tennis shoes. When he realized who it was, his face brightened and called out in a booming voice, "Well, look who's here!"

"Hi, Dad. Leif, can you say 'Hi, G-G-pa'?"

Her father scowled. "Don't teach him to call me that nonsense. If he can't say Great-Grandpa, he can just call me Pa."

"Okay, Dad."

"Well, come on in," her father said, stepping aside. He turned his head and called out, "Mary! Theresa's here!"

Theresa's mother was already in the kitchen, and it dawned on Theresa that it was lunchtime and she hadn't thought to bring anything for Leif to eat. She walked in and greeted her exuberant mother, whose slightly wrin-kled face wreathed in a huge smile. Her long gray hair was confined in a bun, and her bare feet beneath her floral print dress padded quickly across the wood floor. Mary took Theresa's face in her hands and kissed it about five times, and she bent down, picked up Leif, and did the same to him. "What a good surprise!" she exclaimed. "I was just making lunch, so I'll add a little more and then we can eat on the patio. What a beautiful day!"

"Yes, it is," Theresa said. She stood next to her mother and began cutting up an apple for Leif. Her mother added more ingredients to the existing antipasto plate – shaved parmesan, olives, prosciutto, artichoke hearts, endive, and tomatoes. She asked Theresa what brought her over today, and Theresa told her that she would be going back to work soon so Leif would be in daycare, and they wouldn't be able to come and visit. "I wish I had done it more often, Mom."

"Honey, I know you did the best you could. And I'm glad you came today."

"After this I'm taking him to see Anna!"

"That's good. And you must be feeling better," Mary said, raising an eyebrow. "That would take some energy to do two visits in one day. But I'm glad you're going to see her. I'm sure she needs that. How horrible to lose one of your children; I could not even think about it." Shaking her head, she picked up the antipasto plate and walked toward the sliding glass doors leading to the patio. Theresa picked up Leif and followed her.

"Yes, I am feeling better." Theresa had previously talked with her mother about her periodic struggles with depression but had not yet told her about her bipolar diagnosis. It was one of her intended purposes for the visit.

"Joe-love?" Mary called over her shoulder. "Will you please make some lemon water and bring it out?" She walked back into the house and came back a minute later with a tray of glasses.

Leif was about half-finished with his apple. "Mom, I'm going to make him some toast."

Theresa found her father in the kitchen, slicing lemons for the glass pitcher of water in front of him. It probably wouldn't be well-received, but she had to ask. "Are you doing okay, Dad? Can I call a service to help with the lawn?"

"Don't be ridiculous. I can still mow my own lawn. I've

just been a little tired lately." He put the lemon slices in the water and picked up the pitcher. "Another week and I'll be back to normal."

"Okay, Dad." She wanted to say, *I know how you feel. I may be younger, but I know how it is to be at the mercy of your brain chemicals, waiting to get 'back to normal,' lying to yourself that it exists. I know that lie. Or is it hope? That thing that keeps you alive. That makes you keep telling yourself it will get better. And wanting with every fiber of your being to believe it.*

In a few minutes Theresa returned to the patio and set the buttered toast strips in front of Leif. She sat down at the black wrought iron grapevine table and started eating the plate her mother had prepared for her. Mary, in her typical extroverted manner, enjoyed making animated faces at her great-grandson as she encouraged him to eat. When he finished, Joe picked him up, announcing that he had some important things to show him around the yard.

"I want to talk to Bridget before she moves," Theresa said to her mother. "I've been diagnosed with a mental illness that affects my behavior. I've had it since child-hood, just in varying degrees. It's a genetic mood disorder called -"

"That's from your father's side," Mary said, gesturing to the back yard.

"Yes, it probably is, but it's not just about getting angry or being depressed."

"I know, honey. Are you talking about manic-depres-sion?"

"It's called bipolar disorder now, but yes. I know it's not an excuse, but a symptom of mania is heightened sexuality -"

"Your father had that."

"Mom! I'm trying to tell you something. It's not an excuse, but it's what caused me to do what I did with Bridget's first fiancé. I want to apologize to her, but I don't know if she'll talk to me. Every time I've tried in the past, she won't. But I'm so sorry, Mom. Not just for what I did to Bridget, but for how I acted to you. I know I snapped at you and said mean things, like at Kat's birthday party, and at Christmas. Will you forgive me?"

Mary waved her arm as if shooing a fly. "Don't even *ask*. You are my daughter, always my child. I may not understand some of the things you did, but I forgave you the moment you did them."

Theresa's eyes watered and she rose to hug her mother. "Thank you, Mom."

Joe walked up then, holding Leif's hand. "Did you give her something?" he asked Mary.

"Yes," Mary said and smiled. "Unconditional love."

*

An hour later, Theresa found herself sitting at Anna's kitchen table eating frozen chocolate chip cookies and sipping milk.

"If I knew you were coming, I would have taken them out of freezer yesterday," Anna said. Theresa hoped she didn't detect a note of disfavor.

"Ma, don't worry, these are fine. And I'm sorry for not calling, I just didn't plan ahead."

"Well, thank you for bringing my only great-grandchild for a visit," Anna said, smiling at Leif as he gnawed on a cookie. "You want to do *zschooty-zschoomp?*" she asked him with more animation than Theresa had ever seen from her.

Leif looked at her blankly but didn't protest when she picked him out of his chair and carried him to the back bedroom which Marya had recently vacated. Theresa could hear Anna enticing Leif to slide down the back of her old vinyl vibrating recliner chair, as she did with all of Peter's and her children, and probably Anya's as well. It was good to hear Anna's laughter; Theresa hoped that a visit with her great-grandson helped her to set aside her grief for a moment. Leif, by the sound of things, seemed to be enjoying the interaction as well. Or maybe it was just that damned silly chair.

After a few minutes, Theresa heard Anna ask Danika to play with Leif, and Anna came back out to the kitchen and sat down at the table, breathing heavily. "He is wearing me out! Danika will watch him. Would you like tea?"

Theresa stood up and motioned for Anna to stay seated. "Yes, I'll make it." She picked up the stainless steel kettle off the stove and filled it with water. She opened a cupboard to get some mugs and Anna told her where the tea was.

"Are you feeling better since the funeral?" Anna asked.

Theresa's heart thumped. She had already apologized to Anna after the funeral, but she still felt self-conscious about the scene she had made. "Yes, I've been to see a doctor and am taking medication. It seems to be working well for me, and I feel better."

"That's good. Health of our heads is just as important as health of our bodies."

"Very true, Ma," Theresa said, relieved that Anna did not seem to be holding it against her. "So, Peter tells me you're going to Czechoslovakia with Danika in two weeks!"

"Yes, so much packing to do! And my passport should be here any day now. I can't wait to see the rest of my family," Anna said, suddenly breaking down. "It's been so very long!"

"I'm sure they'll be thrilled to see you," Theresa said as she walked back to the table with the steaming mugs of tea.

"Maybe, maybe not." Anna then told her about her sister who had fallen off of the roof because she had tripped over Anna's foot when Anna turned too quickly, after they had argued. "I am responsible for her death," she said, tears streaming down her cheeks.

"Maybe it didn't happen the way you thought it did," Theresa said, handing her a paper napkin. She told Anna that she had thought she hit someone with a car because her mind remembered something differently.

"But I really think she tripped over me because I moved too quickly out of anger. And I don't know how to ask Olga to forgive me." Anna, still upset, put her hand over her mouth.

Theresa reached across the table and held Anna's

other hand. "Maybe in the act of asking forgiveness, it is already given. Maybe that will be the moment we give it to ourselves."

Anna nodded. "You're right, Theresa. I need to forgive myself."

So do I, Theresa thought. *So do I.*

CHAPTER THIRTEEN

Anna winced and tried to ignore the pulling pains in her abdomen. She had never flown before, and she had fifteen hours of flying ahead of her. Her passport had come in with only a week to spare, but it did come, and Peter took Danika and her to the airport, and now they were sitting on the plane waiting for it to take off.

Anna had only been on boats, trains, and cars in her life. Her trip when she emigrated lasted five days by boat and about sixteen hours by train. The night she left, her father brought her in a horse-drawn hay cart from their village to the nearest town, Humenne, over four hours away. But not just Anna. Her cousin's seven-year-old daughter, Helen, was traveling with her. Jana, her cousin, did not have the money saved up to make the voyage. Her husband, Helen's father, was already in America, and he was supposed to meet them at Ellis Island. In Humenne, Anna and Helen boarded a train for Kosice, the nearest city, and then continued on to Bratislava and Prague. From there they traveled through Germany and finally to Hamburg, where they boarded the big ship to America. Thanks to her father's detailed directions, she found her way through various railway stations without much difficulty, except for the frightened little girl in her charge. Helen clung to her the entire time, crying and asking for her mother. Anna, filled with anxiety, wanted to cry with her.

Upon arrival in New York, Helen's father was waiting for them and Helen threw her arms around his neck, saying "Otec, Otec," over and over again. Anna already missed her otec.

After "processing," which didn't take too long because she was American-born and had her birth certificate, she traveled by train again for two hours to her Aunt Mary's home. For many years after that, she traveled only by car. Much later, in 1969, she and Michael took a cruise to Hawaii for their fortieth wedding anniversary, celebrating more their dogged commitment to each other rather than an undying love. They had been committed to their goals and dreams and achieving them together as partners, but they never shared a great love. And as they got older, they interacted and communicated more at the level of brother and sister than lovers. She hated to admit the disappointing truth. There had been passion, for a time, but it was long, long gone. If she had to try to figure out when or why, she didn't think she could pinpoint any one time or incident. But, sadly, it had probably occurred even before their first anniversary. They did respect each other, that much she knew. They both worked hard and invested wisely; they both wanted the same things in life - to instill both American values and Rusyn traditions in their children, to move to California, to own their own business, and to build their own home. And they had achieved all of those things – together. The cruise to Hawaii was more like a company retreat meant to reward the two employees of their marriage. Three years later, Michael had a massive stroke.

They had been having dinner at the home of their long-time friends the Yurkos, whom they had met at their new church when they first moved out to Los Angeles from New York in 1952. The couples had attended the weddings of each other's children, the baptisms of each other's grandchildren, and many barbeques, beach trips, and church functions over the years. That night, Anna and Magda were in the kitchen cleaning up from the broiled chicken and creamed potatoes dinner, and Michael and Stephen were out in the living room watching a Dodgers game. They had been Michael's favorite team since they had originated in New York, and he was a big fan. In the middle of an exciting double play, Michael cheered, went to pump his fist in the air, and then slumped in his chair. He could not move the left side of his entire body, nor could he speak. He told Anna later that at first he was aware of what was happening, although he didn't know why. Then he lost consciousness. Stephen called for Anna, and Magda called an ambulance. They didn't know if it was a heart attack, although Stephen thought not because he hadn't seen Michael grabbing his chest at any point. The ambulance arrived and after a quick assessment, the EMT announced that it appeared to be a stroke, and he was whisked away to the hospital.

The stroke almost did him in. After months of therapy, however, Michael was able to speak again in a hoarse, high-pitched voice, much unlike his robust, hearty voice that had called Anna an angel on the night they met. He was also able to walk with the aid of a walker, but was on permanent disability and was not able to work again. Later, he could walk slowly with a cane. He managed to regain much of his long-term memory, but his short-term memory had been severely compromised. Michael remembered the faces of his grandchildren but had to relearn their names, and even years after the stroke, he could not remember that they had aged, nor that any time had gone by since he'd last seen them. He had thought Marya was still in college.

A few years after the stroke, the Alzheimer's kicked in, and Michael needed more assistance with self-care. He also began forgetting where he was, as in what country he was in. Once, before Anna realized how bad he had gotten, he said he was going for a walk. Three hours later, Anna frantically called the police because he hadn't come home yet. Michael was at the station. He had been picked up because he refused to get off a city bus, saying he was going home to Czechoslovakia.

Anna cried that night, realizing that her partner had forgotten about their American Dream. All that they had worked to achieve – his construction business, her shoe store, their home, college educations for their children – was lost in his mind, or lost *to* his mind, to his oldest memories. She wasn't really sure what he remembered of their life together. They couldn't discuss it well. He mostly talked about people from Czechoslovakia, his childhood, people and relatives from his village whom Anna had never met, some she'd never heard him mention before. He would talk about them as if they were old friends of hers, too, as if she should remember them as he did, and was surprised, almost angry, when she did not. Sometimes she just pretended to remember his old friends, because he did not understand. He never got to see them again. He died four years later, unable to differentiate between his own children. On his deathbed, he thought that Anna was one of the hospital nurses.

We should have gone to Czechoslovakia for that trip instead of Hawaii, before the stroke, Anna thought now, as the plane began jockeying for take-off. *Then he could have seen his friends and relatives – and his village - one last time.* But, she realized, that probably would have confused him even more once the Alzheimer's crept in. It was of no use to worry or wonder about it now.

Anna steeled herself as the engines roared, and Danika reached over and held her hand. Anna's eyes must have been wide, because Danika said, "Don't worry, it always sounds like that," with a reassuring smile.

And then the plane sped down the runway, Anna's body pushed back in her seat, she held her breath, and with a wobble and a shove, they were in the air, climbing higher. She had to admit, it was exciting, exhilarating. Anna watched out the window as they ascended, all the cars, buildings, and freeways getting smaller. She marveled at how all the cars looked just like wind-up toys, still moving. And then, in a moment, they really did look like ants. She had always thought it was an exaggeration, but no. Now she could see for herself.

"What did you think?" Danika asked, leaning over.

"I think I like it," Anna said, looking at the sunlight illuminating the clouds. *This is how I always envisioned heaven. And now they are even serving drinks!*

"So now for three weeks, you will speak only Slovak, Teta," Danika said in English. "That is strange for you?"

"No, I still remember it all. I still dream in both English and Slovak. I am good with learning languages, so it's easy for me to switch. When I was growing up, we spoke Rusyn in our home, which was like Slovak, but some different. And when I went to school, when I was younger, we were taught Ukranian. Then, after war, we were taught Russian in school. So really I know five languages, although Russian and Ukranian I don't remember much," Anna said, winking. Danika giggled.

"So, you did not learn English in school?" Danika asked.

Anna switched to Slovak for a while. "No, in Eastern Europe then, probably all of Europe, they did not teach English in schools. No, my father taught me, starting when I was sixteen. Before I was born and my parents lived in America, there was a six-month strike at the coal mine where my father worked. During that time, he studied and taught himself to speak English. When the strike was over, he became General Manager of the Number 10 mine, because he could speak English. But then the owner of the company died, the son sold it, and my parents had to go back to Czechoslovakia. When I was about fifteen I started to think I wanted to go to America, and so my father started telling me stories about his experiences. And then when I was sixteen, I knew that

I wanted to go, so my father started teaching me English. I remember he told me about black people because I had never seen one before. And he said, 'Don't worry because they look different. They are good people.' He told me that so I would not be scared, but also so I would not develop the prejudice of some Americans, because he remembered when he had lived here that many white Americans were prejudiced to blacks, and he didn't want me to learn that."

"Your father sounds like a wise man," Danika said.

"Yes, he was. I learned a lot from him." *Not just how to keep bees and drive a hay cart, but how to think for yourself, be smart, and stand your ground.*

She remembered how he had told her, after he came home from the war, the story of how he had outwitted some Russian soldiers when their family had come back from America. Anna, her older brother, and their mother had stayed behind at an inn in Kosice while he went to buy train tickets for all of them to get back to Humenne. On the path behind the inn he ran into the soldiers, three of them, probably coming back from a bar. He had hidden his valuable items from America – his wrist watch, shaver, and tools – and they robbed him, threatening him with knives and saying they would kill him. Speaking in Russian, he told them he was Russian, and they demanded he show how he blessed himself, so he made the sign of the cross as the Russian Orthodox did. They continued to quiz him ("What do you call a church?") and due to his good memory, he knew the answers, so they let him go.

"My father is very smart too," Danika said. "He encouraged me to learn English in school so that I could emigrate and find a good job. Oh, I hated to disappoint him! It was awful to call my parents and tell them what had happened. I feel so ashamed of what happened with Eli, the little boy, and I had lied about my visa. And my mother was so upset!"

"She didn't mean what she said," Anna told her. "Parents make mistakes too. And she called you to tell you that."

"I'm glad she called, but I still feel terrible."

"They love you, Danika," Anna said. "I'm sure they'll realize they can't blame you for everything that happened. You were under a huge strain when that boy told you not to come to Australia. That was wrong! You were hurting, alone in New York, scared, unsure of what to do, and so any mistakes you made under the circumstances should not be held against you."

"Thanks, Teta. You are so wonderful."

"And you are a sweet girl. Now I must try to get some sleep, okay?" Anna said, giving Danika a kiss. She pulled down her shade.

They switched planes in New York and flew straight from there to Prague without any problems or delays. Anna thought that she would be a pro at flying by the time she got back home. She learned about gates, tickets, baggage, security checks, and boarding. Airports were such emotional places, full of joyful reunions and teary farewells. Everyone was either hurrying or sitting around waiting, but everyone was transitory. Those metal walls held a strange energy with all the comings and goings, vague and unsettled. Anna liked the planes but not the airports. From what she heard, nobody did.

From Prague, they took a short flight to Kosice, the second-largest city in eastern Czechoslovakia, the side of the country which spoke Slovak as opposed to Czech, and Danika's parents picked them up from the airport when they landed late in the afternoon. Anna saw her niece, Danika's mother, whom she had only seen in photos before, and immediately became emotional because Magda reminded her of her sister. She waited for Danika to greet Magda first, a tearful and tentative embrace. After Magda released her daughter, Anna threw her arms around her and kissed her on both cheeks many times.

"Magda, Magda, you have your mother's eyes!" It was like looking into her baby sister's eyes, all these years later.

"You look like her, too!" Magda said, smiling. "Oh, Teta Anna, she will be so happy to see you!"

Thomas, Magda's tall, thin, and bald husband, stepped forward and embraced her. "My son-in-law is also named Thomas," she told him after she kissed his cheeks.

"He must be a good man," Thomas said with a smile.

Magda's face fell, remembering. "Teta, I am so sorry about Anya," she said, and she embraced Anna again.

Anna, already emotional, let the tears fall. "I wish - " she began, her voice catching. "I wish you could have met each other."

"Yes, so do I," Magda said.

Danika seemed to be much more relaxed, realizing

that her parents were not openly upset with her. "Well, shall we go get the bags?" she asked, starting off in the direction of the baggage claim area.

Thomas picked up Anna's carry-ons, and Magda walked with her while holding her arm. "I hope Danika was no trouble for you?" she asked.

"Oh! Of course not! She is a wonderful girl, and I loved having her stay with me. She was a great help to me around the house."

"I'm glad to hear that," Magda said, and Anna sensed the disappointment in her voice.

"Magda, what happened with Danika needing to leave America was not completely her fault. She made the best decision she could, being alone, upset, and unsure of her options, and not wanting to disappoint you. It can be very difficult being an immigrant," Anna said.

"Yes, Teta. I'm just frustrated because I told her not to go to Australia in the first place. I could see that boy she liked was not devoted to her. But she wouldn't listen. And the plane ticket to Australia – very expensive for us – was wasted."

"I understand, my neter. But Danika had to follow her heart. She would have always wondered if she hadn't tried. She says she's going to work and pay you back the money, and I'm sure she will. She feels terrible about disappointing you, she really does. She's not taking it lightly."

"Yes, she did apologize, and I know she feels bad. I just wish she had listened to me," Magda said.

"Children have to find their own way eventually,"

Anna said as they approached the baggage claim area.

"Oh, Teta," Magda said, hugging her. "You are so wise."

*

That night for dinner, Magda made a big tray of halupki and served it with a spinach salad. "We like the traditional food but try to be concerned with our health," she explained.

Anna took a bite. "It's delicious. Is this your mother's recipe?"

Magda confirmed it was how Olga had taught her. Plans were then discussed for when they would go to see her the next day, and Anna felt a pang in her stomach at the thought.

Her youngest sister had been only eight years old when Anna left for America. She remembered saying goodbye to her, embracing her and kissing her plump cheeks, cold because it was nearing winter. Anna told Olga she loved her and she wanted her to come to America when she was big. Her father gave her his small English dictionary, and her mother gave her clothing to bring to her Aunt Mary and all the cousins. For weeks before she left, Anna had made beaded necklaces from colored glass beads to give to all her new relatives. She packed them, the clothing, the dictionary, and some food in a big cloth bundle which had been used to carry wheat to the village mill. It was tied over one shoulder and around the neck, diagonally. She wore four dresses, one on top of other, so she wouldn't have to carry them in the bundle. Her mother had tears in her eyes and could hardly look at her as she helped her to put the dresses on. Anna could understand now how heartbreaking it must have been for her, to have yet another child, one of only two left, to leave, knowing she would probably not see her again. But at seventeen, wanting to put as much distance between herself and a mother she felt ashamed of, Anna couldn't possibly understand.

Years later, she deeply regretted the way she had left her mother. Not because she had left in the first place, but because she hadn't hugged her as lovingly, as sincerely, as she could have. "Goodbye, Matka," she said with little feeling, as if she were saying goodbye to one of the parishioners at church whom she didn't know well. As if her mother were one of those gossiping women of the village and Anna was politely saying goodbye, an expected obligation. Her mother, tears streaming down her face, kissed both of Anna's cheeks. She should have told her mother that she loved her, that she would miss her and keep her in her heart forever. Why didn't she? Why did she have to reject her mother, even on the last day she would ever see her? She withheld her love from the one woman who did nothing but cherish her, and that painful mistake, like a disease which has no cure, could never be undone.

Her father drove the hay cart to Anna's cousin Jana's house to get Helen, who sobbed inconsolably as her mother embraced her and told her little girl she would see her soon. Anna knew it would be at least two years before Jana's husband could save up the money for the ticket.

Thus began the long, jostling trip to the train station early that still-dark morning, during which time Helen slept some, much to Anna's and her father's relief. They arrived four hours later, happy the weather had accommodated them. But this small bit of good fortune was soon forgotten when it was time to say goodbye. Anna's father kissed her, told her he was proud of her, admonished her to be careful, and to enjoy her exciting new life. He clutched her to him and wiped away the tear that had begun to roll down her cheek. Anna threw her arms around his neck in one last desperate embrace and then slowly let go. She watched him walk back to the cart as she sat down on a bench with a quiet, resigned Helen in her lap. Before her otec left, he looked at her and held his hand over his heart. It was one of many times she had questioned the feasibility - and the worthiness - of her dream.

An hour later, Anna boarded the train with a deep breath, a firm resolve, and Helen's hand in hers. They had to switch trains three times, blessedly without incident, especially since they'd had to spend the night on a bench at the train station in Prague. Finally they arrived in Hamburg.

The boat voyage lasted five days – quick, fortunately, even for a steamer. During that time they listened to others wretch and vomit, and several times Anna felt like she would as well. They were given oatmeal, bread, and potatoes with some meatish gravy, but Helen wouldn't eat, no matter how Anna tried to coax her. She would quietly cry and buried her head in the folds of Anna's dress. Anna put her arms around Helen and sang songs to help her sleep. Anxiety plagued her – what if Helen's father wasn't there? What if they couldn't find him? What if she got on the wrong train? What if someone tried to rob her? She prayed for everything to work out as God intended. That angels would protect her, and she had done the right thing.

It seemed like weeks before they reached the harbor with its welcoming statue. An interpreter got them off the boat, found Helen's father, who was waiting for them, and put Anna right on a train to Pennsylvania. Because she was American-born, Anna didn't need shots. But she wished she could have stayed longer at Ellis Island anyway because she didn't get a bath. She got called "Greenie" on the train and wondered what that meant, but she didn't want to dig around for her dictionary to find out.

*

Danika felt a strange combination of relief and disappointment to be back in her old bedroom. It was the same small room she had shared with her sixteen-year-old sister Varina before their brother Thomashka left to go to college, when Varina moved into his room two years ago. The familiarity was good, welcome - a reprieve from having to move around so much after the accident. Danika sat on a pink knit coverlet which must have been from when she was a baby. It barely covered the top of the single bed. Her blue hooded sweatshirt hung from the metal post of the headboard, and the top of the brown particle-board dresser held her doll collection and pink jewelry box with the pop-up ballerina. Next to that was her small, white, wooden desk with her books on it and an old wooden chair in front painted to match. Her posters of tropical islands still adorned the walls; her parents hadn't changed anything. Maybe they believed she would return. And she'd had to – because she failed.

She still couldn't get her mother's words out of her head – *never want to see your face again*. It hurt more than anything. Danika began to cry. About the little boy, about having to come back, about what her mother said. How could she have been so heartless? At least she called to apologize, to say she didn't mean it, and she let the anger get the better of her. But she did that a lot while Danika was growing up. When Danika was ten years old, a boy at school gave her a note saying he wanted to have sex with her. She barely knew what sex was; she felt violated by the mention of it. She wanted to write him a response as insulting as he had been to her, but she couldn't think of anything to insult him about except for his new glasses. She wrote that they made him look ugly, and then she put the note in the freezer so it would be cold when he read it, which sounded like a good idea at the time. Her mother found the note, of course, and, without asking why she had written it, called Danika a snake and yelled, "Get out of my sight!" So she did, without getting to explain herself. The note was never delivered, and Danika told Damek about it, at which point Damek, who had a crush on her, punched the boy at school on the playground.

She knew at some point during her ninety-day stay in Czechoslovakia she would have to see Damek; their parents were friends, after all. Damek liked to say they knew each other before they were born. But that was just it – they were friends. Yes, they dated for a while, but she wanted different things in life. And she would be going back to those different things.

Danika had stopped crying and now smiled over how different Damek and Eddie were. Not just physically, but in their interests. Eddie was a Mexican who worked in a restaurant and a mechanic shop, hoping to own it someday. Damek was a Slovak who was going to school to become a dentist. At least, that was the last she heard. Eddie liked music and cars, Damek liked sports and the outdoors. And teeth, apparently.

Her thoughts careened back to her mother, how negatively she reacted when Danika told her she wanted to go to the United States and Australia. Was it because she was jealous, or fearful? Going to miss her? Maybe it was all of those things.

Danika, startled by the knock on her door, called out *Come in*, and Varina opened the door. She entered wearing jeans and the black and silver "Hollywood" T-shirt Danika had bought for her, long blond hair in a ponytail, carrying some small plastic bags full of glass and metal beads and a spool of fishing line.

"Last night Teta Anna told the story of how she brought beaded bracelets for gifts for her relatives when

she went to America. So I decided to make beaded bracelets with you when you came *back* from America!"

Danika smiled and got up to hug her sister. They sat
down cross-legged on her bed and pulled back the knit
coverlet so they could work on the smooth surface of the
light pink sheets. Between the two of them, Varina
opened and set up the bags of one-eighth-inch diameter
beads – dark red, deep cobalt, shiny gold, wine bottle
green, brushed silver, and matte black.

"Where did you get these?"

"At a new store near the cathedral."

Danika said she'd love to see it, and Varina suggested
they could go on the weekend. "Yeah," Danika said. It
would be interesting to see what else was new since she'd
been gone. She decided to do one bracelet with random
colors, and another with the green, silver, and black. Varina started one with blue, gold, and black.

After a minute of stringing, Varina said, "I'm glad
you're back. I'm sorry about what happened, but it's so
good to have you here. I hated it being just me, Mom, and
Dad. Dad's always working and Mom's always yelling. I
wish I was out of school and could go with you."

"I wish you could too, Rina. Does Mom yell at you or
at Dad?"

"Both."

"I'm sorry. She always yelled at me too."

"I remember," Varina said, stringing another bead. "If
she doesn't stop, she'll drive everyone away and then
she'll be alone."

"Maybe that's what she wants."

They both stopped to think about that for a while, and then Varina changed the subject. "So! Tell me all about Eddie!"

Danika smiled and told her about his thick hair, his warm eyes, and his romantic nature. She said what a good work ethic he had, and how determined he was to succeed, and how attentive he was to her.

"And you are in love with him?" Varina asked as she tied off her bracelet.

"Yes, very much," Danika said as she held up her string of beads. But the end knot had unraveled during the time she had been stringing them, and the beads all fell off onto the bed.

"Oh no!" Varina said and started giggling.

Danika joined her, trying to make the uncertainty go away, the unwelcome doubt that inexplicably crept in, as it often did when she thought too long about Eddie, when she acknowledged that love, like life, offers no guarantees.

CHAPTER FOURTEEN

Zbudske Bela still felt the same after over sixty years. Anna's village where she had grown up looked a bit different now, but it still felt the same – quiet, as if everyone there were holding their breath, waiting for something to happen.

I didn't wait, Anna thought. *I left so I could make something happen.*

The creek still ran through the village, the one that everyone fell into when the ice cracked during the Epiphany ceremony. The gaggle of geese still congregated under the oak tree by the creek. How many generations have passed for them? The church still stood on top of the hill that the paska and pysanky had rolled down one Easter morning, but at some point a cement stairway had been built up to the entrance. The old one- and two-room cottage family homes from her childhood had been replaced by two-story townhouse style homes that had been built after the Second World War. But some of the old *budas* – homes – still stood, including the one that belonged to her family.

Olga, heavier than Anna, eight years younger but with undyed gray hair pulled back under her navy blue babushka, wearing a flower-print dress-apron over her white button-up blouse and black lace-up shoes with thick two-inch heels, led Anna through the backyard of her townhouse-style stuccoed home to their old family home where their mother had lived until her death in 1948. It seemed so small, and poignantly pastoral with its thatched roof, the one from which her sister had fallen to her death. Anna walked through the creaking wooden door of the light blue stuccoed cottage and waited for her eyes to adjust to the interior.

It was like a dream, seeing the white-stuccoed walls and oven-stove, and the exposed wooden beams overhead that she remembered from childhood. All of her mother's china plates were still on the wall, her icons, and the big crucifix hanging between the wooden framed windows on the back wall. The wooden table and benches that they sat at for meals were still there. She remembered how their father had kept an ax under the table to chase devils away from the house, but other families did that as well. Rusyns tended to be a superstitious people, craving ritual, ceremony, and tradition. That is what sustained them through cold winters, uncertainty, and the boredom of eating cabbage for weeks on end.

Anna went and sat on the bed she had shared with Mary, and then Olga, before she had left for America. It still had the red coverlet on it that their mother had embroidered so long ago. In the middle was a white deer, symbolizing wealth and prosperity, and the border was embroidered with pine needles, representing eternal life. A flood of memories, in the form of flashes and smells, came to her as she brushed her hand across the old, musty fabric. It was too much for her, and Anna, with a lump in her throat, got up and walked over to the kitchen table, where she noticed a basket of pysanky.

"Did you make these?" she asked Olga.

"I made some of them, but most are Matka's. Would you like to take some home with you?"

Anna's tears fell then. "Oh, yes, Olga. Thank you." She looked through the basket and could tell which were their mother's, and not because they were older. The designs were tighter, better executed, and more detailed. Olga's were indeed beautiful, but did not display the same level of skill as their mother's. Anna selected one of Olga's, painted with flower designs, and three of their mother's, elaborately decorated with eight-pointed stars, triangles, and more pine needles.

"She would want you to have them," Olga said. She paused then, acting as if she had something to say but wasn't sure how. "Anna," she began, "come sit down with me a minute. I want to tell you something." She motioned Anna toward their parents' old bed - small and sagging, covered with a yellowed wool blanket - in the other corner of the cottage.

Anna experienced a strange sensation, like feeling someone's pain. But it was old pain, distant. And then she realized that it wasn't Olga's pain. It was their mother's. And it was Anna's own – the pain of loss and guilt. She, too, had something to tell. Something that she had kept inside all these years. She sat on the bed, turned toward Olga, and listened to what she had to say.

"Matka died on this bed. She went in her sleep. I don't

know if it was 'peaceful' or not, but I hope so. She had told me after she'd had supper with us one night in the big house that she didn't feel well and was going to bed. I walked her back here, said goodnight to her, and went back across the yard. The next morning I found her dead.

"She had told me something a few months before she died. She came to me one afternoon in my kitchen while I was making halupki. She shuffled in through the back door, and it was then that I realized how shrunken and frail she was. There was a look on her face that was the same as when Otec died, and she said, 'Olga, I need to tell you something. We could not talk about it before Ilya Bicko died, because of the shame. But I must tell you now, because you should know. Ilya Bicko was your father.'" Olga said, imitating their mother's soft voice.

"Ilya Bicko is your father?" Anna said. It all came back to her now, the way the other village women treated her mother, the way her mother would just take it. It was emotional blackmail!

"Yes. I was surprised too, but it made sense. I remember sometimes when I was growing up, some women in the village always looked at me, stared at me, when I walked by, and Ilya Bicko always went out of his way to talk to me, said I was a neter to him, and told me to call him 'uncle.' Matka said that when you and she and Marya returned to the village while the war was still going on that she was very sad about our brother John dying. And then she was told that Otec had been killed in the war, and then the baby was born sick and died, and she said that the only reason she did not hang herself in the barn was because she had you and Marya. And then, because Ilya Bicko started coming around."

"I remember that," Anna said. "He started coming over for supper, and helping out around the farm." More memories flashed in her mind. Ilya sitting next to her mother on the wooden bench at the table, chopping wood in the backyard, baling hay, trying to resuscitate the beehive.

"Well, I guess they were getting pretty close, and Matka said that they were in love and going to get married in the spring. And then Otec came back, and Matka had to stop seeing Ilya Bicko, of course. A few weeks later, she found out she was pregnant. I'm sure Otec knew that I wasn't his, but he was always loving to me, and treated me like his own. It must have been so hard for Matka, being in love with one man but having to live her life with another," Olga said.

Yes, Anna thought. *I know what that is like. All those years, married to Michael, I still thought about John Nagajda.* "Well, thank you for telling me," she said. Anna could not recall if Ilya ever spent the night at their home, but now that they were talking about it, she had a faint memory of her mother going out the door late at night sometimes. This was shortly before her father's miraculous return. "A lot of things make sense now. And knowing about it helps me to understand Matka better now, at least the way that I remember her." Anna told Olga about how the village women treated their mother and how at the time she couldn't understand why their mother never stood up for herself. She thought about how horrible it must have been to endure their insults about her cooking and having to do their laundry.

"How awful for her," Olga said. They embraced each other then. Olga, teary-eyed, continued, "I didn't know what you would think!"

"I think that our matka was a very strong woman, and we are, too. And now I have something to tell you also, that I never told anyone because I was ashamed," Anna said, trying not to cry. Every time she talked about it, she would feel her anguish again, she could see her sister's body pitching head-first off the roof, could see her twisted neck where she lay on the ground, her lifeless face, blood seeping out of her mouth and nose. She remembered how Marya had started to scream as she fell, and how it had stopped with that terrifying thud. Her heart pounding in her chest, Anna rushed over to the ladder, somehow climbed down on shaking legs, and ran to her sister's side. Her own desperate scream still echoed in her head.

"I am your sestra. You can tell me anything," Olga said, looking into her eyes.

"Oh, Olga. It is about Marya. It was an accident!" Anna broke down and sobbed, hiding her face.

"Yes, yes, of course it was an accident. It was a long time ago," Olga said soothingly.

"But it was my fault! She tripped over me! We were both on the roof; Otec told us to clean all the leaves off, and I was not being careful because I was angry about something, because she told me that Matka said her embroidery was better than mine, and I thought Marya was the favorite. I said that to her in a mean voice -" Anna stopped as she stifled a sob. "I was on my stomach and I quickly turned the other way just as Marya was walking behind me, and my legs tripped her, and she fell head-first! Oh, Olga, please forgive me!"

Anna had screamed Marya's name as she felt her sister's last seconds of fear and pain, and her own pain of guilt and remorse. Marya's neck had snapped; she died instantly. But Anna had lived with the guilt for over sixty years.

"Anna, Anna, shh. There is nothing for me to forgive. You can't blame yourself. You did not push Marya. Surely God will forgive your impulsiveness. I'm sure He did when it happened."

"Olga, I'm just so sad that I robbed her of her life. And took away another child of our parents'. And a sestra from you. I wanted her to come to America. I wanted you to come to America, too." Olga handed Anna a handkerchief out of her apron pocket, and Anna wiped her face.

"Well, it was not so bad, living here. After World War II, our village had a little more autonomy. Then I married Nicholas, and he did well with horse breeding, like Otec did. And Matka needed me here," Olga said, effectively changing the subject.

"Yes, you're right. But I should have sent you money so you could have come to visit, at least. I love you, Olga. I am so glad that I made this trip and that I could see you and your beautiful family. And it is good to see the village again, and Czechoslovakia." *It is good to come home, to breathe this air again. To come clean.*

Olga hugged her. "I love you too, Anna. And it's good that you came now," she said, standing up and straightening her apron-dress. She walked to the door, and Anna got up and followed. "The national historical registry wants to move the house to the skansen in Svidnik, because it is one of the only traditional homes left in the village, and is in such good condition."

Skansens, outdoor museums laid out as the old villages were originally set up, were similar in idea to the Old West towns preserved in America. About a dozen stuccoed, thatch-roofed cottages were moved there from various Rusyn villages in the area, as well as original one-room schools, barns with sleighs and hay carts, food storage buildings, chest-high fences woven from branches, beehive racks, handsome, dark wooden churches with wooden onion domes on top, sometimes a mill with a water wheel, and even an outhouse or two. Food concessions and souvenirs – books and postcards, mostly – were available. Within a month, Olga said, their original family home would be moved and put on public display. Strangers would see the roof from which their sister had fallen to her death.

Later, Anna walked through the church cemetery of Zbudske Bela and stopped in front of her parents' graves, and next to them, those of her siblings. The tombstones were stucco-covered, Ten Commandment-shaped tablets with crosses on top, exactly as Anna remembered them. John had been buried first, then Michael, born during the war, then Andrej, Olga's stillborn twin brother, then Marya and their father, and lastly, their mother. The

Petrovich plot was the largest in the little churchyard; before Anna's mother died, the village cemetery had been moved to a hillside at the east end of town, with a rusted gate and a broken down car at the entrance.

Anna's relief filled her. She had finally admitted to someone other than God that she had been responsible for Marya's death. She felt freer, younger somehow. That afternoon, she and Olga sat on the couch in Olga's living room and showed each other their photo albums. They talked about their husbands, both now gone, their children, grandchildren, and their great-grandsons (each had one). They talked about their lives, and what they had done for sixty-two years. One had gone to another continent and the other had stayed in the same village, leaving only for day trips to Kosice. Both decided they were happy with that.

Danika came and picked them up to take them back to Kosice to have dinner with her family. Anna loved seeing Olga's other grandchildren, Danika's older brother Thomashka and younger sister Varina. Thomashka came with his wife Kassia and their one-year-old son, Mattous. Olga's son Nicholas also came with his wife and two teenage children, a boy and girl who reminded Anna of her own grandchildren.

Anna was the center of attention, regaling stories from her emigration experience through her cruise to Hawaii for her fortieth wedding anniversary. She talked about everything from feeling earthquakes to going to Disneyland to being robbed. And they told her plenty of stories too. Stories of weddings and wars, births and deaths. There was nothing like family, even those she'd never met before. They were such loving, welcoming people. She truly felt at home – again, after so very long.

And she had a glimmer of hope for something else. At one point early on in the evening, before the extended family had arrived, she was in the kitchen helping Magda and Olga with food preparation when Danika walked in with a bag of groceries and said, "Oh, Matka, guess who I ran into at the store – Damek Nagajda. He works there. You should have told me!"

Anna's skin prickled. *Nagajda? Could he be related?*

Magda said, "He was always so nice, Dani. I don't understand why you broke up with him."

"Because he was going nowhere. He had different goals, and I wanted to get out and travel. Besides, I'm going to be going back to America and marrying Eddie now," Danika said as she walked out of the room in a huff.

"Oh, sometimes she is so hot-headed," Magda said under her breath.

Anna's heart quickened again, just at the possibility. "This Nagajda boy," she began, "does he have a relative named John Nagajda, from Zbudske Bela?"

"Yes, Teta, that's his grandfather. Did you know him?" Magda asked.

Did? Anna's heart fell at the use of past tense. "Yes, I knew him when I was growing up. When did he die?"

"Oh, I think he's still alive. At least he was two years ago, when Danika was dating Damek," Magda said.

"Yes, I remember him," Olga said, peeling potatoes. "Wasn't he that boy you dated for a while? I remember one time I saw you kissing behind the barn!"

"Yes. I wouldn't marry him because he didn't want to go to America with me. I guess Danika gets that from me!" Anna said, chuckling with these two women she had not seen in decades, and one not at all. *John Nagajda! He could still be alive!* "Whatever happened to him? Did he get married and have a family?"

"Yes, he married Aleksandra something – I can't remember her last name. They had four children. One son died in a car accident many years ago. And his wife died of breast cancer a while ago. I think last I heard he was in a nursing home here in Kosice. He has Alzheimer's," Olga said, shaking her head. "Sad to think that."

"I'm sorry to hear that," Anna said, washing her hands. She knew what that meant.

"Teta, if you want to try to see him, I can have Danika find out from Damek where he is," Magda said as she put the pan of halupki in the oven.

*

Anna kept thinking about the kissing behind the barn. She remembered what it felt like to hold John's hand, the calloused skin of a farmer's son chafing against her own - softer, but just as hard-working. He smelled of earth and animals, an adventurous, loamy scent that made her swoon, made her want to travel the world with him, to always be by his side. Out of all the girls in the village, she was his and he loved her. She felt certain that they would have an amazing life together in America and couldn't

wait to talk about her plans. She loved him and everything he represented – truth, discipline, and, admittedly,
excitement. They went everywhere together. Most people in the village assumed that the next wedding would
be theirs. She could think of no other person she'd rather
spend the rest of her life with.

Five days later, Magda dropped off Anna at the nursing home where John Nagajda lived. She wore a corn-
flower blue knit skirt and matching short-sleeved top and
curled her dyed, short brown hair. She clutched her
brown leather purse in front of her as she walked up to
the front desk to ask for John's room. She glanced around
at all the couch-ridden people watching TV, wondering
if that was her fate.

She tried to prepare herself for the possibility that he
would not remember her. Even Michael forgot who she
was at the end. And she hadn't seen any photos of John,
so as she walked down the hallway to his room, she wondered how he would look. She remembered his cheekbones and his blue eyes, and his full lips. She remembered
that face as it watched her ride away in the cart the morning that her father took her to the train station to go the
ship that would take her to America. John was standing
behind the barn, but she saw him.

Anna walked in tentatively. The room smelled of for-
maldehyde, sharp and unpleasant, so she tried to breathe
as shallowly as possible. There he was – was it really him?
John sat in a wheelchair, seated at a small table next to a
hospital bed. A checkerboard was set out in front of him.
He was wearing plaid flannel pajama pants and a white

T-shirt. His bald head shook slightly as he turned to look at her.

She recognized him immediately, even though over eighty years of life were etched on his face. As she approached, she could see that his blue eyes were cloudy, and he did not have glasses on. It only took seconds to see his appearance, but she wondered more about what she couldn't see. Was there pain? Was there resentment? Was there still love? She sat down at the chair across the table from him, unable to believe that after all these years, she was looking into John Nagajda's face. Had she broken his heart the way she had broken her own?

"Who are you?" he asked in a neutral, albeit scratchy voice.

Anna's heart flapped. "I am Anna Petrovich, from Zbudske Bela."

He took in a breath, but did not seem to recognize her. "Hmm," he began, rubbing his chin. "I remember there was a girl named Marya Petrovich, and I heard a story that she made black pysanky! Hee-hee!"

At least he didn't say that she was the one who fell off the roof and died. "Yes, John, that was my sister Marya. I told you how she did that, how she left the eggs in the black dye too long and it seeped under the wax and the eggs came out black. Do you remember I told you that story? *I'm Anna. Anna Petrovich. You have to remember me, John. I'm the one who told you that story.*

And then she saw something in his eyes, some recognition. But his face quickly turned dark. "Anna Petrovich left to go to America. She thought she was too good for

Zbudske Bela. She thought she was too good for *me* because I didn't want to go."

Oh, John, is that what you thought all these years? "No, John, I didn't think I was 'too good.' I thought I wouldn't be good enough. I thought I wouldn't be a good wife for you, because I couldn't be a farmer's wife."

"Anna..." John whispered, tears building in his eyes. "How could it be? Am I hallucinating?"

"No, I'm really here, John. I came from America for a visit, after over sixty years. I was visiting my niece, and her daughter knows your grandson, Damek."

John smiled. "Oh, Damek is a good boy. He visits me and plays checkers." He tapped his finger on the board in front of him.

"That's good, John," Anna said. She told him about Mike, and her great-grandson. They talked about their children, and John, through tears, mentioned his son who had died in a car accident one icy night, coming home from college to visit for Christmas. They talked about the deaths of their spouses, and how they had cared for them at the end.

"Sometimes I think about that black pysanky," John said wistfully. "I think about how my life is sort of like that – something that didn't turn out the way it was supposed to. Something that was supposed to be beautiful."

"But some of it was beautiful, wasn't it, John?" *Oh, John, surely the love was beautiful, wasn't it?*

"Yes. But it wasn't the way it was supposed to be," he said, looking out the window.

Anna realized that she had lost him. She remembered

that Michael had often reacted this way, and would also become negative and unreasonable. The irony was not lost on her that, had she stayed in Czechoslovakia, she would have married someone who would have ended up the same as the one she married in America. That in the end, she had chosen well. She had chosen her dream, and that is what she loved.

"John," she said in an upbeat tone, "would you like to play checkers?"

*

Danika hung up her apron, washed her hands, craned her neck to pop it, grabbed her purse, and walked out of the café where she had been waiting tables for the past month, the same one that she had worked at when she was in high school. She was half-way through with her three-month waiting period for the K-Visa and anxious to get back to what she believed would be a better life in America. She and Eddie talked twice a week on Tuesdays and Fridays. It was torture being apart, but they were de-termined to get through it. She needed to save up the money to fly back to America anyway.

She had been invited to the Nagajda home for dinner that night. Damek's mother had always been nice to her, encouraged her to reach for her goals even though it meant that Danika probably wouldn't end up being her daughter-in-law, because she would be in a different country. She had told Danika a year ago that if she didn't go, she'd always wish she had, always wonder 'what if?'

But as the weeks wore on in Czechoslovakia, she was beginning to feel like Eddie's and her determination to make it to the end of the three month waiting period was more to prove a point. She thought they loved each other, but she had thought that she and Brian loved each other too. Why did love have to be so uncertain? Eddie had called her the day before, and he seemed rushed, talking quickly because he was on his lunch break between jobs. It always made her feel stupid when he talked like that because she had a hard time keeping up. The more time went by, the less she could understand. The more time went by, the more distant he seemed. But that was just it – he was over six thousand miles away.

Danika took the bus back home to shower and get ready to go to dinner at the Nagajda's home. Her mother smiled when she told her where she was going.

"Damek's just a friend, Matka! I have dreams to follow back in America," Danika said, going up the stairs.

Dinner at the Nagajda home happened to be Danika's favorite Rusyn food – pieroghies with prune butter. She ate so much she felt greedy and worked it off helping with dishes. The warmth of their home, somewhat large by Kosice's standards, was evident in the family's jovial, loving nature, but also in the steam from Beata's – Damek's mother's – savory repertoire, which clouded the panes of the sweltering kitchen and wafted its way through the house. Beata bustled about, her round, red face framed by short brown curls and punctuated by a smile of yellowing teeth. Brahm's *Symphony No. 1* played on the stereo, and Alexje, Damek's father, hummed along as he sat on their sage green velveteen couch and sipped Jagermeister with Andrej, Damek's older brother. Andrej inherited many of his mother's features, although he was grateful to have surpassed her in height. A manager at a local American-themed restaurant, he was twenty-five and, much to his mother's dismay and his father's curiosity, had never had a girlfriend.

Damek took after his father, a doctor at a local clinic, both in looks and interests. Alexje, relieved that his love of medicine had rubbed off on at least one of his sons, applauded Damek's earnest, worthwhile goal of becoming a dentist.

After the kitchen had been cleaned and Beata forced veternik (a cream puff pastry) on everyone, Danika and Damek went for a walk, enjoying the warm summer night and each other's company. Damek had gelled his hair and looked a lot better than he did in his grocery clerk uniform. It looked like he was trying to impress her. *He better not try to hold my hand,* Danika thought, but almost wished that he would.

They had driven to the downtown part of Kosice and walked around the beautiful, evocative St. Elizabeth's Cathedral, one of the last Gothic cathedrals to be built, and the eastern-most one in Europe. They walked around it, admiring its ornate, classic design, complete with iron scrollwork on the tall wooden doors, steep spires, and gargoyle water spouts. The inside lighting cast a magical orange glow that emanated into the night. They sat on a bench in the courtyard in front of the cathedral, and Danika spotted the bead store Varina had told her about, but it was closed.

"Danika," Damek began. "Even if you weren't going to marry Eddie, what would be your motivation for going back to America? You already lived there for five months. Aside from Eddie, what do you need to go back for?"

Danika wasn't sure where Damek was going with this, so she just answered. "To follow my dream of owning my own business."

"People own businesses in Czechoslovakia," Damek said.

"But they are more successful in America!"

"I don't think America is the answer, Dani. Education is the answer. That's why I'm going to college for dentistry. What kind of business do you want to own?" Damek asked.

"A travel agency," Danika said, her tone defensive.

Damek took a deep breath. "Dani, look at it this way. When you were in high school, your main goal was to go to America to live. *You did that.* You did it for five months. You followed your dream and achieved your goal!"

"Yes, but I failed! I got sent back! I was a failure. I have to make up for that. I have to try again."

"Dani, you know how you like to say that everything happens for a reason?" Damek said, looking her in the eye.

"Yes. I believe that."

"Well, if you truly believe that, then you wouldn't be afraid of failure, or regret failure, because it also happens for a reason," Damek said. He held out his arms to give her a hug. "And for what it's worth, I really don't think you failed at all. I'm proud of you. You lived and worked in a foreign country for five months! Most people never do that! You did it, Dani! Don't you see?"

"Yes, but now I'm back where I started. If I don't go back and marry Eddie, I'll miss out on so many opportunities."

"We don't always know where opportunities will come from. Look at our school. That's an opportunity," Damek said.

"What do you mean?"

"An opportunity for you to start an exchange program, so that secondary school kids can have the *opportunity* to study abroad for six months. I'm sure there are lots of other people who have the same dream you did. You could start a service that does that, sort of like a travel agency. I mean, I know you're going to marry Eddie, but I'm just listing that as an example of the opportunities that could be here, since we were talking about that." Damek stood up and stretched. "Well, do you feel like some gelati, or are you still full after that dinner?"

"I've always got room for gelati," Danika said, smiling.

It felt so easy being with Damek. He always supported her, never judged her. He talked to her, made her think. He was one of her oldest friends. And she had to admit that she liked his idea about starting an exchange student service at their school. Maybe she could organize trips, like to Egypt or Greece. And now that she spoke English fluently, she could be an interpreter. Or a tour guide. Why hadn't she thought of that before?

She did love Eddie, and she knew that he loved her. Why else would he still call, still say that he couldn't wait for her to come back? Unless – was he just trying to do the right thing? Trying to be the opposite of Brian Leech because he knew how hurt she had been by him? Why was he doing this? They had only known each other for two months when he asked her to marry him. And, she realized, they didn't really know each other at all. By the time she returned they would have been apart longer than they had been together. What if they got married and things didn't work out? Where would she be then? Was it worth the risk, just to prove a point? Just to do the right thing?

CHAPTER FIFTEEN

"Look, Ma, they even have a knitting club," Peter said, pointing to a page of the color brochure in his hand.

It was two o'clock in the afternoon on a warm July Saturday, two weeks after her return from Czechoslovakia, and Peter had taken Anna to view and tour another "retirement residence." Anna had to admit that they were much more desirable places to live than nursing homes, and this way she would be protected from break-ins, and she would have care options when the time came that she could not take care of herself. And she did not want to be a burden to her children, of that she was certain.

She knew what it was like to have an elderly mother-in-law in her home, and even though she would not be mean and negative like *her* mother-in-law, her *svokra*, had been, she did not want to be underfoot in Theresa's home. She did not want her presence to be merely tolerated, or even resented.

Michael's mother, Olga Sopkova, arrived in America in 1942, when Peter had been born. Her husband had been killed in World War I in 1918, as had her older son, and she was a bitter woman with a permanent scowl on her face who tried to make everyone around her as miserable as she must have been. Anna tried to be pleasant and appreciative, but Olga, who unfortunately had the same name as Anna's beloved sister, constantly insulted her cooking, criticized her clothing and housekeeping, and lambasted her parenting ability. Anna soon recoiled at the thought of leaving her children with this woman while she was at work in the shoe factory, but that was why she and Michael had agreed to send for his mother – to watch the children while they worked during the day. And now, they had her to support as well.

When, on the day that she arrived, her mother-in-law found out what village Anna was from, she said, "Zbud-ske Bela is full of nothing but drunkards and idiots. Too much inbreeding. Good thing you married someone from Strocin. Much smarter people. This way maybe your children will be smarter than you." She had said it first thing in the morning while sitting around the break-fast table, after Michael had gone to work. Anna was still home with Peter, who was one month old. She planned to go back to work within a month, but now considered going back sooner.

Anna bit the insides of her lips as she stared at the pot of oatmeal she was stirring. She did not want to be alien-ating her husband's mother who would be taking care of their children, and she didn't know how to respond to this insult. But she remembered how the women in the village had treated her mother and remembered her own vow to be different. She took a deep breath and turned around from where she had been standing at the stove.

"Well, this surprises me. With the way your son is, and other people I have met from Strocin, I would have never guessed that people from Strocin were so negative," Anna began, shaking. Her heart pounded as she continued, "You are here in my home. If you do not want to be here, then we will earn the money to send you back. But as long as you are here, you will not say such things. Or you can take your negativity right back to Strocin."

Her *svokra* looked at her then, eyes narrowed. Anna could tell that she had not been expecting a response like that. "Watch your tongue, girl. In Strocin, elders are not spoken to in that manner."

"We are not in Strocin," Anna calmly retorted. Baby Peter began to cry, and Anna left the room to tend to him.

For seven years Anna coexisted with this disagreeable woman in their two-bedroom house. She figured that her svokra must have alienated so many people in Strocin that no one wanted her to return. As it turned out, Michael wrote to his sister in Strocin to tell her that they might be sending their mother back, and his sister responded telling them *not* to send her back, that her husband would leave if their mother returned, and furthermore, when she dies, bury her body there in New York and do not send it back to Czechoslovakia.

Finally, after seven long years of insults and resentment, the woman died, apparently of a stroke, which did not surprise Anna. She came home from work one evening and found her dead on the kitchen floor. The children had covered her with a blanket because they thought she was sleeping. So much malice in one person could not be good for the body. Anna believed that her svokra had manifested the stroke with all her negativity and mean-spiritedness. She could not have guessed then that her husband would one day also have a stroke.

Olga was buried at a cemetery in Binghamton, New York, a lone Rusyn amidst a plot of Irish. Perhaps some of them had been drunkards, Anna mused.

Peter and Anya were in school, but Marya was three years old, so Anna and Michael paid an older lady to watch her so that Anna could continue working. E-J was a wonderful company to work for, but they were tired of factory work and had saved as much money as they could. Michael wanted to start a construction business, and Anna wanted to open a shoe store. Within three years they felt they had saved up the money to at least start the construction business, but they had heard that there were better opportunities in Los Angeles, with a growing population of almost one million in 1952. The war was over and business was booming as quickly as the babies supposedly were. It was a good time for a big move.

They would live in Van Nuys, ten miles west of Los Angeles, because there was a Byzantine Catholic church there, and that was the best way to connect with other Rusyns. They knew that being in a new area they would need a support system, just like when they were teenagers and emigrated to America.

And it felt like they were emigrating again. It took five days to cross the Atlantic by boat, and it took them five to cross the United States by car, heading first to Chicago and then traveling on Route 66 for the rest of the way. Most people took longer to savor and enjoy the roadside attractions along the Mother Road, but Michael and

Anna just wanted to get to their destination as quickly as they could, making jokes about the possibility of gypsy blood in their families of origin. They got lost (took a wrong turn in Tulsa), they argued (over Michael spending too much time in a bar in Missouri, whether they would make it to the next gas station in New Mexico, and having to see the Grand Canyon, the Petrified Forest, *and* the Painted Desert, when the Grand Canyon alone would have sufficed), they were tired (on day three they drove thirteen hours and the radiator overheated), but the five of them made it. And they loved California. They drove all the way to Santa Monica, lured by their first scent of the Pacific, and took off their shoes to walk in the sand and wade ankle-deep in the foamy gargle of the waves. They got back in the car, and as soon as they traversed the hill into the San Fernando Valley, they knew they would be happy there. They had never seen palm trees before and were enchanted by the exotic fronds bending over the streets, intoxicated by eucalyptus trees and orange blossoms, and even entertained (in Rialto, earlier in the day) by teepee motels.

They found a little house just half a mile from the Byzantine church and started looking for work and registered the children in school. After much deliberation, they decided that it would be best for Michael to not start the construction company right away, and he went to work for a contractor while he "got his feet wet," a metaphor that would have perplexed them if they hadn't dipped their toes into the ocean the day of their arrival. They became familiar with their surroundings and made new friends at their church. While the children were in school, Anna drove around to find a good location for her shoe store. She found an opening in a mall prototype in Sherman Oaks and decided to own a Florsheim franchise. She had learned how to make good shoes, and now she would sell them. At first, customers asked her to repeat what she said when she described the craftsmanship of the shoes, and she realized that her strong accent would affect sales. She asked Peter to help her with her pronunciation, and customers no longer gave her questioning looks. She rode the wave of Florsheim's success, as company sales in general doubled between 1953 and 1963, and Florsheim controlled over seventy percent of the market. Within three years Michael was able to start his construction company.

And now their hard-earned money would be used to pay her monthly rent until she died. She wanted to leave more for her children and grandchildren, not just what was left over after her stay at the Geezer Hilton. It would be expensive, and it bothered her to think that if she could still live in her own home, which had been paid off ten years ago, there would be so much more to inherit upon her death. But everyone wanted her to be safe and well-cared-for, she knew that. And it would be much easier for her to not have to be dependent on others to drive her to the grocery store every week for food, as there was a dining hall there that served three meals a day. She had cooked since she was ten years old. It would be a nice break.

"What do you think, Ma?" Peter asked, gesturing

around the main entrance hall. The air-conditioned, high-ceilinged room boasted a twelve-foot-high river rock fireplace with several floral print couches and up-holstered rockers surrounding it. A few residents walked or rolled around, and out the windows at the back of the large room she could see a fountain and gardens. It re-minded her of the hospital where Anya had died, and she felt a wave of sadness. She didn't know if she could live at this place.

"It's nice, Peter," she said, wringing her hands.

"Let's go take a look at the sample one-bedroom unit," Peter said as he walked toward the elevator.

Anna turned to follow him, but she turned too sharply, twisting her ankle while her upper body still had the momentum of movement. She fell sideways so quickly that she was not able to break her fall. She landed on the same hip that had been hurt when the robber had pushed her to the floor in her home six months ago. The pain seared through her much worse than it had the first time. Anna tried to mentally distract herself from the pain that caused her to cry out. She focused on her breathing and thought of Anya. Her beloved daughter had suffered such dreadful pain. The memory - coupled with her own crippling injury - overwhelmed her, and Anna began to weep.

"Ma! Ma!" Peter cried, running back to her and crouching by her side. "Did you trip? What happened? Are you okay?"

"Peter," she gasped as her face wreathed into a gri-mace. "It's too much pain...I can't move..."

"Let me help you sit up," Peter said. He tried to raise her shoulders, putting pressure on her hip and making her cry out.

Peter lowered her back down. "Okay, Ma, you just lie there and I'll have them call an ambulance. Or maybe they have a doctor on staff."

Peter ran off to the front desk, and Anna lay there looking at the ceiling, willing herself to put the pain out of her mind. *I don't care if I can't move my arms or legs as long as I can remember my name.*

And soon enough a flurry of people were around her, including a doctor who announced that she had probably broken her hip, and then she felt the pain surge again as she was lifted onto a stretcher and taken out to an ambulance. She closed her eyes and bit the insides of her lips.

"I'm right here, Ma," she heard Peter's voice. "I'm going to follow the ambulance to the hospital."

She feared that it would be the same one where her daughter died and prayed that it wouldn't be. But then she remembered something that disturbed her even more than which hospital she was going to. She remembered hearing a statistic that people in their eighties who break their hip are usually dead within a year.

Oh, well. At least that way there will be enough money left for everyone. I want to leave them a legacy. Something for their own American Dreams.

*

A month later, Anna sat at a table in the dining hall of

the Geezer Hilton. She had spent two weeks in the hospital, and then went to a rehabilitation center for two weeks, where she healed enough to use a walker. Peter had put her house on the market and it had sold within two weeks. He brought her back to the house for a day so that she could say goodbye, trudging in the walker through her twenty-year-old home, remembering how excited she and Michael had been while watching his crew build it. They had done what they set out to do. They had left their world behind and they became Americans and *this is what they built.* Pride and sadness surged through her as she watched Peter and her older grandchildren pack up the house.

Marya took two weeks off of work to come out and sort through everything. So much of it Anna couldn't keep; there just wouldn't be room. "It's called 'down-sizing,' Ma," Marya told her as she carried another box of old clothes out to her car to take to Goodwill. Anna made sure it did not include her box of pysanky, especially the ones she had brought back from Czechoslovakia.

She had actually been stopped in customs at the New York airport on her way back home because of the pysanky. She found it odd that she had been stopped that time, but that she had not when she arrived at the age of seventeen so many years ago. They whisked her through Ellis Island and put her right on the train to Pennsylvania. This time, after she had lived in the United States for almost seventy years, she got detained because of some pretty painted eggs. Apparently there was a bird flu virus causing concern. "Some of these eggs are over eighty years old," she explained to the customs officer. "Ma'am, we still need to have them evaluated," she was told. The whites of the eggs had evaporated long ago, leaving a hardened yolk to roll around inside, as the officer discovered when he shook them.

"Please be gentle," Anna asked. "My mother made those long ago."

That seemed to have some effect. The officer replaced them carefully in their box and handed it to Anna. "They seem to be all right, Ma'am," he said with a respectful look. "Thank you for your cooperation."

And now, along with some of her own pysanky, they sat in an engraved crystal basket on the coffee table in the living room of her new apartment. She was able to bring her old couch and her rocker, but unfortunately the baby grand piano had to go, as well as the beautiful cherry wood dining room set that she had owned for decades. It saddened her to see it go, as if her memories of Easter dinners around that table would go with it.

Now her table was a round, fake wood formica-covered imposter that she shared with three other old women, down in the dining hall. She had been there a week and was trying to fit in, to make friends. They were all widows at the table. Agnes used a walker like Anna; she had also broken her hip, six months earlier. Marjorie used a stylish wooden cane, and Betty walked alone, but slowly. None of them were immigrants, and they found Anna's stories to be enchanting, like fairy tales. She told them that she had recently gone back to Czechoslovakia for a visit, and that she had gone with her great niece, who had also immigrated. The ladies found it interesting to think about how different Danika's experience must have been – fifteen hours by plane as opposed to Anna's five days by boat.

Anna thought about the letter she recently received from Danika, who had decided to remain in Czechoslovakia. Danika sounded like she was trying to justify her choice, almost as if, with writing it down on paper, she were trying to convince herself that she had made the right decision by not returning to America. Anna wanted to reach through the letter to cradle the girl's face in her hands and tell her, *You know in your heart what is the right thing to do at each moment.* That was what Anna's father had told her the night before she left for America, and she still carried that with her, after all these years. She wanted Danika to know that she supported her completely. That she wasn't giving up on a dream; she had found a new one.

Anna turned her attention back to the women at the table. Marjorie, who still dyed her chin-length hair blond and wore makeup and a sleek black pantsuit, was talking about her husband's death of a heart attack five years ago, while they were on vacation in Mexico. He had climbed to the top of Kukulcan Pyramid, the tallest of the Mayan ruins in the Yucatan Peninsula. He climbed all the way back down, and then collapsed at her feet, clutching his chest.

Then it was Betty's turn. Her tight white curls framed her youthful face, which feigned a quick look of concern for Marjorie before launching, as if with a piece of neighborhood gossip, into her own death-of-a-husband story. "Oh, that's terrible! You poor thing! Al had a stroke in the middle of the grocery store, and I wasn't with him when it happened. Some ignorant young clerk found his number in his wallet and called me and said, 'Hello, I work at Ralph's on Sepulveda Boulevard, and we've got Al Granger lying here on the floor in the middle of the produce department. I think he's dead.' Can you believe the audacity? The insensitivity?"

They all murmured clucks and sounds of shock and agreement. As Agnes, the oldest and most somber of the group, told about the morning that she discovered her husband had died in his sleep, right next to her, Anna thought about the fact that this was such an odd thing to bond over – sharing stories of their husband's deaths. *This is where we are. Stories are all we have left of our lives.* She bit the insides of her lips as everyone looked expectantly at her.

"Michael had had a severe stroke, but he didn't die until eleven years later. It took him many months to learn to talk again, and walk with a walker. But his mind was never the same. I think he had Alzheimer's, although back then we called it senility," she said, and the three women nodded. "He kept wanting to go back to Czechoslovakia, and even tried to once, by bus!" The women chuckled politely, and Anna continued. "Then he really started to deteriorate. He could no longer bathe himself or go to the bathroom himself, so I had to help him. I was much stronger then, so I could do it. Finally, the Alzheimer's was really bad, and he couldn't tell his own children apart, and he wouldn't eat, so we put him in the hospital. And most of the time he was delirious or not conscious, but he was awake for a little while on his last day, and as I sat with him, holding his hand, he said to me, 'I feel very weak. Bring my wife to me.' And so I said, 'I am your wife,' and he said, 'No, you are the nurse,' and I told him again, 'I am Anna, your wife,' and he said, 'Yes, Anna is my wife, please get her.' Anna's lower lip began trembling as she continued, "And so I got up and went out into the hall, and then I came back in a minute, and his eyes were closed, and I sat down and took his hand and I said, 'I'm here, Michael. It's Anna, your wife,' and then I knew that he was dead."

Then the tears rolled freely down her cheeks, and Agnes gave her a handkerchief, and a young male server came and took her plate away.

*

It was a sunny July day in eastern Czechoslovakia, and Danika sat in a small rented rowboat in the middle of Vinianske Lake, about an hour from Kosice. Damek stood up in the boat and playfully acted like he was going to jump into the water.

The lake's serene, dark, blue-green, mirror-like surface reflected the low Carpathian Mountains to the north and a few cotton-ball clouds above. Clusters of hornbeam surrounded the lake, looking from afar like a group of green hippos standing onshore, where Varina sunbathed, read, and napped. But Danika's eyes were fixed on

Damek, shirtless with a pair of navy blue swim trunks sitting on his hips. How could she have forgotten? She had seen him with his shirt off once before, playing soccer, but his physique wasn't something she took much notice of then. And really, it wasn't the important thing now. All Danika could think about was how much she finally realized that she loved him.

Damek dove in, surfaced, and Danika play-applauded and smiled. Then he started doing slow laps around the boat. As she watched his rhythmic strokes she thought about how different her life would be now, how different it already was. She loved being with someone with whom she didn't have to think so much – every minute – to feel comfortable. She didn't have to constantly search her brain for the correct word in a foreign language or hope she got the verb conjugation right. And there were the benefits to having a history with someone. In addition to the welcome familiarity, Damek knew exactly what she needed – to do, to hear, to believe. She didn't have to try with Damek like she did with Eddie.

She first realized it the night that she had dinner at the Nagajda's home, and not just because of Damek. It was his family. They liked her, welcomed her, appreciated her. She was home. And Damek was right – she could find ways to build a career out of traveling, and helping others to do so. Her heart knew she needed to stay, but her mind wasn't ready to accept it. How could she tell Eddie? How could she step on his devotion? How could she let Peter think all of his efforts on her behalf meant nothing? But how could she go back when she knew exactly where she needed to be?

She had to tell Eddie soon. He usually called around 9:00 PM her time (noon his time) on Sundays and Wednesdays, and the next time he did after that dinner with the Nagajdas, she tried to approach the issue logically with him. She tried to tell him that it wasn't about emotion (but in the end she realized it was all about emotion). She could lay out all kinds of reasons: By the time I return, we will have spent more time apart than we were together, we're just trying to prove a point, you're just trying to do the right thing. And yes, there was love there. But was it enough to sustain a marriage? Was it enough to start a life together?

Eddie resisted at first, valiantly ("I do love you! A love like ours isn't easy!"), but in the end he agreed with her. They needed to let each other go. Danika realized it had gotten a little harder to speak in English now that she had been back in Czechoslovakia for a month. But she told Eddie as best as she could that he would always be in her heart, a special friend.

Eddie, choking up, said he would miss her even more and always remember her. "My heart was like a loaf of bread rising out of the pan, and you were the oven."

Danika said, "And you are like a prince on a horse." Prince? She couldn't remember the word for the other regal-looking guy with the hat of metal that goes in front of the face. That's what Eddie was. And she would always be grateful to him.

So what was Damek then? As he climbed back into the boat, trying not to spray water everywhere, he looked at her and she smiled. Then Damek smiled and she realized that he was her mirror, reflecting back the best parts of her – her love of family, her adventurous spirit, and her true self.

"You seem thoughtful today," Damek said, sitting down next to her.

"I still have to tell my teta and cousins that I decided to stay. I don't want to seem ungrateful, after everything they did for me."

"I'm sure they'll understand, especially Teta Anna."

"But Peter - he did so much for me!"

"He did it because you're family, and he loves you."

"He even picked me up at the police station after the accident." Tears sprang to her eyes. "I don't know what I would have done without him."

She started to cry and Damek wrapped his damp, sheltering arms around her. He knew that she was crying about the little boy, that there was nothing she could have done, and nothing to ever make her feel better about it. She sobbed unreservedly then, out there in the middle of the lake.

"I should have never gone to America!"

"Dani, Dani," Damek soothed. "If you hadn't gone to America you would have been miserable."

"I'm miserable now!"

"You're grieving, and you have regrets, but that's a part of life, Dani. You are not your mistakes. Your past does not define you. And it doesn't own you," Damek said as he gently rubbed her back.

She sobbed even harder. "He almost died! And his life

is forever changed! And that of his family!"

"It wasn't your fault."

"I shouldn't have taken them for a walk!"

"Dani, you can't change what happened. You have to let it go."

"I don't know how!"

Damek held her in his arms and brushed the tears off her cheeks. He looked lovingly at her and said, "You spend each moment focusing on the time that we have now. Because that's all we can be certain of. That's what we've been given. That and each other."

Danika let out one last hiccupping sob and half-way pulled out of Damek's embrace. She looked into his gray-blue eyes, squinting from the bright sun, and knew that he was right, that he knew her and what she needed, that he always would. That no matter what mistakes or hurdles life threw her way, she could get beyond them.

"Okay," her voice croaked, and she nodded slightly. "Okay."

CHAPTER SIXTEEN

"I feel like I'm invisible," Theresa said, close to tears. Her black cotton sweater shrouded her body as much as her anxiety, and her graying limp hair sat, unmoving, on top of her shoulders. The lithium kept her from going full manic, but she seemed to be stuck in an agitated mixed state, debilitating sadness on one hand, and head-churning with mania on the other, often at the same time. She looked sideways at the floor and yanked at a hangnail on her thumb. Peter, seated next to her on the shiny brown leather couch, had accompanied her to a therapy session with Dr. Tucci.

"Of course you're not invisible," Peter said, taking her hand. "You're a vital part of the household. I wish you would realize that." It was difficult to be supportive without lying. A vital part of the household, yes, but lately not a pleasant one. He knew she didn't feel right; he couldn't hold it against her. But it was disappointing that she was on medication now and she still had issues. And he missed Anya intensely, like the void of a freshly pulled tooth, filled not with blood but with grief. The ache of her death, knowing how devastating it was for his mother, brother-in-law, niece and nephew, tore at his heart.

"I know I'm not invisible to the household. I don't care

about how I seem to the *household*, Peter! I feel like I'm invisible in our marriage!" Theresa's face contorted. "You make it a point to spend time with everyone but me!"

Peter opened his mouth to object, but then realized that she was right. He had started coming home early on Wednesdays to babysit Leif while Mike and Heather both worked. Now that he was three, they had put him in daycare, but Peter felt strongly about spending some one-on-one time with his grandson, so he picked him up from daycare a little early once a week to do so. Tuesdays and Thursdays he helped coach Kat's softball team and went to her games on Fridays. Saturday mornings he got up early and had a cup of coffee with Mike, and in the afternoons he played a game of chess with Joseph. He was starting to feel more connected with each of his children.

Kat's softball surely took up the most time, but it was worth it. It was working. She talked to him more, smiled more, and even seemed nicer to her little brother. Most shocking of all, however, was that while they were driving home from practice one day, she actually told Peter about a boy she liked. "He's on the baseball team, and he's really nice. He's in my English class too. I try to talk to him and stuff, and I hope he asks me to prom. I think you would like him, Dad." Peter felt elated – this was the first time she had opened up to him about anything more personal than needing help with her algebra homework. He sensed that he was finally building a relationship with her. *Parenting is as much a journey of wit as of love.* He dared to think that she liked him.

He loved playing chess with Joseph, his quiet, intellectual son. Peter was glad that Theresa reminded him that Joseph enjoyed it, that it made him feel confident, and important. He had told Peter last Saturday that he wanted to be an engineer when he grew up – he wanted to design bridges, like he did with Lego. "But I want to design *real* bridges, Dad," he told Peter. "I think that's a perfect career choice for you, Joe." For his son to have such insight at the age of nine amazed Peter.

His talks with Mike on Saturday mornings were beneficial. It was during one of them Peter discovered that Mike hadn't liked Little League at all when he was a kid; he just did it because Peter encouraged him to. He was glad that he had learned early on with Joe, and not pushed it. The fact that neither of his sons was athletic but his daughter turned out to be amused Peter. He enjoyed meeting them at their level, getting to know them as individuals, not just as his children.

He felt glad that Mike seemed comfortable telling him things like how he never liked Little League (well, ten years after the fact, but that was okay). He told him his concerns that although he really loved Heather and they got along fine, they had different priorities and interests, and he was starting to think that he'd made a mistake in marrying her. He had fallen into the "it's the right thing to do" trap – they both had. They had talked recently and Heather actually felt the same way, and they didn't know what to do about it.

"You don't have to do anything about it right now, Mike," Peter had advised. "If it's a marriage of convenience for a few more years until you can get through college while taking care of Leif, that's okay."

"No, it's not, Dad. It's living a lie, and that wouldn't be fair to either Heather *or* me," Mike said softly.

Peter realized that his nineteen-year-old son was right. He was proud of Mike for standing his ground and telling him how he really felt, and he told him so. Then Peter said, "Well, my son, if it's divorce you're after, you've come to the right place," and they both laughed, sipping their coffee at the kitchen table as the sun poured through the windows.

"Maybe in a few months," Mike said. "You are right about not needing to do anything right now. We're not fighting or anything, just not...in love."

Peter wondered if he and Theresa were at that point. Not of divorce, but of not being happy any more. Theresa felt invisible, he felt stretched, and although he was connecting with his children better than he had in years, maybe better than he ever had, it was clear that he and Theresa were at their worst point. *Isn't that normal though?* Peter wondered. *Every marriage goes through low points. But not every marriage deals with mental disorders and teen pregnancy. I think we're not doing too bad, all things considered. Maybe not too bad, but it could be better. And I want it to be better. It's better with the kids. Why can't it be better with her too?*

"I'm sorry, honey, I'm sorry. I was just feeling like the kids were getting more and more distant from me, and I had to do something about it. I didn't mean to neglect you," he said as he looked into Theresa's wet eyes. He had wanted to say, *You? Invisible? Honey, that is the last thing you could ever be*, but that would not have been a good idea. That would be a step backward to say the least. Definitely would be misinterpreted at best. "Let's start doing something, just the two of us, every Saturday night. We'll make it a rule that Saturday nights are our night, okay?"

"Saturday night's not good, because then we have to get up and go to church the next day," Theresa said. "We'll have to come up with some other time."

Peter had a brainstorm. It had been festering and brewing for months, and now, it hit. "Let's stop going to church!" He practically jumped out of his seat. He smiled and his eyes were wide, like a psychosomatic manic moment. "Let's just not go to church anymore!"

Theresa must have thought he was being sarcastic and lowered her voice. "*I'm* not complaining about church, Peter. I have *never* complained about going to church, so don't act like it's that."

Dr. Tucci leaned forward and opened his mouth to intervene, but Peter quickly said, "I'm serious, Theresa, I'm totally serious. I've been doing a bit of thinking lately, and I've realized that I just don't feel spiritual going to church. I've always done it because I thought I should, because it's the 'right thing to do,' because it was expected. Because our parents expected it. I've been feeling like a hypocrite lately because going to church is not a true conviction for me. And, I think you might feel the same way. Do you?" His pulse raced as he finally vocalized something that had bothered him for a long time, the lie that he had been living.

Theresa looked stunned. "Yes," she said tentatively. "I

didn't realize you felt that way. I had no idea -"

Peter continued, "It's not that I don't love God and appreciate the many blessings in our life. It's just that, more and more, I'm thinking of myself as more of a spiritual person and less of a religious one. I'd rather do something as a family during that time than go to church."

"Peter, I just – I didn't expect any of this. But I think that sounds good. I think that would be good for us."

"Well, since Anya's death, I've been realizing that we never know how much time we have with our loved ones. Life is so fragile."

Theresa's face fell. "Oh, Peter. I realize that I wasn't there for you when Anya died. I was -" she broke off as she began to cry.

"I know, honey, I know. You were needing medication and we didn't know it. You don't have to explain," Peter said, holding her.

"But I was so – I don't even know how I was. All I know was that the day before your sister died I thought I had hit someone while driving, and I couldn't think about anything else. And then I made a scene at the funeral. I'm so sorry! I was – not well," Theresa said, still crying.

"It's okay, honey, you don't have to apologize. I don't hold it against you. We survived. And you're better now, and that's the important thing."

"I love you so much," Theresa gasped as she embraced him.

"I love you, too. I always have."

After a moment, Dr. Tucci leaned forward and said, "Wow, you two don't even need *me*!"

Theresa laughed and said, "Oh, yes, we do. Well, I do, for sure."

Dr. Tucci continued, "But don't you see how well the two of you do communicate when you finally sit down to talk? That was amazing! Peter, you really should pursue your goal of only doing family mediation counseling. You're a natural. And Theresa, I'm *very* proud of you. You are working so hard on yourself. I have seen plenty of bipolar patients who think that as long as they take their medication, that's all they need to do. That their personal relationships will take care of themselves. But you have such a strong drive to work on yourself, Theresa, and it's evident in how much progress was made in this session. And it also helps tremendously that you have such a supportive spouse. It's a joy to work with both of you."

Peter and Theresa thanked the doctor and collected themselves. It had been an emotional afternoon, and even the positive ending left them both drained, but they were optimistic. They walked out to the car with their arms around each other, and the magic continued for a few minutes. Peter felt that the bridge between the two of them had been rebuilt, fortified. An aura surrounded them. Everything would be all right.

"Honey," Theresa began after Peter started backing out of the parking space. "I feel so terrible. I don't even know how bad it was with me, but I know it was bad, I know it was hard. And it was for a long time. I wish I had gotten help and gone on medication sooner."

"Sweetheart, stop. I married you for better or for

worse, and there were some worse times, but now it's better. Let's move forward, okay? Let's go home and hug our kids, and let's plan what we're going to do Saturday night! We've been married twenty years, honey. Now that you're feeling better, we should try celebrating again," Peter said.

They had gone to Palm Springs for a weekend for their twentieth anniversary a few months ago, and it was during one of Theresa's depressive states. Peter had left work early on a Friday afternoon, dropped Kat and Joseph off at Theresa's parents' house, and came back to pick up Theresa, who hadn't finished packing yet. Peter shouldn't have rushed her, he knew, but he was anxious to get out of town early and start the two-hour drive before the rest of L.A. got on the road. "It's two nights and one and a half days, Theresa," he had said to her in exasperation, helping her pack. She sat sullen-faced in the car the whole way there and would barely answer any questions that Peter happened to inconvenience her with. When they arrived, she stayed in the car while he checked in, and when he came back with the key, she went directly to the hotel room and would not leave it the entire time they were there, brief as it was.

Peter swam in the pool alone, reflecting on his more than two decades of knowing Theresa. He tried to pinpoint a time when she had changed, but it had been gradual. Their wedding, held at a country club in Newport Beach, was lovely, and she was gracious, the bride of his dreams. Stunning, really. Mild-mannered, no sign of mania. Personable, no sign of depression. They enjoyed a romantic honeymoon in Hawaii, holding hands while snorkeling. And they came home and started their life together, and Mike came along soon, a honeymoon baby. They thought that was romantic too.

But if Peter had to pick a time when it started, it started with Mike. Not just post-partum depression, but also "partum." Theresa did not "glow" during pregnancy. It was like she was a different person. Peter could only imagine, of course, the hormonal and physical upheaval on her body, and so he patiently hoped that she would feel better once the baby was born. But, of course, the hormones of pregnancy were traded for the hormones of lactation, and Theresa seemed to slip into an even worse frame of mind. Why didn't he get help for her then? Did he just not think of it? Maybe he just kept thinking in the same pattern. When the baby's born, she'll be okay. When the baby gets on a schedule, she'll be okay. When the baby can sit up, she'll be okay. When she weans the baby, she'll be okay. Maybe Theresa just wasn't happy with babies. At least her frame of mind improved once they were toddlers. But then it wasn't long before they had another one and the cycle would start all over again. She loved the kids, though; Peter had no doubt of that. She held them, kissing their precious heads, rocked them and sang her own made-up songs to them. She baked Christmas cookies with them, decorated Easter eggs, and made their Halloween costumes (the octopus had been the most challenging, Peter recalled). She read them bedtime stories (they had read *The Chronicles of Narnia* books twice) and played board games (Parcheesi was a favorite).

She cheered for them when they succeeded and consoled them when they didn't. But it was more than just doing things with them or for them, out of obligation. She did it with pure love.

Peter went back into the hotel room; Theresa was in bed. He put on some clothes so he could go out to get some lunch, and he brought back a chicken sandwich for her. She wouldn't eat it so he put it in the mini fridge in the room and went back out to the pool.

He dove into the soothing water and let the air out of his nose as he surfaced. Peter loved to swim. He wished they could have a pool at home, but their hillside lot precluded that from happening. He had learned to swim the first summer after his family had moved from New York to Los Angeles and they started going to the beach. He'd later tried surfing and never could get the hang of it, but swimming he could do. He would stay in the water long after his fingers began to prune. He had taught all three of his children to swim, and tried to instill his love of water in them. Water was life, and life-giving. He realized, as he thought about it now, that swimming in the ocean made him feel much more spiritual than he ever did enclosed in the four walls of a church. He was glad that on impulse he'd spoken his mind and decided to no longer "live a lie," as Mike had put it. He felt exhilarated by his decision to stop going to church.

He hadn't gone to church that weekend in Palm Springs, and he hadn't missed it. Instead, he'd spent as much time in the water as possible, wishing that his wife of twenty years would "snap out of" her depression and join him. He went in the room again when it was time for dinner, and Theresa had at least conceded to eating the chicken sandwich. She told him that was all she wanted. All she wanted. After twenty years, that was all she wanted.

When he came back from his solitary crab leg dinner, he asked Theresa if she wanted to go in the hot tub with him. She said no, and he went alone. But the suggestion must have had some appeal to her, because when he came back in, she was out of bed, taking a bath. A glimmer of hope flashed in Peter's mind, and he offered her a massage, with an ulterior motive. She accepted, and later he actually made love to his wife that night.

And then, while driving home from the therapy session, he had another brainstorm, his second in the same hour. "I know! You know how you love baths? Let's get a hot tub! I don't know why we never got one before! What do you think?"

"I think that's the second greatest idea you've had in a long time," Theresa said, smiling.

*

He's practically giddy, Theresa thought, glancing at Peter as they entered the freeway onramp. He's acting like the stereotypical description of mania – talking rapidly, eyes wide, can't sit still.

But Theresa knew now that mania went beyond that. That for her it could involve hallucinations and uncontrollable, senseless, racing half-thoughts. It could involve sleeping with your sister's fiancé. She remembered that night, how her skin felt, what she wore, how Jim looked at her. She tried not to remember it, but it was a real memory, not imagined, and all the details were still there. And all the regret.

It was summer; she'd spent the day at Hermosa Beach with Mark, who was trying to teach her to surf. She didn't feel patient enough for it, but she loved being in the water. She could feel the salt in her pores and walked deeper into the waves until she was up to her shoulders in the ocean. She would move with the tide as it rhythmically pulled and pushed her, back and forth, outside of her control, but not enough to pull her away. Then she came back on the shore and reclined on her Hawaiian print towel, her black tank bathing suit soaking up the sun as she watched her brother surf. She ate a tuna sandwich and thin, salty potato chips.

That night their parents had all of them over for a family dinner. At the time, Bridget had an apartment in Burbank, where she was an elementary school librarian. Jim Harding, her fiancé, was an investment banker who lived in Beverly Hills. Mark was still in college and living at home, and he brought his girlfriend Carrie. Theresa was "between boyfriends," as her family liked to joke. Her mother made her specialty chicken parmesan, and Theresa exclaimed that it was the best she had ever made. The flavors exploded in her mouth, the bread smelled divine, the vinegar in the salad seemed especially enticing, and the wine seeped through her veins. She sat at the dining room table in her turquoise halter sundress, feeling her air-dried, windblown hair grazing her shoulders, smiling and talking with her family, and she couldn't remember ever feeling so good.

After a dessert of her mother's luscious tiramisu, Jim, thirty-two, handsome, charismatic, and, it turned out, calculating, suggested that they go out for drinks, and insisted on driving. Mark and Carrie had both recently turned twenty-one and were excited to go. Theresa thought that it would be the perfect way to top off the day. Bridget complained that she wasn't dressed for going out, in her "clam digger" pants, pink cotton blouse, and flat shoes, but Jim, in his slinky black dress shirt and slacks, assured her that she looked fine.

They piled into Jim's silver Mercedes-Benz, and he drove directly to a second-floor cocktail lounge in an old brick building. Theresa loved the dim, swanky ambiance; they sat on plum velveteen-upholstered chairs and leaned across darkly stained teak tables. Jim regaled them, buying a couple rounds of drinks and telling stories of his rise to success from starting out as a teller in Des Moines. Theresa ordered a Pink Lady and savored each sip of the creamy liquid as she listened to Jim. She noticed the light lines beginning in his forehead, the piercing blue of his eyes, the straightness of his teeth, the unobtrusive nose, the determined jaw. She felt him look at her, somehow felt heat from his intermittent but definite gaze in her direction.

Mark, probably wanting to equalize himself even though he was nowhere near Jim's financial arena, picked up the next round. They all took turns talking about The

Beatles, commenting on President Johnson and the Civil Rights Act, and impressing each other with their social progressiveness. Jim bought another round of drinks, effectively sealing the deal. By the time they stumbled back down the stairs (having already consumed a good deal of wine with dinner), Bridget could no longer mask the sullen look on her face, Theresa felt better than she had in her entire life, and Carrie was so drunk she had to be carried.

Jim drove Mark and Carrie back home, where they would stay in separate bedrooms at their parents' directive, and Carrie threw up as soon as she got out of the car. Jim wiped the back of his hand across his forehead in mock relief, and Theresa, now captivated by his every move, laughed with abandon. Bridget expressed concern over the vomit drying on the walkway and Jim assured her that it could easily be hosed off. "Not that I have any experience with that sort of thing," he said, sending Theresa into another fit of laughter.

He dropped Bridget off next, walking her to the door in a futile attempt at chivalry, probably telling himself that he was being attentive, considerate, perhaps even loving, even though Bridget could obviously sense what he was doing. Upon his return to the car he invited Theresa to move to the front seat, and she willingly obliged, smiling, feeling the warmth again. It mixed well with the cooler night air that enveloped her skin. She felt beautiful and euphoric.

Jim jockeyed a couple of freeways until he got off at Santa Monica Boulevard and headed toward Santa Monica, where Theresa lived. But as soon as he got to Beverly Hills he turned right and said, "I need to make a quick pit stop at my place, if that's okay?"

"Sure," Theresa said, wanting to sound breezy and carefree.

He pulled into a parking garage behind an expensive-looking apartment building and encouraged her to come inside; he wanted to show her something. And had she not been manic, bells would have gone off inside her head at that moment and she would have said, *Sorry, I'm really tired, I'll just wait here.* But perhaps bells did go off, different kinds of bells, and that's why she felt her whole body tingle and said "Okay" and got out of the car and walked next to Jim, feeling the night air embracing her bare legs as she walked in her cork platform sandals, and her legs felt longer and sleeker than they ever had in her life.

And then Jim was opening the door to his penthouse apartment and they were walking in and the only light was what came in through the living room windows, the sultry, seductive lights of the city, and after Jim shut the door he slowly backed her up against the hallway wall. And the bells went off again, the right ones this time, or probably both kinds, and she opened her mouth to say something, anything, *Wecantdothisyouremysistersfiance,* but as soon as it started to come out, his mouth was on hers and her knees almost buckled and the tingling turned into a jolt, a tidal wave of ecstasy. She took a deep breath and let him kiss her, surrendered to the moment, regardless of the grave consequences, which no longer grazed the surface of her manic mind.

He then untied the knot of her halter dress, and it fell down to her waist, rendering her half-naked. At this point the thought of stopping did not exist. Jim lightly dragged his hand over her chest, around her breasts, and fingered her nipples. She gasped and quivered; every inch of her skin felt like litmus paper, absorbing every breath, every touch, pulling it all in until it was saturated to the point of falling apart. And so, her heightened sexuality at its peak, Theresa fell apart in his arms, and he carried her to his bed, and it was a done deal.

She didn't sleep that night. Regret had not yet taken over as mania was still in the driver's seat: racing, random half-thoughts assaulted her tired-but-wired mind until the sun rose. While Jim slept, she found her clothing and put it on, hating to feel that dress against her skin now. Jim's apartment was about half a mile from Santa Monica Boulevard, so she didn't have too far to walk before being able to catch a bus to get home. Of course her car was at her parents' house. She would get Mark to come and pick her up after he recuperated from his hangover.

Theresa had blisters from her platform sandals by the time she finally got back to her apartment, but that pain was nothing compared to the shame. She waited a day before she called Bridget, whose lack of surprise was accompanied by supreme anger.

Howdareyoudosuchathingtome.

Whatkindofapersonareyou.

Whatkindofasister.

A few months after that, Theresa met Peter, and after the first Christmas at her parents' house, she had to tell him why her sister wouldn't talk to her. She blamed it on the alcohol, for years, but that was because she didn't have the awareness of bipolar. Regardless, it ruined her relationship with Bridget.

Peter exited the freeway, and Theresa thought about the counseling session. The not going to church – her parents wouldn't approve, but they didn't have to know. Thank God they didn't go to the same church. Suddenly she remembered something Peter had said during the session.

"What did you mean by now that I'm feeling better we should try celebrating again?"

Peter sighed. "Our anniversary trip. Aside from lying in bed together that night, I felt like I had gone by myself."

Theresa had to admit it was true. "I know. I was just so depressed. But you're right, we can try going again."

"I would love that," Peter said as he pulled in the driveway. "After I change, I'll pick up Leif from daycare and take him to the park for a bit. Would you like to come?"

"Thanks, honey, but I have a couple of things I need to get done before dinner," Theresa said as she got out of the car. She went into the kitchen to wash some potatoes and take out the chicken to defrost.

After Peter left she got out her phone and address book and laughed at the sad fact that she didn't know her own sister's number. Bridget worked mornings as a part-time librarian, so Theresa thought she might be home. She dialed, and Bridget picked up. After exchanging neutral pleasantries, Theresa said, "I was hoping we could see each other before you move."

"Oh, I'm sure we'll run into each other at Mom and Dad's before then."

"I mean I'd like to see you alone." Theresa knew she had ventured into thin-ice territory. But she hoped that after so much time, a pampering husband, and two beautiful, intelligent daughters, Bridget might be open to reconciliation. Theresa took a deep breath. "I'd like to clear the air after all these years," she said solemnly. "You're my sister, Bridget."

Bridget's finger-pointing, angry tone sounded exactly as it did twenty-four years ago. "Yeah, that's what I could never believe! You think just because *you* want to clear the air, because *you* have guilt and want to get it off your chest, that I'm okay with dropping everything to talk with you. I don't need to clear the air, I'm not the one who made it stale. You did it, you live with it. Just have the respect to keep your distance, why don't you? Goodbye, Theresa!"

CHAPTER SEVENTEEN

When his children were each six years old, Peter taught them to swim. It was important to him for safety issues, of course, but also because swimming was something that he wanted to share with them. He wanted them to feel water glide across their skin, to experience the sensation of moving through its tempered viscosity as it enveloped them. He wanted them to enjoy it but also respect it.

Kat was the easiest, being the most athletic of the three, Mike was a little more difficult, but he eventually got it, and Joseph had the hardest time. He pointed out to Peter that if humans were meant to go in the water "we would have gills."

Three evenings a week, after dinner Peter took Joseph to the pool in their gate-guarded community. The first session, all Joseph would do was sit on the edge of the shallow end and dangle his feet in the water. Peter talked to him about the importance of water safety and that it was necessary for him to learn to swim. The next session, Joseph got in the shallow end and walked from one end to the other. Then he practiced putting his face in and holding his breath. They did that for a whole week. After that, Peter took him out to the middle of the pool to teach him to tread water. Joseph was terrified, even though Peter held his hands the entire time. After two sessions, Joseph let go of Peter's hand and tried it on his own. When he realized that he didn't have to be frantic, and that the small movements he made actually kept him afloat, he said with a nervous smile, "Dad, am I doing it?"

"Yes, Joe, you're swimming."

"I don't have to do that windmill thing with my face in the water?"

"No, you don't have to do that. I just wanted you to be able to stay afloat if an accident ever happened and you fell out of a boat or something."

"Well, treading water's not so bad. I guess sometimes things aren't as hard as you think they're going to be, huh, Dad?" Joseph said as he reached out to hang onto the pool wall.

"That's right, Joe," Peter said. "But *you* thought it was going to be hard, and I'm proud of you for doing it anyway."

And now, in San Diego for a Labor Day Weekend trip, Peter watched as Kat rode the waves in on her boogie board. Joseph lay on his stomach on a towel while reading a book, right next to Peter. Theresa lay on the other side of him, on her back, a wide-brimmed straw hat perched on top of her face, her signature sleek, black tank-style bathing suit wrapping her torso.

She had reclaimed herself, and Peter felt so much pride and love for her that he became emotional just thinking about it. They sat down in the living room one night, about a month after Dr. Tucci had given her the diagnosis, and explained it to the kids.

"I wish we had known sooner," Kat had said. "Then we would have been able to understand why you had those days when you stayed in bed all day."

"I thought you just didn't want Leif and Heather and me to be here," Mike said. Heather was at work that moment, and Leif played with a train set on the floor in the kitchen.

"I thought you had cancer, like Aunt Anya," Joseph said.

"Oh, honey, I'm so sorry you thought that. It had nothing to do with the three of you. It was just me not knowing what was wrong and not having the strength to find out," Theresa said, reaching across the couch to touch Mike's hand.

"Well, I'm glad you're not going to die," Joseph said. "That was really sad when Aunt Anya died."

"Yes, that was very sad. But I'm not going to die, sweetheart. Not anytime soon, I hope!" Theresa said as she put her arm around him.

"I'm going to take psychology as an elective next year so I can learn more about bipolar," Kat said. "Is it genetic?"

Peter answered, glad that their announcement had been well received. "There is a genetic component, but it could also be environmental. It's a psychotherapist's job to work on that with their patients."

"That sounds like an interesting job. I might want to major in psychology in college," Kat said.

"Yeah, I'm thinking about minoring in psychology," Mike said.

"I'm happy you guys are interested," Theresa said. "That encourages me!"

"Aw, Mom," Kat said, leaning over to hug her. "We're here for you."

"Yeah," Mike and Joe chimed in.

Peter, relieved, remembered how he and Theresa had agonized over how to tell the children, what they would think. Would they think their mother was going crazy; would they be afraid or ashamed? Would it upset their children in some other way they hadn't thought about? He should have guessed that they would love and accept their mother no matter what. It was just as Joseph had said – *some things aren't as hard as you think they're going to be.*

Like Theresa finding a job, for instance. Even though she hadn't been in the workforce for almost twenty years, she found that her prior education and experience was still worth something. Peter had said that they could easily create a secretarial position at his firm, but Theresa insisted on finding her own job, and she did. For the past month she had been working as a legal secretary for a circuit court judge, and enjoying it. She was like a different person now. She couldn't possibly go back to the person she had been when Peter had met her and fallen in love. In this freeway life of theirs, too many cars had gone under the overpass since then. But she could take the person she had been and merge her with the person she was uncovering in therapy and go from there. It wasn't easy, but it gave her something to strive for. She told Peter that her new job was just like riding a bicycle, except a newer, fancier bicycle with new laws and ordinances to learn. But she felt appreciated there, and doubly appreciated at home.

With Theresa's earnings, Peter was able to reduce the amount of divorce cases he needed to take and instead focus on starting his family mediation business. It was sort of a 'full-service salon' approach. Couples having problems could come in for a few mediation sessions and see if they could work things out. If not, he could start the divorce process for them. He no longer wanted to take on the cases where one spouse was out to get the other spouse; he wanted to focus on amicable divorces. Some of Peter's colleagues laughed, calling his idea an oxymoron. "Not necessarily," Peter responded. He believed that even if a couple comes to the conclusion that it would be best not to continue the marriage, they could still divorce respectably and walk away with their dignity intact. He figured most people would prefer that.

Unfortunately, his first clients were his son and daughter-in-law. Mike and Heather had decided to go through with a divorce instead of waiting until they no longer wanted to be friends. Peter was sad that his son would go through a divorce so young, but then he didn't think that they were mature enough to get married in the first place, so it wasn't exactly a surprise. But divorce always saddened Peter, maybe because he had seen so much ugliness in it. At least Mike and Heather did not fall prey to that. They diplomatically decided that they would continue with the joint custody arrangement they had already been living with, except that Leif would spend most of his nights with Heather, who still worked during the day as a manager at a clothing store in the local mall. Mike would still live at home until he was finished with college in two more years, and Heather agreed to wait until he was finished and then she would start on her business and marketing degree, and their custody arrangement would switch. Peter began to realize that perhaps they weren't as immature as he had originally thought. They actually had a pretty good plan in place. Leif, now three, seemed happy at daycare and adjusted well to going back and forth between homes, since it didn't happen every day. Mike took classes during the day, worked nights as a manager at Del Taco, and had Leif on weekends.

This Labor Day Weekend was one of them. Peter chuckled as he saw Leif run across the sand and trip head-first into it. Mike, right behind him, picked him up and wiped the sand out of his mouth. Peter was glad to have both of them along on this family trip. It was good to all be together.

His hot tub idea proved to be a winner. Almost every night at least two members of the family used it. Not only was it relaxing, it encouraged a lot more talking than they had done in the past. One night, when he and Theresa were alone, she told him that she had still been wondering what might have happened to the body by the side of the road. Through her own research, she discovered that it had been a drug-related murder, that the man was twenty-six and did not have any children. That was what Theresa had been so concerned about, that someone's daddy had been killed. She was glad to find out that was not the case. "But he *was* someone's son," she had said.

"Yes," Peter said. "But they might not have been close to him. Not everyone is as lucky as we are."

Peter was referring to their relationship with their children, but he was also referring to his relationship with his parents. His father had been gone almost eight years. Peter had difficulty *not* remembering how his father was at the end, although some days he was fine, and Peter would come into the nursing home and play cards with him on Saturdays, and they would remember when they played baseball in the neighborhood park in New York. When Peter was eight, one day he pitched the ball to his father who hit it into an adjacent warehouse, breaking a window. Michael yelled, "Son of a bitch!" and Peter, mouth open, looked at him. "Don't tell your mother!" And they laughed there in the tiny old room with the wood paneling on the wall and paintings of bass jumping out of the water, hooked on a line. A twin bed with a gold Vellux blanket on it was pushed into one corner, a particleboard dresser in the other, and a small wooden table with two metal and plastic chairs had been placed under the window. The room looked like a cheap motel room stuck in the 1960s. And this was where his once bold, industrious father spent the last few months of his life.

One day Peter pulled one of the chairs beside the head of Michael's bed and read *The Grapes of Wrath* to him. Peter read for about an hour, then spoon-fed his father some applesauce, and resumed reading. Anya walked in at that moment, carrying a plate of crescent roll cookies. She apologized for interrupting them, but the cookies were fresh out of the oven, and she wanted to bring them over right then. Peter said it was no problem, got up, and walked over to look out the window at the weed-ridden lawn so that Anya could sit down next to their father. Then Peter heard his father greet Anya and say, "Who's that man over there? He's been here all day."

Although painful to witness, Peter reminded himself that it was a short time in such a full life. His father had accomplished everything he set out to do – go to America, get a good job, have a family, build a home, and own a business. He even took a cruise and bought lavish gifts for his wife.

Peter's mother "might be a bit materialistic," he liked to say, "but that's why she has a heart of gold." He felt much better with her living in the retirement residence, knowing she was always safe, she was always fed, and someone checked in on her daily. He and at least one of the kids went to visit her every other weekend.

Last weekend, she had told him about the letter she received from Danika that she had decided to remain in Czechoslovakia and not return to America to marry Eddie. It didn't bother him that he had paid all her court fees, researched immigration law, and it came to naught. She was family, and she had needed help. It did surprise him, however, because it seemed that Danika and Eddie had been so determined to get through those three months. But maybe they had put all their energy into proving their love when it wasn't that strong to begin with. What amount they had was not enough to stand the test of time – even if it was only three months. Or maybe Danika realized that her sense of self was in Czechoslovakia, and five months in America had been enough for her, especially after the traumatic end. Maybe she wanted to leave all of that behind her. And maybe that was just as well.

He was glad that his mother had also made some good friends at the Geezer Hilton. He wondered how that would feel, knowing that on any given day you could come down to eat breakfast at the dining hall and find out that one of your friends had died in the night. He guessed that they just dealt with it. It was the nature of the place. Someday, like his mother, he would probably be there.

And he missed Anya terribly, could not believe he would never see her at Easter again or talk to her on the phone. He kept going over in his mind how senseless her death was, but ultimately he realized that life doesn't make sense. That sometimes we spend our days being jettisoned around like a little silver ball in a pinball machine, but then there are days when we can sit on a beach and listen to the waves and close our eyes and feel like God is there, and it doesn't matter if life doesn't make sense.

For now, Peter enjoyed a warm sunny weekend in San Diego with his family. Kat had come in from the water, dried off, and opened a Pepsi. The afternoon was waning, and they decided to head back to the hotel, which was just a few blocks away, to clean up before going out to dinner. On the way they passed a small park with palm trees surrounding several picnic tables. The sunlight filtered through the palm fronds and cast dancing shadows on the grass below, which was covered with pigeons.

"Birds!" Leif exclaimed, pointing, straining to break free from his father's hand.

Mike scooped him up. "Leif, if you run up to them, they'll get scared and they'll all fly away. So let's walk up to them quietly and then we can feed them, okay?"

"Okay, Daddy," Leif said, smiling. "What do they eat? Worms?"

"Maybe. But they also like bread. And we have some bread in that bag that Grandpa's carrying," Mike said, pointing.

They stopped at one of the picnic tables and Peter set down the paper grocery bag, reached in and pulled out the plastic bag full of half a loaf of bread, leftover from their sandwiches that day. He distributed a piece to everyone. He watched as Mike showed his son how to tear off bits of bread and toss them out to the pigeons.

The pigeons all began to walk towards the six of them, nodding their bald little heads in the funny way that pigeons walk. Theresa reminded Joseph of the Sesame Street song, "Doin' the Pigeon," and the two of them walked around, singing the song and acting it out. Theresa's grin lit up her face, and Peter swore that he fell in love with her all over again. But really, he had been in love all along.

A group of pigeons crowded around Kat, and she said, "Hey, Dad, could you hand me another piece of bread? They're frantic!" She looked down at the birds as Peter handed her a slice. "Hey, guys, relax! There's enough to go around!"

Peter breathed deeply. *Yes, there is.*

*

Why Bridget had wanted to go to lunch in Santa Monica, Theresa couldn't guess. There were so many other Mexican restaurants closer to where either of them lived. But Bridget had thought it would be nice to be near the beach, and Theresa wasn't going to argue. A lump formed in her throat as she drove past the street where she used to live.

Bridget had called her the night before, telling her that the house was in escrow and she wanted to see Theresa before she moved to Boston. Bridget asked if she could meet her for lunch on Saturday. Hopeful, but not daring to get too optimistic, Theresa said yes.

She got off the phone and stood alone in the kitchen. Peter was not home from work yet, Joseph was at a friend's house, Kat was at her summer job scooping ice cream, and Mike was at his job. Theresa looked at the kitchen floor and remembered the time she sat on it and fell apart because she discovered that someone had eaten the last of the tuna salad. She remembered how it felt to vacillate between bursting into tears and wanting to throw her head into a wall. She marveled that a daily pill could change all of that, could make her trust herself again, believe in herself. That she could sit in a hot tub with her husband and children and enjoy the moment, the quality time, instead of feeling the chlorine seep into her pores and wanting to rock herself. That she could lie in bed next to Peter, close her eyes, and not feel like stadium lights had been switched on the inside of her forehead. Medication brought relief even beyond what she knew she needed.

How did I get so far away from myself that I couldn't realize how bad things had gotten?

Her brain no longer felt like gelatin, now that she was working again. She hadn't realized how desperate her level of intellectual stimulation had become from not working for twenty years, from losing her identity. It was like a brush with death. Of course, she had read a ton of books in those twenty years, and she enjoyed talking with Peter about all of his cases, but the fact was that in returning as a legal secretary she felt like a dishwasher at a restaurant trying to learn to wait tables. Everything had changed – legislation, policies, people. Her boss, a cigar-smoking gentleman with a combover, was nearing retirement, and a saint, she'd said, in taking her on. "Don't be ridiculous," he huffed when she thanked him. "I know you'll work harder because you feel you have something to prove. But you don't. It's like swimming. Shallow, deep – doesn't matter. As long as you can swim, you'll still float." So she did, learning new strokes as she went along.

But isn't that all we ever do in life? We keep learning. We survive. We try to laugh more than we cry.

It was a huge change going back to work. Theresa had to buy a new wardrobe full of "power suits" and pumps, wear makeup and curl her hair every morning, and run out the door with a briefcase instead of watching the morning news in her pajamas with a toddler on the couch. But she wanted that change, wanted to reclaim her identity. Was there anything more fragile than that?

Near Tres Hermanos Restaurant, Theresa found an on-street parking space, an act of God for a Saturday afternoon in Santa Monica. She took that to be a good sign. Bridget's car, a red Fiero, was parked across the street. Bridget always had a red sports car. What was *that* about? Perhaps that was her identity, and just as fragile.

Theresa braced herself. Bridget had said that she wanted to talk, but what did that mean? Usually when someone wants to meet at a restaurant, Theresa thought, it's because they have bad news and they figure if they deliver it in a public place the recipient will be less likely to make a scene. But if Bridget had wanted to say something negative she would have done it over the phone.

Bridget was not in her car so Theresa walked up to the glass door of Tres Hermanos, saw her reflection, and wondered if she had overdressed. Her work suits gave her some level of confidence, so she had worn a beige linen pantsuit with a peach silk blouse. She opened the door and there stood Bridget in the foyer, dressed in lilac pedal-pushers, sandals, and a white sequined tank top. Any confidence Theresa's suit had afforded her went right out the glass door.

"You look so business-like!" Bridget commented, giving her the usual obligatory hug they exchanged on holidays. But this time, Theresa felt Bridget hold on a second longer. Was it a second of pity? Of forgiveness? Maybe even a second of love?

"Well, I've been getting used to these things again after so many years," Theresa said, feeling completely self-conscious.

"You look good! How's the job going?"

Theresa let Bridget's enthusiastic *You look good!* echo in her mind. She couldn't remember the last time her sister had said those words to her. Still affected by that realization, Theresa responded in a hesitant voice, "Thanks; it's going really well."

"Great!" Bridget exclaimed. "Let's go get our table before the rush hits." She had always been the shot-caller.

A handsome, young Latino man wearing a white shirt and black pants led them to their table along the wall, which featured staple-gunned Mexican blankets and a black and gold velvet sombrero in the middle. Theresa asked how Bridget had heard about this place, and she said one of her colleagues at the library had recommended it. Fortunately there were a few other diners present; a couple at the front window and a party of four in the middle of the restaurant.

They sat down and ordered margaritas like old friends on a lunch date, like they did it every month. The air between them was pregnant, full, ready to pop, but only Bridget could do the popping. The young waiter didn't seem to notice and informed them with an inviting smile that he would be right back with their drinks. Theresa looked at the plastic coated menu, even though she knew she wanted a chicken tostada.

"I think I'll have a shrimp tostada," Bridget said in a tone that solicited approval. "That sounds refreshing." She put the menu down and took a sip of water.

"That's funny," Theresa began, hoping she didn't sound fake. "I was going to have a chicken tostada!"

Bridget looked at her. "Yeah?" she said with a light laugh. "Funny."

The waiter returned with their drinks and took their orders, initially recommending they try the chicken enchiladas, saying that those were their specialty. He said that they were his ex-girlfriend's favorite, and she was from Eastern Europe.

Bridget tried to make a joke. "Ex? Are you sure it wasn't the enchiladas?"

The waiter politely laughed. "No, she had to move. It was okay. What would you ladies like?"

A flash of recognition pulsed in Theresa's mind. She remembered Danika telling her about her fiancé, Eddie, working at a Mexican restaurant in Santa Monica, and wondered if this could be him. How many other young, Eastern European immigrants had boyfriends who worked in Mexican restaurants in Santa Monica? Theresa almost wished he could sit down and talk with them so that she could tell him what a good person she thought he was, so dedicated, so disciplined. She wanted to look into his deep brown eyes and tell him that no matter how noble one's intentions, love still wasn't going to be easy, but she was sure he knew that by now. What he didn't know, what he couldn't possibly know yet, was that no matter the outcome, it was always worth it. There was always something worthwhile to come from love.

Theresa gazed after him as he whisked himself away. She desperately wanted to delay what was coming. It was time. No more pleasantries. No more jokes and light laughs.

Bridget took a quick sip of her margarita and began. She looked at the corner of the table. "I've been reading this book on...forgiveness and it...has some exercises in it that have helped me to realize that I've been punishing you for twenty-four years, and I don't want to do that anymore. I want to let it go," she said through a quivering mouth.

Theresa gasped and began to cry. "Bridget, I'm so, so sorry."

A sob racked Bridget's chest, and she got up to embrace Theresa. "So am I." They clung together then, quietly crying, and Bridget whispered, "I forgive you."

The sound system mariachi music played on and the other patrons went about the business of ordering and consuming their food, talking, clinking glasses and scraping plates, seemingly unaffected by the two tearful women near the back of the restaurant. Sometimes love is a roar, loud but volatile, bold and sudden, but more often it is a gentle breath, quiet and patient, soft but sure, only wanting to be heard.

CHAPTER EIGHTEEN

The last time Anna ate a meal in the dining hall of her retirement residence, which was breakfast that morning, she looked around from her place at the fake wood table where she sat, one of perhaps twenty tables, and she thought, *All we're doing is sitting around waiting to die.*

Our spouses have died. Some of us even have children who've died. We've seen all we wanted to see, done whatever we could do that we wanted to do. We've gone back home and stared down our demons. We've said goodbye to people we'll never see again. Our estates are in order. We've apologized for our mistakes. Some of us have broken our hips. Even our children have approached us to tell us their secrets - that they're lesbians or no longer going to church. *All we have left to do is die.*

It's not that learning about her children's secrets made her want to die. It's just that it seemed to be another step, perhaps the last one, a part of the end-of-life process that people went through. Marjorie, one of her friends at the Geezer Hilton, had mentioned that a few months ago her son approached her to tell her he was gay. Betty's daughter had recently told her that she'd had an abortion back in the sixties. Agnes's son, in tears, confessed that he had stolen money from her when he was a teenager. And last week, when Peter had come to visit Anna, he took a deep breath and told her that he had stopped going to church. Then he immediately pointed out that he still *believed* in God and prayed, but that he had discovered that he would rather spend time bonding with his family every Sunday than attend church, which was "too stressful" for all of them, and not something that made him feel very spiritual. Then, obviously nervous, he looked at her as if waiting for a courtroom verdict.

"Just as long as you have my funeral service in church," Anna said.

Peter coughed and said, "Of course, Ma, of course! And we'll all be there, singing and crying, you can be sure of that. I just wanted you to know that I'm not going to church on Sundays. It's not about being lazy or 'rebellious.' I just think we need to spend more family time together, and Sundays is when we can do that."

"Peter, you're grown man with own family, and grandchild even. You know what is best for you. You don't have to explain yourself to me!"

"Well, I just wanted you to know. I didn't want to keep it from you," Peter said.

"Okay, Peter, okay. And don't worry - I'm not going to write you out of the will!"

He laughed then. "Thanks, Ma. This place has really brought out your sense of humor!"

"You have to have sense of humor to live here, otherwise you just sit around and wait to die," Anna said, scrunching her white crocheted blanket in her lap.

"Are you unhappy here, Ma? I thought it was working

out okay for you."

"Oh, it's fine. I guess it is better than sitting at home, alone and dependent on everyone," Anna said.

"The food is okay, and they treat you well?" Peter asked.

"Yes, everything's good. I just meant that you have to have positive outlook here or it's easy to get depressed. Nobody knows how much time they have left, and it tends to wear on people," Anna said. Her white blanket comforted her, and it reminded her of Anya.

No one thinks they will have to bury their child. But even if you have to think it, nothing can prepare you. Nothing can fill the void or extinguish the pain. You can adopt a numbness, wrap yourself in surface memories, put on your "I'm functioning" mask, and feel guilty the first time you laugh about something after they are gone. Or you can cover yourself with the white crocheted blanket that you made when your daughter was still alive, and you wait to die so that you can be with her again.

"I'm sorry, Ma. I can imagine how hard that must be. Someday I'll be in that position, and I'll understand. All I can tell you now is how much we all love you and that we can't wait to celebrate your eightieth birthday next weekend!"

Peter had planned a big party at his house for Anna's birthday, and her sister Olga and niece Magda had flown out so that they could attend. Anna had decided that she needed her sister to meet her family and finally see America. She paid to have the two of them fly out, and paid for them to stay at a nice hotel nearby. Marya drove out from

Arizona and offered to chauffeur them around when Peter was at work. On her second day there, after taking them sightseeing around Los Angeles to see the Queen Mary and a half day at Disneyland, and out to dinner at an Italian restaurant, Marya dropped them off at their hotel and then took Anna back to the Geezer Hilton.

After she walked her mother up to her room, she sat down on the couch and said, "Ma, there's something I want to talk to you about, and I don't know when we'll have another chance to be alone."

"What is it?" Anna asked as she pulled her white blanket across her lap. Her joints were sore from walking around all day, especially her hip, and her back felt as if it would crumble like an old building in an earthquake. She and Olga had used wheelchairs at Disneyland, but she still felt exhausted. They shouldn't have done so much in one day, she decided with a sigh. Anna just wanted to sleep and hoped Marya didn't want to talk for a long time.

Marya folded her hands in her lap and looked up at the ceiling. "Well," she began, "I wanted to stop living a lie. I want you to know that I'm a lesbian – you know, gay – and I'm not going to be getting married -"

Anna chuckled, remembering Peter's recent revelation about not going to church. "You think this shocks me? I'm eighty years old, Marychka. Nothing surprises me now. I figured this for a long time. And you are just like your cousin in Czechoslovakia – her name is Marya, too. You should visit her sometime."

"So, you're okay with it, Ma?"

"Yes, Marychka. I know it is how you are. I don't know

why you waited this long to talk to me about it."

"I guess because I was afraid," Marya said. "I was afraid that you wouldn't accept it, wouldn't accept *me*."

"Acceptance is something I've become very good at," Anna said, and Marya embraced her.

*

"God grant you many years...God grant you many years...God grant you many blessed years! In peace, health and happiness...in peace, health, and happiness...God grant you many happy years!"

Anna smiled and sang the Old Church Slavonic song with her family as she sat at the head of the dining room table at Peter and Theresa's house. A luscious white-frosted poppy seed and raspberry-filled cake sat in front of her, and she blew out the two candles on it. The room erupted into applause and shouts of "Na zdravie!" which literally translated as "Your health!" but was often used as a congratulatory phrase. Anna had heard it and the Slavonic song at every wedding, baptism, and anniversary throughout her life.

Is there a word that means 'love of a culture'? Anna wondered. She loved being American for so many reasons. One was because she could also still be Rusyn.

Olga came up to her then and kissed her on both cheeks. In Slovak she said, "You have a beautiful family, sestra. Just look at all of them!"

Anna glanced around the room at her son and daughter, her daughter-in-law, who was cutting and serving the cake, her son-in-law, her five grandchildren and her great-grandson. They had all given her the blessed, happy years they sang about. And then she looked at her niece and sister all the way from Czechoslovakia. Anna realized she had fulfilled her last wish.

"Olga, do you remember long ago when I left for America, I said to you that I wanted you to come to America some day? Do you remember that?"

Olga closed her eyes for a moment. "Yes, sestra, I remember when you left. I was eight years old. I remember you had four dresses on at once and a bundle tied across your chest. I remember you said you wanted me to come to America when I was bigger." She smiled. "I guess I am big enough now!"

Anna and Olga shared a hearty laugh. "Thank you, sestra," Olga said. "I am glad to be here with you."

"I am glad you are here, too. You are the only one to see my American life! I wonder what John Nagajda would think," Anna said, eating a bite of cake.

"Oh, Anna, John Nagajda died, I think about a month ago. I'm sorry to tell you the sad news at your party," Olga said.

"Don't worry, Olga. I could tell when I saw him that he would not live much longer. He reminded me of Michael before he died," Anna said. *The two men I have loved,* she thought. I loved them both completely but for different reasons. John was my earth, enveloping and holding tight to a deeply rooted tree. Michael was my ocean, providing an unwavering current, carrying a fragile shell and gently guiding it to safety on an unfamiliar shore.

"Well, they are both at peace now," Olga said, patting Anna's arm.

Peter walked up, holding his paper plate with his piece of cake. "Ma, do you like your cake?"

"Yes, it's good," Anna said quietly as she poked it with her plastic fork.

"What's wrong, Ma?" Peter asked, pulling up a chair and sitting down next to her.

"I think…after eighty years, my heart is holding too much emotion. Maybe only now it is finally breaking," Anna said, swallowing hard.

"Oh, Ma, I miss Anya too. I wish she could be here with us."

Yes, Peter, I am sad that Anya died. I am sad that your father died, and sad that John Nagajda died. But it's not the dying - it's the letting go. That's the hard part. And it's hard to love and let go of someone I could never tell my children about. I would never want you to think that I didn't love your father just as much, and in some ways more. And so, even mothers have their secrets.

Anna bit the insides of her lips, trying not to let the tears spill out of her eyes. "What is word for happy and sad at same time?"

"That's life, Ma. That's just life."

"Then I am living. I am laughing, I am crying, I am living," Anna said.

"That's good, Ma," Peter said, putting his arm around her. "You keep on living as long as you like."

ACKNOWLEDGMENTS

I am indebted to my colleagues who have graced this book with their generous reviews and critiques: Laura McHale Holland, Carrie Wilson Link, and Michelle O'Neil. My appreciation for your time, attention, and support is beyond words.

My early readers have my undying gratitude: Monica Shapiro, Alexis Savko, Eric Werner, and Emma Werner. Your suggestions and encouragement mean the world to me. This book would not have evolved without you.

Thank you to Toni Tesori for designing the cover to be lovelier than I could have imagined. And to Faye Smedley for proofreading - I appreciate your efforts in what must have been a daunting task.

I am grateful to Madeline Rose, my mother. I started writing books because of the ones you read to me when I was little. And you typed my first novella. You supported my dream and I know you always will.

Many thanks to Mary Savko, my grandmother. *Enough to Go Around* is a fictional account of her experiences growing up in Czechoslovakia and her immigration to America. All my life her stories have intrigued, entertained, and inspired me, and I am honored to share them.

Most of all I wish to express my gratitude and love for Michael Savko, my father, who helped immensely with the research for this book. He believed in it and he believed in me. He died of cancer before it was finished, but I know he would have been proud.